9·90

Sweet Punish[ment]

"Since you have invaded my territory unchaperoned, it occurs to me that I know exactly how to punish you," Marcus said.

His hands came to Gwenyth's shoulders, and as she stared up at him in wide-eyed shock, he drew her slowly toward him.

Gwenyth's mouth was dry, but the only fear she felt was dismay at her own responses. She ought to slap him, she told herself. She ought to resist. No true lady would just stand there, mesmerized, waiting, her blood racing through her.

His lips touched hers, gently, his kiss feather-light. With a moan, she pressed upward, rising on her toes, as she urged him to get on with it, to stop tormenting her. If he were going to punish her, then let him do so, now, at once. . . .

AMANDA SCOTT, winner of the Romance Writers of America's Golden Medallion Award (*Lord Abberly's Nemesis*) and the Romantic Times' Award for Best Regency Author and Best Sensual Regency (*Ravenwood's Lady*), is a fourth-generation Californian who was born and raised in Salinas and graduated with a degree in history from Mills College in Oakland. She did graduate work at the University of North Carolina at Chapel Hill, specializing in British History, before obtaining her MA from California State University at San Jose. She now lives with her husband and teenage son in Folsom, California.

SIGNET REGENCY ROMANCE
COMING IN OCTOBER 1990

Michele Kasey
A Difficult Disguise

Mary Balogh
An Unlikely Duchess

Evelyn Richardson
Miss Cresswell's London Triumph

Lord Lyford's Secret

by

Amanda Scott

A SIGNET BOOK

SIGNET
Published by the Penguin Group
Penguin Books USA Inc., 375 Hudson Street,
New York, New York 10014, U.S.A.
Penguin Books Ltd, 37 Wrights Lane,
London W8 5TZ, England
Penguin Books Australia Ltd, Ringwood,
Victoria, Australia
Penguin Books Canada Ltd, 2801 John Street,
Markham, Ontario, Canada L3R 1B4
Penguin Books (N.Z.) Ltd, 182-190 Wairau Road,
Auckland 10, New Zealand

Penguin Books Ltd, Registered Offices:
Harmondsworth, Middlesex, England

First published by Signet, an imprint of Penguin Books USA Inc.

First Printing, September, 1990
10 9 8 7 6 5 4 3 2 1

Copyright © Lynne Scott-Drennan, 1990
All rights reserved

 REGISTERED TRADEMARK—MARCA REGISTRADA

PRINTED IN THE UNITED STATES OF AMERICA

Without limiting the rights under copyright reserved above, no part of this publication
may be reproduced, stored in or introduced into a retrieval system, or transmitted,
in any form, or by any means (electronic, mechanical, photocopying, recording, or
otherwise), without the prior written permission of both the copyright owner and the
above publisher of this book.

BOOKS ARE AVAILABLE AT QUANTITY DISCOUNTS WHEN USED TO
PROMOTE PRODUCTS OR SERVICES. FOR INFORMATION PLEASE WRITE
TO PREMIUM MARKETING DIVISION, PENGUIN BOOKS USA INC., 375
HUDSON STREET, NEW YORK, NEW YORK 10014.

To William Douglas, M.D.,
his dozen doughnuts
a small price for life

1

"Oh, Gwen, f-forgive me," stammered the young lady in lavender sprigged muslin standing uncertainly beside Lord Tallyn's stately butler upon the threshold of the front drawing room at Tallyn London House.

"Pamela!" Slender, flaxen-haired Lady Gwenyth Traherne threw her book aside and leapt up from the glove-leather sofa in the window embrasure to move with light, quick steps toward her visitor, her hands stretched out in welcome. "My gracious me, what are you doing in town?" Without waiting for a response, she said to the butler, "Marwyn, bring refreshments at once. Miss Beckley looks ready to faint from hunger."

Self-consciously pushing a shining raven lock back under her fetching lavender bonnet with one hand while she released the ends of the lacy shawl she had clutched to her generous bosom in order to take one of Gwenyth's hands with the other, Miss Beckley said anxiously, "I know I ought not to have come to you like this, but I could not think what else to do."

"Don't be a goose," Lady Gwenyth Traherne said, giving Miss Beckley's small lavender-gloved hand an affectionate squeeze. "I have been bored to distraction, for my aunt has long since deserted me to visit her widowed mama-in-law in Berkshire, and the last gala at Vauxhall was rained out on Friday. Even the Italian opera has closed, so with nothing of interest to do until the new theater at Covent Garden opens for the king's Jubilee celebration next month, I am very glad to see you. But how is it that you are here without so much

7

as a word to warn us of your coming? I had thought you still fixed at Miss Fletcher's school, though why you should be, in summer and at your great age, I'm sure I don't know.''

Glancing over her shoulder and clearly taking courage at finding the butler gone and the drawing-room doors firmly shut behind him, Pamela said dramatically, ''I have run away! I came up to town on the common coach, and I depend upon you, Gwen, to stand my friend, for matters have come to a dreadful pass. Cousin Marcus has said I am not to make my come-out at all this year, even in the Little Season, though Papa promised, and''—she dissolved into tears—''and, oh, Gwen, he has said he will not consent to my m-marriage!''

Gwenyth, three inches taller, looked down at her in bewilderment. ''Marriage? But how is this? You have written of no one for whom you feel even the slighest tenderness.''

Pamela's violet eyes grew wide beneath their heavy dark lashes. ''Oh, no. Why, how should I have formed an attachment when Miss Fletcher never lets us near any gentleman to whom we are not quite firmly related? I never had the courage to sneak out of school like you and some of the others did.''

''Hush, goose,'' admonished Lady Gwenyth, her light blue eyes atwinkle. ''My brother Tallyn is at home and you will confirm his worst opinion of me if you prattle such revealing stuff to him.''

''As if I would,'' exclaimed Miss Beckley in consternation. ''I would never . . . My dearest friend . . . And after you were so kind as to take me under your wing when I was so lonely and unhappy. But you have been gone two years now, and then Papa died, and oh, how I have missed you!'' With these words she cast herself into Gwenyth's arms, sobbing gustily.

Gwenyth made no immediate attempt to free herself, though she was certain her rose muslin morning gown would be drenched by the girl's tears. At last, however, knowing that Marwyn would not be long in returning with the refreshments she had ordered, she said quietly, ''That's quite enough now, Pamela. You know Miss Fletcher would not approve of such a complete show of emotion as this. Take my handkerchief and dry your eyes."

Obediently Miss Beckley straightened up, making a visible effort to stem her sobs as she accepted the cambric handkerchief Gwenyth extracted from beneath her wide embroidered sash.

"I must look a sight," Pamela said a moment later, dropping her shawl onto a nearby chair and, with a singularly graceful gesture, lifting her hand to twist a dusky curl as she peered anxiously at Gwenyth.

Stifling a sigh of envy, Gwenyth said, "Not at all, my dear. Come, sit with me on the sofa, and we will have a talk."

When Pamela continued to regard her uncertainly after they had sat down, she chuckled. "It really is too bad of you, you know, that your eyes do not even grow red when you weep."

"But you would not wish them to do so unbecoming a thing as that, would you?" Pamela asked, staring at her in surprise.

This time Gwenyth's sigh was audible. "Tell me why you came to London, Pamela."

Dabbing her eyes one last time, Pamela settled her hands in her lap and drew a long breath, only to let it out again—whether in frustration or relief, Gwenyth couldn't tell—when the doors to the drawing room opened and Marwyn entered. He was followed by a tall footman in the Tallyn green-and-silver livery, who bore a silver tray containing a pot of tea, a bowl of fruit, buttered toast, elegant china plates and cups, and silver cutlery.

"Will there be anything more, m'lady?" the butler inquired.

"No, thank you." When the servants had gone, Gwenyth turned back to her guest to discover that Pamela was now looking about the opulent drawing room with visible awe.

"Theatrical, is it not?" Gwenyth said with a smile. "My sister Meriel hates it. She cannot decide if it looks more like the anteroom to a king's palace or to a Greek bordello."

Pamela gasped. "What a dreadful thing to say! One doesn't expect such elegance, you know, when approaching Tallyn

House from the street. It looks like any other house on Berkeley Square, except for Landsdowne House, of course," she added conscientiously. "But one enters the beautiful stair hall—so much magnificence in so small a space—and then ascends to this." She held her arms wide, shaking her head in wonder.

Gwenyth followed her gaze with amusement. The front drawing room at Tallyn House was indeed spectacular, rising one and a half stories to a coved, tunnel-vaulted ceiling, coffered and gilded, and bedecked with inset paintings depicting, in a three-dimensional effect, Greek gods and goddesses whose figures were repeated in a collection of marble sculptures of various sizes decking every chest and table in the room. The plasterwork and furnishings were equally ornate, and the chamber's splendor was reinforced by a magnificent Oriental carpet, its rich dark colors matching those of the paintings overhead.

Pamela stood up, pulling off her gloves as she stepped toward the white marble fireplace opposite the door and gazed curiously at the large painting above the chimneypiece. It showed, through a light mist, a huge sprawling stone house set at the base of a lofty snow-capped, twin-peaked mountain.

"That is Plas Tallyn," Gwenyth told her, "our home in Wales." There was softness in her voice, and she found herself gazing at the painting with an unexpected surge of longing. "I never think I shall tire of London," she said, "but sometimes I surprise myself. I do love the mountains so."

"That place looks a bit lonely," Pamela said, turning back and setting aside her gloves in order to help herself to a plate from the tray. "Would you like me to pour out?"

"No, I'll do it," said Gwenyth, moving to suit action to words. "You just sit down again, my girl, and spill your tale, as my little brother, Davy, would say."

Pamela sat, but shot Gwenyth a look of curiosity. "You have told me about your brothers and sisters before, and though I tend to get them mixed up in my head, I should have supposed Davy to be rather larger than you are by now.''

Gwenyth laughed. "Indeed he is, for he is eighteen now and presently enjoying the long vacation from Oxford.''

"Then he is here?'' Pamela's voice vibrated with interest.

"No, he is not,'' Gwenyth said more sharply. "He is with a friend somewhere in the Lake Country on a walking tour. Enough of this, Pamela. Tell me about Cousin Marcus and this marriage he will not allow, and with no more roundaboutation, if you please, for my patience is no longer now than it ever was.''

Pamela took a bite of toast, but upon seeing the gathering annoyance in her hostess's face, she chewed and swallowed quickly. "I told you,'' she said, lifting her chin. "Marcus has said I am not to come out. But Papa promised me I should do so in my seventeenth year, and now I am past seventeen. Why, I shall be eighteen next May, and quite upon the shelf.''

"Thank you very much,'' Gwenyth said with a wry look.

"Oh, but I did not mean to imply anything about you, dearest Gwen. I know you must be nearly twenty by now, but surely you are unwed by choice, not for lack of suitable offers! You always said you meant to take London by storm and be a lady of fashion, but that you meant never to surrender your freedom to a husband.'' She sighed. "I have never had any freedom to speak of, you know, although darling Papa nearly always let me do as I pleased.''

"Except when it came to sending you away to school,'' Gwenyth pointed out with a smile.

"Yes, but that was the only time, and he did it so that I might make proper friends,'' Pamela said with a toss of her head. "I could nearly always manage Papa otherwise.''

"But your cousin is different? I collect that he must be your guardian now that your papa and mama are both deceased.''

"Oh, yes, and my trustee as well, and it is the most dreadful state of affairs, for he hasn't got a penny of his own, you know. Here he has inherited a stupid earldom, which one might think to be a good thing, but the estates that go with it are all encumbered and things are in a tangle, so he says he hasn't got time to look after me and I must simply stay at school until he can be bothered to arrange my life for me. Only I don't want him to arrange my life! I want to make my come-out and meet all the eligible young men in London and choose my own husband from amongst them.''

"You seem certain that you will have your choice," Gwenyth said, seeking to bring her back down to earth.

"Oh, but don't you think I shall?" The violet eyes opened very wide. "I was always the prettiest girl at school. You know I was. And that hasn't changed, Gwen, I promise you, so I am certain I shall find a dashing, eminently suitable young man."

"You certainly haven't learned the worth of modesty," Gwenyth said tartly, "and I must tell you, Pamela, you sound exactly like my sister Eliza used to sound before she met her husband and settled down to raise children in Shropshire. She lived in the pages of the idiotish books she was used to read, and tumbled head over ears in love with every unsuitable young man who passed before her eyes. She was Lydia Languish to her toenails. I should hope you have better sense."

"I never can keep your family straight in my head," Pamela said. "Is Lydia Languish a cousin?"

"She is from a play," Gwenyth said, gritting her teeth. "A character so foolish as to be ridiculous. My family doesn't enter into this matter at all."

"Well, I know one of your sisters married a Sir Something, here in London, but didn't your other one marry a Frenchman? How can she live in Shropshire?"

"You forgot one. My sister Nest married the Frenchman. Meriel—the one married to Sir Antony Davies—is the eldest, and she lives more in Maidenhead now than in London. Then comes Nest, then Eliza in Shropshire, then me. Joss—that is, my brother Tallyn—is the eldest of all of us, of course, and Davy the youngest. But again you change the subject,

Pamela, and I warn you, it will not do. I mean to have the whole tale out of you. You did say you need my help, did you not?''

"Yes, for Marcus will surely come after me once Miss Fletcher tells him I have left school. I think," she added with a grimace, "that he means to marry me himself, Gwen. For my fortune, you know."

"Are you such an heiress, then?" Gwenyth asked with a smile, certain the young girl must be exaggerating.

But Pamela replied complacently, "Oh, yes, for there is no one else, you know. All of Papa's money came to me. I think Marcus expected to get some of it, for his mama was my Aunt Margaret, Papa's sister, only Aunt Margaret displeased Papa through some cause or other, or Marcus did—I am not certain which it was—and then of course Aunt Margaret died of the consumption before ever Papa did, only he did not die of consumption, of course, but of an apopletic seizure, even though he had the mildest of tempers, except of course—"

"Pamela!" Gwenyth cut in sharply. "I promise you that I shall indulge in an apoplectic seizure of my own in a minute. I do not know when you draw breath. Where is your cousin now?"

"Why, I don't know," Pamela said. "His new estate is an abbey or castle or some such thing, located in Berkshire somewhere along the River Thames; however, I believe—"

"An abbey on the Thames?" Gwenyth frowned, attempting to capture an elusive memory.

"Yes, I do remember that much, though I never can remember the name of the place, but I think he is somewhere else just now on business, anyway, maybe even here in London." She shivered dramatically. "Only think if I should have encountered him! He did write to me, but his letter was not at all amusing, only telling me that I must be patient and do all I might to help Miss Fletcher when the new girls arrive, just as if I were a junior mistress or some such odd thing, so I paid no heed to the rest."

"His wanting you to stay at school does seem odd,"

Gwenyth agreed. "Could you not have gone home to Beckley Hall with a lady chaperon instead?"

"Oh, yes, but I did not want to go there even if Marcus had not said it was too far away to be convenient for him to look after me. 'Tis in Norfolk, Gwen, practically on the coast, and as lonely as that place yonder in the painting, I daresay."

"Gracious, you make them both sound a million miles away," Gwenyth said, laughing. But when Pamela opened her mouth to reply, she held up a hand to silence her. "No, never mind. I do understand why you preferred to come to London. But what is your purpose in coming to me? I cannot help you evade your rightful guardian, you know. 'Twould be very wrong of me."

"You never bothered your head much about right and wrong at Miss Fletcher's," Pamela pointed out with a mischievous smile.

"But, really—"

"No, don't say it, Gwen. I don't want you in the suds on my account, but surely you can help me teach Marcus a lesson, show him I have some protection against his wicked designs."

Gwenyth studied her face for a long moment before she said, "Are you certain he has such designs, Pamela? I remember you were used to exaggerate quite remarkably whenever it suited you to do so, so I hope you are not making up this tale merely to obtain my sympathy."

Pamela looked wounded. "How can you think such a thing? Have I not told you he has no money? Only imagine what it must be like for him to be forced to look after a tremendous fortune like mine and to have a huge estate to put in order, as he does, without being able to touch the first to aid the second." She paused long enough to allow that argument to sink in, then added, "The simplest answer to his plight is clearly to marry me. Why else would he say he will not countenance my marriage to anyone just yet, and why else would he keep me shut up at school, where he knows I cannot even meet any eligible young men, if it is not so that he might one day make me Countess of Lyford?''

"Lyford?" The elusive memory took form with a snap. "Your cousin is not just Marcus Beckley but the tenth Earl of Lyford?"

"Well, I don't know about tenth," Pamela said defensively, "and his family name is Hawtrey, not Beckley, but he is certainly the Earl of Lyford. Why does that make you frown so? Do you know him? Oh, Gwen, you won't take his side?" She burst into tears. "Promise me you won't!"

"I don't know him at all, and of course I shan't take his side," Gwenyth said, unmoved by her weeping. "Not without hearing it, in any event. Do try not to be such a widgeon."

"But I am desperate," Pamela insisted, blotting her tears with the damp handkerchief as she added with a soulful sigh, "If you won't help me, I daresay I shall have to set out alone, and most likely I shall be taken prisoner by bandits and forced to Herculean efforts to protect my honor and fortune."

"Stop that, Pamela. You will make me ill. Let me think."

Obediently, and not without a glimmer of hope in her expressive eyes, Miss Beckley dropped the handkerchief distastefully onto the table and turned her attention to the bowl of fruit. Selecting a ripe red apple, she sank her white teeth into it, ignoring the knife provided for her use.

The drawing-room doors opened again just then, and a very broad-shouldered, light-brown-haired gentleman of three-and-thirty years entered, his head thrust forward, his dark brows beetling, his mouth set in stern lines.

"Gwenyth, I find that I must leave London today, at once, in fact, and—" He broke off in surprise as his gaze encountered the lovely Miss Beckley. Straightening, he appeared for a long moment to have been struck speechless.

"Pamela," Gwenyth said, amused, "may I present my brother Tallyn. Joss, this is Miss Beckley, a friend from Miss Fletcher's. I believe I have mentioned her name to you upon one occasion or another."

"Never did," Tallyn said, making his bow with more care than she was accustomed to seeing in him. "I'd remember.

Do you make a long stay in London, Miss Beckley?''

Pamela had risen to her feet as she spoke and, having wiped her hands daintily upon a linen napkin, made her schoolgirl curtsy, but his question brought such a look of confusion to her face that Gwenyth took pity on her and said composedly, "Her plans are unsettled, Joss. Indeed, we were just discussing what she ought next to do.''

"Good, good,'' Tallyn said, still staring appreciatively at the younger girl.

Gwenyth experienced an unfamiliar urge to prick him with a pin. "Did you wish to speak to me?'' she inquired politely.

"Speak to you?'' He glanced at her, then took control of himself and said more sharply, "Yes, yes, indeed, I did.''

"Oh, dear, what have I done now?''

"Not a thing,'' he replied impatiently. Then, looking at her more carefully, he added, "Nothing that I know about, in any event. Is there something?''

"No, sir. Do come to the point. People seem most anxious today to *say* they wish to speak to me, but then they waste an unconscionable amount of time before they actually do so.''

"Well, if you would pause long enough in your own speech-making to let a fellow get a word in,'' he retorted unfairly, "I would tell you I am off to Plas Tallyn for a forthnight, maybe longer. A letter from my steward by this morning's post informed me of matters there requiring my presence. Nothing serious, but I have not set foot on the place since February, so a trip is certainly in order. I cannot leave you here alone, of course.''

"Don't be nonsensical, Joss. I am twenty years old, and I have Marwyn and the other servants to look after me, not to mention my own Annie Gray, all stuck in London just as we are.''

"We could have gone home.''

"And left poor Meriel? What if something had happened, and us a million miles away in the north of Wales?''

"Poor Meriel is at Maidenhead with her children, her house, and her husband to occupy her,'' Tallyn said, "and that makes her a most unsuitable chaperon for you now, my dear, particularly in her present delicate condition with Antony away on one of his many little journeys. If he were home . . . But since he is not, I think I must insist upon your accompanying me to Wales.''

Knowing from experience that to argue with him would produce no result other than a loss of his temper and her own, and not wishing to present the spectacle of a Traherne family squabble to her guest, Gwenyth collected her thoughts rapidly while Tallyn pulled at his lower lip and gazed at her. Then, just as it looked as though his mind were made up and he really was going to insist, she said calmly, ''I believe you are right, Joss. For me either to stay with Meriel or to require her chaperonage just now would be too great an imposition. Perhaps you would not object, however, if I were to pay a visit to our aunt in Berkshire.''

''Berkshire? What the devil is Auntie Wynne doing in Berkshire?''

''Now, Joss, she was there from the first of October, after the old earl died, till late January, as you must remember very well, and after she left us to visit Meriel, she went back to stay with the ancient dowager.'' She glanced at Pamela as Tallyn chuckled, just as she had hoped he would.

''Forgot about that,'' he said. ''Wrong of her to call her the old countess so, of course, but one can certainly understand the provocation. Auntie Wynne can't much enjoy being cooped up in Berkshire with that old harridan.''

''She believed it was her duty.'' She smiled at Pamela. ''As I told you before, my aunt, the Viscountess Cadogan, is bearing company to her mama-in-law, who was widowed last September. It will be just the thing for us.'' She watched Pamela closely this time to see if the date or her aunt's name drew any sign of recognition. They did not.

''Wait now, Gwen,'' Tallyn said, shaking his head. ''I aim to take ship from Portsmouth and sail up the coast, so I don't travel by your route, and it ain't fittin' for you to go there alone, even if you take your woman with you.''

''I shall take Miss Beckley with me,'' Gwenyth said

casually. "She was telling me just before you came in that she has been feeling the heat of the city, and we were seeking a way for her to find relief. A visit to Berkshire will be the very thing."

"But she's only a child." Tallyn beamed at Pamela, who lifted her chin and rewarded him with a sunny, demure smile. "A very pretty child," he added, "but one who needs protection as much as you do, my girl. Still, I suppose if you take her maid as well as your own . . ."

"No doubt we will take our nuncheon at Davies Manor," Gwen said, not wishing to encourage discussion of Pamela's nonexistent maid, "so I daresay I can ask Meriel to lend me her pistol if that will make you more comfortable."

He glared. "Less of that, my girl, or it's Wales for you."

At the same time, Pamela, who was staring at her in astonishment, said, "your sister has a pistol?"

Gwenyth chuckled. "When you meet her, you must ask her to tell you about her adventures when she went into France six years ago. 'Tis a rare tale, right enough."

" 'Tis a tale best left untold," said Tallyn grimly. "Don't bid farewell to me, Gwenyth, thinking I shall turn a blind eye to any such activities on your part. If Miss Beckley's family does allow her to accompany you, I do not wish to be regaled upon my return with complaints about your lack of care for her."

"Oh, that would never happen," said Pamela ingenuously. "You see, my family—"

"Her family," said Gwenyth, cutting in swiftly, "knows perfectly well that I would never allow harm to come to Pamela."

"Very well, then," he said, "but mind, Gwen, your coachman is to take one of the grooms along, armed with a blunderbuss. I don't want the pair of you attacked by footpads or worse."

"We will be very careful, Joss, I promise. Do tell everyone at home that we think of them often."

He nodded, favoring her with a long look, which she met

steadily, and then, with another bow, he took himself off, leaving Gwenyth to breathe a sigh of relief.

"He is very handsome for an older gentleman," Pamela said thoughtfully into the silence that followed his departure.

Gwenyth grinned at her. "Doddering old man that he is."

"Oh, I didn't mean that," Pamela assured her. "He thought I was beautiful, didn't he? I can tell, you know. He looked at me much the way our last drawing master did before Miss Fletcher dismissed him. He had a wart on his cheek, though."

Gwenyth ignored this tangent, saying, "You nearly let the cat out of the bag, Pamela. We are fortunate that Joss is in a hurry and did not ask more about your parents or maid. Had you told him you were here on your own, he would have put an end to any plans of ours and sent you straight back to Miss Fletcher."

"Oh, he would not be so unkind!"

"I assure you, he would. His sense of duty is strong, and he can be very strict. I know to my cost, believe me."

Pamela looked at her. "Then I suppose it is as well that we did not tell him. Do you really mean to take me to your aunt?"

"Yes, indeed, but there is one thing you ought to know before I do, my dear. You did hear us say that her mama-in-law is a dowager countess, did you not? Widowed within the year?"

Pamela nodded, bewildered.

"I was a ninnyhammer not to have seen the connection at once, of course," Gwenyth said. "Do you not think the coincidence of two earls dying within the same span of time might have occasioned rather extraordinary remark within the *beau monde*?"

"Why, I suppose it would, but what is that to the purpose?"

"Only that my aunt's mama-in-law is the Countess of Lyford."

"Oh!" Pamela stared at her in dismay. "Then we must not think of going there. Why, Marcus—"

"You must face him sooner or later," Gwenyth pointed out, "and at Molesford Abbey you will have my support, my aunt's, and no doubt Lady Lyford's too. According to Auntie Wynne, the dowager says little in favor of the new earl. Moreover, you said your cousin had gone elsewhere on business, did you not?"

"But he will return," Pamela exclaimed, wringing her hands together, "and when he does—"

"When he does, we will simply explain the situation to him," Gwenyth said matter-of-factly.

Pamela let out a long breath. "Are you certain that your aunt will be willing to help us?"

"Of course she will. She will have any number of good ideas as to what must be done to foil your wicked cousin."

"Well, he is wicked," Pamela said, relaxing again and picking up her apple. "He has no business to be telling me what to do and saying that I cannot do what dear Papa promised, merely because it is inconvenient to him. We must show him that I can manage perfectly well on my own. Do you think perhaps your aunt might be induced to sponsor me, Gwen? Just for the Little Season, of course, for I should not expect her to present me, and Almack's will not be open, will it?"

"No, the subscription balls are held only in the spring, though I daresay we might attend concerts and lectures there."

"Oh, well, concerts are well enough, but I have had enough fusty lectures at school to last a lifetime, I promise you."

Chuckling, Gwenyth told her to drink up her tea. Then, a moment later, when another thought occurred to her, she said, "I say, did you bring any of your belongings with you?"

Learning that Pamela had managed to carry away no more than a nightdress and a few sundries in a small satchel, Gwenyth rang the bell and ordered her coach to take them to Leicester Square. "For you will never fit into my clothes, and you must have several gowns, at least. My dressmaker

will accommodate us at once, even if it means altering something she has already finished for someone else, and while
she is attending to that, we will shop for other necessities.
As we go, you may tell me all about the new Earl of Lyford.
If we are to fight him, I must know as much about him as
you can reveal to me.''

But, as she discovered in the coach, other than that Cousin
Marcus was a harsh and unfeeling man who wanted her
money, Pamela could divulge little more. "He went to school
here in England, I believe, but I know he has lived somewhere out of the country too, for he was away when Papa
died. In fact, he did not return until just before Christmas,
which was nearly a year afterward."

"Goodness, perhaps he lived in the American colonies for
a time like my brother Tallyn did. How old is he?"

"Oh, as old as your brother, I daresay, though he seems
older since he's always so stern and crotchety. But I do not
think it was America," she said doubtfully. "Did your
brother truly live there?" When Gwenyth nodded, Pamela
said, "He looks as though he could do almost anything, but
Marcus would no doubt have got scalped by one of their wild
Indians through trying to tell him how to manage his affairs."
Giving a dramatic shudder, she added, "He may very well
scalp me when he sees me."

Giving up in the belief that Pamela could hardly be
expected to view the man objectively, Gwenyth decided to
wait and judge him for herself after she had had the privilege
of meeting him. He sounded like a worthy opponent, if he
could make Pamela fear him even a little, as it seemed she
did. Miss Beckley's experiences with her papa having led
her to believe that all men would dance easily to her piping,
her cousin Marcus must have come as something of a shock.

Glancing at her friend as the carriage drew up before the
modiste's establishment, Gwenyth decided with a complacent
smile that she herself, having nothing to lose, would be much
better able to deal with the earl.

2

Rising early the next morning, the two young women took their leave of Berkeley Square, with amiable, modestly garbed Annie Gray sitting opposite them in the hired post chaise.

"Very kind of Lord Tallyn, I'm sure," the plump middle-aged abigail said approvingly as the chaise lurched forward over the cobbles. "Two boys and a full team. Very pleasant indeed."

"Joss arranged for the chaise before he left," Gwenyth told Pamela. "I fully expected us to have to lumber along in that old coach we used yesterday, because he is using his own chaise himself, of course. You can imagine my astonishment when Marwyn told me this morning that Joss had ordered a post chaise and four, as well as a pair of armed postilions, for us."

"How very kind he is to you," Pamela said. "How lucky you are to have an older brother to look out for you."

Gwenyth chuckled. "I have a notion, however, that this time he did it not for me but to impress you."

"Goodness," Pamela said, tossing her head, "I cannot think what you mean."

Annie looked sharply at Gwenyth and raised her eyebrows in the sort of silent query that would have been intolerable in any maidservant who had not known her mistress from birth.

Gwenyth laughed. "She sent him to grass, Annie. He tumbled just like every other doltish man Miss Beckley has ever met. Why do they do it, do you suppose?"

Hiding a smile, Annie pretended to examine Pamela, then shook her neatly capped head. "I cannot imagine, m'lady. So ugly as she is, so common in her manner, so—"

"Oh!" Pamela's squeal of indignation caused her companions to cover their ears in protest. "Gwen, make her stop!"

"Very well," Gwenyth said, laughing, "but if you expect me to sing your praises, you are out, for I shan't do any such thing. To my mind, you are as conceited as you ever were, and that is your greatest fault, next to your fascination for Drury Lane drama. Frankly, I must tell you I am still uncertain as to the truth of all you unfolded to me yesterday."

"Well, but . . ." She glanced uncertainly at Annie.

"We needn't discuss it now," Gwenyth said kindly, knowing that however much she might trust her abigail, Pamela would find it disconcerting to discuss personal matters before any servant. "Tell us instead how you left Miss Fletcher."

Pamela blinked. "On the common coach. I told you."

"Don't be blockish. You know perfectly well what I mean. Does she still wear flowers in her hair to Sunday dinner?"

Miss Beckley had no objection to telling her all the news of Miss Fletcher's academy for young ladies in Tunbridge Wells, and that pleasant topic and various tangents thereof occupied them pleasantly all the way to Maidenhead, where they left the main road to take a tree-lined private drive, drawing up shortly thereafter before an elegant three-story manor house nestled in a thick grove of trees. A few moments later, Annie having been borne off to visit friends in the nether regions, the two young women were escorted into Lady Meriel Davies' drawing room.

Their hostess sat comfortably before her hearth, becomingly attired in a cheerful pink morning gown, her matching cap trimmed with mint-colored ribbons and creamy, elegant lace. She greeted their entrance with undisguised pleasure, her smile setting dimples to dancing in a face grown plump from three previous confinements, as well as her present interesting condition.

"Goodness, Gwen," she exclaimed without rising, "what a marvelous surprise! Do you come to stay? Who is your lovely friend?" When Gwenyth had introduced Pamela, Meriel said apologetically, her gray-green eyes atwinkle, "Forgive me for remaining seated, Miss Beckley, but I have been threatened with dire consequences if I overtax my strength."

"Meri, what is it?" Gwenyth demanded, instantly concerned. "Are you ailing?"

Shooting her a glance brimful of amusement, Meriel said, "Not ailing, only in the family way, as you know perfectly well."

Gwenyth frowned. "But this is not your first confinement, and it is not like you to coddle yourself. What's amiss?"

"Nothing, I promise you, only I had the misfortune after a particularly tiresome day to swoon at Antony's feet just before he left for Oxfordshire, and although Dr. Knighton—hailed forth from London with scarcely time to snatch up his coat—pronounced me perfectly fit, the result is as you see. Antony made me promise to do nothing strenuous while he is away if I do not wish to be packed off to his Aunt Selena in Dorset. Since I do not care for Dorset or for Aunt Selena . . ." She spread her hands.

"But surely you ought not to be alone," Gwenyth said.

"Alone? With three children, their nursemaids, a butler, a housekeeper, and a dozen other servants in the house? You have no idea how much I sometimes yearn to *be* alone!"

The door flew open just then, and a towheaded little boy of five in nankeen breeches and a wrinkled blue coat dashed in, glancing over his shoulder as though he feared pursuit.

"Mama!" he exclaimed, dashing to Meriel's side. "Please, Mama, you must tell Daisy I am not to have runner beans for my dinner. You promised, Mama, not for a whole week, but Daisy says that's nonsense, that greens is good for me."

"They *are* good for you, Tony," his mother said gently, "but I will speak to Daisy. Do you turn about now and make a proper bow to my callers, if you please."

He whirled on his small heels and bounced his head forward, looking up almost immediately with his blue eyes dancing. "It is Auntie Gwen," he said. "Do you like my bow? I practiced."

Gwenyth's heart turned over as it always did when she beheld her little nephew, and she held out her arms to him, hugging him tightly when he ran to her. "Ah, Tony, you are a gentleman born," she said, delighting him, "but you did not greet my friend Miss Beckley."

Straightening, he turned and executed another quick bow. "I do one lady at a time," he explained. "How do you do, ma'am?"

A plump, red-faced maidservant appeared in the open doorway just then and gasped apologetically, "Beg pardon, m'lady, but I turned my back for just a twink and he disappeared. I've run down all them steps, and 'tis a wonder I didn't fall and break my neck. And his little sisters sitting proper at table like the precious angels they be. What this young scamp needs—"

"Yes, Daisy, but I did promise him he need not eat runner beans for a week. I ought to have told you, but I forgot. Do you take him back upstairs now, and he will behave himself just as he ought. Will you not, Tony, my lamb?"

"Yes, Mama, I always do," said her lamb with wide-eyed innocence as he placed his small hand in Daisy's. "We'll go up the stairs slowly, Daisy," he added consolingly, "so you can catch your breath again. You oughtn't to run. It ain't proper for a female to run. Ain't you always telling the girls?"

Hiding a smile at the nursemaid's disgruntled snort, Meriel turned back to her guests, but Gwenyth saw nothing to smile about. Barely waiting until the door had shut again behind the pair, she said, "Do you think that woman ought to be trusted with Tony, Meri? Will she really—"

"No, of course she will not," Meriel said, "though he must tempt her sometimes beyond all reason, for he is the veriest imp. Even Antony cannot always control him. The unfortunate thing is that he makes us laugh just when we ought to be scolding him. Davy was much the same, you'll remember.''

"Well, if you are certain that she will not mistreat him," Gwenyth said, unconvinced. "He may be a devil, but he is much more entertaining than the girls, however angelic they may be.''

"What you need, sister mine, is a dozen such little devils of your own," Meriel told her roundly. " 'Twould teach you to appreciate a woman like Daisy, if you were ever so fortunate as to find another willing to put up with such mischief.''

"As much as I should like to be surrounded by children," Gwenyth said firmly, "I am not ready to relinquish myself to any passing gentleman merely to get some.''

"So I should hope," Meriel said with another chuckle.

"You know what I mean." Gwenyth turned to Pamela. "My family wants nothing more than to see me wedded. Even Meriel, though she values her own independence, desires to see me riveted to some fool man who would order my every movement and thought.''

"Good gracious, Gwen," Meriel said, "surely you don't think Antony orders me about like that.''

"Observe," Gwenyth said, indicating her reclining position. "When Antony says, 'sit,' you sit, do you not?''

Meriel laughed. "You know very well that he rarely exerts himself to such purpose. Normally he is the soul of languor.''

"What about when he forced his way into your bed-chamber?''

Meriel smiled reminiscently. "The fact that you have to go back six years to find a second incident proves its own point, and poor Antony insisted that it took him the first two months of our marriage to recuperate from that exertion. He would have stayed in bed the whole time, too," she added with a wicked look, "had not other duties beckoned him forth. But you have not yet told me why you are here. I hope you mean to stay long enough at least to take a nuncheon with me.''

Gwenyth assured her that they would be glad of food.

"Joss has gone to Plas Tallyn, and we are on our way to Molesford. Though I know that any house in which Auntie Wynne resides will be prepared to receive guests at any hour, I believe it is as well to take no chance of starving."

"Gluttonous girl," her sister retorted. "You never change. Do you ring that bell, and I shall prove that I, too, am prepared to feed unexpected guests."

In response to a request from Pamela, Meriel entertained them with tales of her exploits in France until her butler announced that their meal had been served in the dining room. But when they had seated themselves at the table, she said after a long, thoughtful silence, "I have a notion, Gwen, that you have not completely explained this sudden visit of yours. Are you in the briars again?"

Glancing at the hovering servants, Gwenyth replied airily, "No, of course I am not. What a thing to suggest!"

"You are very glib," Meriel said with a searching look. "Is there something you are not telling me?" When Gwenyth remained silent, she glanced at Pamela, who blushed and looked away. Dismissing the servants with a wave of her hand, Meriel said firmly, "You had better tell me the whole, you know, and at once, before I imagine worse things than the truth."

Briefly Gwenyth considered prevaricating, but she knew it wouldn't answer. Meriel knew her too well, and besides, Pamela was looking as guilty now as a child caught out in mischief. Sighing, she told her sister everything.

When she had finished, Meriel said, "Did you explain this farrago to Joss? He might be able to help, you know."

"No, for he was in a great hurry to leave London." In response to a skeptical look, she added hastily, "I want to do this myself, Meri! I was bored to tears in town, but now I can have my own adventure—well, mine and Pamela's."

With a reminiscent gleam in her eye, Meriel gazed at her thoughtfully for a moment before she said, "Very well, then, but mind you do nothing to fling us all into the suds, Gwen. Antony may not exert himself often, but I'd as lief he not find out that I was the least party to this if you make a muck of it. His temper when he does exert himself is not pleasant to behold.''

Reaching out to squeeze her hand, Gwenyth said gratefully, ''I knew you'd understand. And you won't tell Joss, will you?''

''Good gracious, do you think me a ninnyhammer? I shall plead ignorance to everything if I see him before you do. No doubt you will have Miss Beckley's problems solved long before then anyway, and will be longing to leave Molesford. You can stay with us then if you like. Antony will be home in a sennight, I daresay, or a fortnight at most.''

''Did you say he went into Oxfordshire?'' Gwen said. ''Is that not unusual?'' Glancing at Pamela, she added for that young lady's benefit, ''He is something marvelous in the government, you see. Usually he doesn't say where he goes at all. Is this family business, Meri?''

''Pray, do not ask me to explain, for I know as little as you do, though I do know it is not family. I think he has been looking into something for the Customs and Excise Service.''

''In Oxfordshire?''

''Well, I thought that's what he said,'' Meriel said with a shrug. ''He doesn't tell me much, Gwen. You know that.''

''Secrets,'' Gwenyth said, wrinkling her nose. ''How dreadful to have to live with them all the time. I should hate it.''

''I know,'' Meriel agreed with a chuckle. She looked at Pamela. ''Gwen prefers gossip to secrets. She will no doubt grow up to be just like one of those eccentric Berry sisters.''

Pamela wrinkled her brow. ''Who?''

Meriel shot Gwenyth a teasing look, then said to Pamela, ''They are two elderly ladies who live near us in London. If I tell you that they extinguish the lamp over their door whenever they have had a surfeit of lady callers and will then admit only gentlemen, will that describe them sufficiently?''

''But how rude!'' Pamela said. ''Why, I should think no one at all would visit them when their lamp is out.''

''Oh,'' Meriel said, ''the gentlemen know they are always welcome, and the Berry sisters' receptions are very popular.''

Gwenyth sighed wistfully. "Those ladies may be a trifle peculiar, but they have exactly the freedom I hope to have myself one day. If only Joss would permit it, I should set up my own household at once and hold my own receptions. I am certain they would quickly grow to be as popular as any in London."

"But no lady can do such a thing alone," Pamela protested. "And surely, whatever you say, you must wish to marry a handsome, titled gentleman and have his children and look after his household. That is every lady's sweetest dream, is it not?"

"Not Gwen's," said Meriel with an amused look at her sister, who was grimacing as though she were in pain. "But," she added more briskly, "you had better be thinking about departing soon. You will want to allow plenty of time to deal with accidents or other delays on the road."

They agreed, but when they had collected Annie and were in the front hall ready to leave, Gwenyth looked carefully at Meriel. "Are you sure you would not rather we stay a few days?"

"Don't fret about me," Meriel said, patting her arm. "I enjoy what little solitude I can steal."

Having not considered the matter in that light, Gwenyth nodded slowly. "If you are quite certain . . ."

"Off with you," Meriel commanded, laughing, "and give my love to Auntie Wynne and the countess."

The chaise was soon off, back to the main road, then on through Maidenhead Thicket and Hare Hatch to Twyford. Five miles more found them in Reading, the county town of Berkshire, known in better times for its considerable trade in corn and flour, for it was here the River Kennet met the Thames. Both were alive with traffic, including not only a vast number of mill barges carrying barrels of wheat or sacks of flour, but also barges laden with lumber, hogsheads of ale, and less easily identifiable crates, barrels, sacks, boxes, and bales. Swimming alongside many of them, oblivious to the bustle, were a number of graceful white swans and other, less elegant waterfowl.

"Goodness," Gwenyth said, "I recently heard Antony tell Joss that we have begun receiving shipments of grain from India to alleviate the English shortage, but I didn't think the rivers would be so busy again already. How nice if everyone can soon have bread again without having to pay a small fortune for it."

"Does bread cost a fortune?" Pamela asked. "I shouldn't think most people would be able to pay so much."

"No, of course they cannot," Gwenyth said. "Did you learn nothing at school, Pamela? The war has sadly depleted our grain supply, you know, and many people must go without."

"Well, I did not find history and such subjects amusing," Pamela said, lifting her chin. "They were never so diverting as drawing and music, so of course one paid less heed to them."

With a sigh, Gwenyth drew her companions' attention to the Chiltern Hills rising in the eastern distance. The chaise left the main road to travel parallel to the south bank of the Thames, though not by any means alongside it. The property between road and river being occupied by magnificent mansions and estates of men in power in London, it was not, in fact, until two hours later, when they reached the town of Pangbourne near the Goring Gap, that they were able to gain a direct view of the Thames and watch a barge being towed upriver through a pound lock. From the road, the operation looked like a veritable tangle of horses, men, and cables, but so experienced were those in attendance that the barge moved nearly as swiftly up the river as the chaise did through the congested streets of the town.

Once their vehicle was free of town traffic, Gwenyth said on a note of anticipation, "Not far now. I hope they are not vexed with us for failing to send word. I never thought to do so."

Pamela said, " 'Tis too late to worry about that now. Surely your aunt will not turn us from the door."

"No, but if you will recall, it is not precisely her door, and in your cousin's absence, the ancient dowager may decide to take a pet if she is as crotchety as Auntie Wynne says she is.''

Grimacing, Annie Gray said, ''You'd best stop calling the countess 'the ancient dowager' in that heedless fashion if you wish to retain a place in her good graces. She won't thank you if even the word 'dowager' slips from your lips. Nor will Lady Cadogan, I'm thinking.''

''But if Marcus's grandmama is a widow,'' Pamela said reasonably, ''surely she is likewise a dowager.''

''But she needn't be called so if she doesn't wish to be,'' Gwenyth replied. ''Custom permits her to retain her previous title so long as her husband's heir remains unmarried. And, as you pointed out earlier, your cousin has not yet taken a wife.''

Pamela bit her lower lip but said nothing, and Gwenyth returned her attention to the road ahead.

''Auntie Wynne has described the abbey to me any number of times,'' she said. ''The property occupies two full miles and more of the riverbank, I believe, and she said it lies no more than three miles from Pangbourne.'' Several moments of silence passed before she said in a voice of satisfaction, ''That high wall just ahead with the thick trees showing beyond it all the way to the river—I'll wager my best gown that that is Molesford Abbey.''

Pamela had been looking increasingly nervous for some time, and after the carriage had rattled along for several minutes more, she said in a small voice, ''Perhaps we are making a dreadful mistake, Gwen. Perhaps we ought to go back to Maidenhead to look after your sister instead. Marcus would never find me there, and truly, I do not wish to see him.''

''Nonsense,'' Gwenyth said, glancing at Annie to see that she had turned her attention to the road and was carefully pretending not to listen. ''It is no use fidgeting yourself, Pamela. You know that Miss Fletcher must have communicated with him—''

''But that is just the point! Don't you see, he will already be out of temper. Would it not be better to stay away for a time at least, long enough for him to . . . to . . .''

"To what? Call out the Bow Street Runners?"

"Oh, he wouldn't!" Pamela squeaked. "Oh, my goodness, I never thought about such a possibility as that!"

"Well, he won't have done so yet," Gwenyth said practically, "but it will do you no good to put off meeting with him, so you might as well make up your mind at once to do so."

"But I can't," Pamela wailed. "Call to the postboys, Gwen, please. I want to go back to London right now."

"Too late," Gwenyth said grimly as the chaise drew to a halt before a pair of tall iron gates. The lead postboy spoke to the lodgekeeper, and a moment later the gates were opened and they swept on, up a long, winding, floral-bordered gravel drive to the house, a great Carolean mansion built of mellow brick, its front entrance designed in the Palladian style with a tall pediment carried on slender Ionic columns above broad white marble steps.

"It doesn't look like an abbey," Pamela said, peering out the window anxiously. "Are you sure this is Molesford, Gwen?"

"I'm sure. It was used to be a Cistercian abbey, my aunt told me, but I believe the original building was demolished by a Puritan earl who built this house, or the better part anyway. Auntie Wynne was used to speak of it often, when she thought she would one day be mistress here. Only then my Uncle Cadogan died before his papa did, so she is destined to remain a viscountess, which is a constant sorrow to her."

"What if Marcus is here, after all?" Pamela said desperately, looking truly frightened at last.

"We cannot turn back," Gwenyth said firmly. "It is four o'clock now and would be midnight before we got back to London."

There was no time for more debate, for the front doors of the house had been flung wide and two liveried footmen were hurrying down the steps to meet the chaise. The near-side door was opened and the steps let down. Within moments the three occupants stood upon the gravel drive.

"I am Lady Gwenyth Traherne," Gwenyth said to the footman who had assisted her. "Lady Cadogan is my aunt."

The footman bowed. "Your gear and your woman will be taken up immediate, m'lady, and Mr. Frythorpe will announce you to Lady Cadogan. Lady Lyford is not receiving, but no doubt she will order supper put back to give you time to refresh yourselves after your journey." Inside the vast high-ceilinged stair hall, he turned them over to the butler, who informed them that Lady Cadogan would receive them in the Chinese drawing room.

Following him up the wide spiral staircase, Gwenyth found herself fascinated and a little apprehensive, for although the white stairs were obviously fastened to the walls of the hall and soared up four stories to the top of the house, she could discern no visible means of proper support. It was as though each step had simply been stuck end-on to the wall. The ornate openwork wrought-iron banister added to the illusion of swooping flight.

At the second-floor landing, they turned down a long arched corridor between a wall solid with portraits and another boasting tall red-velvet-draped windows that overlooked a large central courtyard. At the end of the corridor, a pair of white-painted doors opened into one of the most amazing rooms Gwenyth had ever seen. It was with difficulty, when the butler announced their names, that she dragged her gaze from the elaborate hand-painted wallpaper, seemingly alive with trees, birds, dragons, and butterflies, across the equally busy, brightly colored carpeting to the lady occuping one of a pair of Chinese Chippendale chairs flanking a round lacquered table in the center of the room.

Lady Cadogan, approaching her sixties, no longer made any attempt to cover the bits of white and gray that peppered her auburn locks. She was thin now, rather than slender, and her fingers showed knobby traces of the rheumatism that plagued her from time to time, but Gwenyth knew they still moved as quickly as ever when she knitted or plied her needle to a tambour frame such as the one that, at the moment, was held motionless above her lap while she stared in surprise at the newcomers.

"Merciful heavens, Gwenyth," she said in her strident but carefully cultivated tones the moment the butler fell silent, "what new start is this?"

Chuckling, Gwenyth hurried forward to hug her, then stepped back to introduce Pamela, adding, "I do hope you and the countess can find it in your hearts to forgive this impulsive intrusion. I confess I even failed to remember until the footman mentioned putting supper back that you would be keeping country hours."

"Pish tush," retorted Lady Cadogan. "You are most welcome, my dear, and your friend as well. Frythorpe will inform Almeria's cook, a most accommodating man despite his being French, and all will be well." With an imperious gesture she dismissed the butler.

Taking a seat and motioning Pamela to another, Gwenyth said, "The countess's footman told us that she is not receiving. I hope she is not indisposed."

"No, only primping," Lady Cadogan replied. "Invited a man to dine, so she's gilding the lily as best she might. You won't be as entertained as you might otherwise be, however, for she don't consider Sir Spenser Newton suitable husband material."

Pamela exclaimed, "But, ma'am, I am not on the lookout for a husband yet, and nor is Gwen!"

"You?" Lady Cadogan regarded her with a cool, appraising look, then relaxed and said with a chuckle, "Good gracious, child, I wasn't thinking of you. Almeria considers her own need far greater than that of any younger woman, I promise you."

Gwenyth smiled. "Surely you jest, ma'am. She is still in mourning, is she not, or half-mourning, at least?"

Lady Cadogan clicked her tongue. "She hasn't let a little thing like that stop her. What she's looking for is some ailing, wealthy gentleman stuck in a Bath chair, and a handy cliff to tip him over the moment she is safely riveted to him and can claim a second widow's portion or more. But never mind that,'' she went on, clearly enjoying the astonished looks on their faces. "You will wish to tidy yourselves before we dine. Pull the bell.''

A moment later, as they stood to follow the butler from the room, Pamela whispered urgently, "Gwen, what about—"

"Oh, yes," Gwenyth said calmly, turning back to her aunt. "Miss Beckley has come in search of Lyford, ma'am, on a matter of private business. He is her guardian, you see. Have we perhaps been so fortunate as to find him at home?"

"Oh, dear, no," Lady Cadogan said, eyeing Pamela with undisguised curiosity. "He has gone to London to confer with someone at Bow Street, I believe, but—"

"Bow Street!" both young women exclaimed at once.

"Well, yes," Lady Cadogan said with a distasteful grimace and a pointed look at the hovering butler, "but you needn't say anything to Almeria if you please, for she thinks he has merely gone to town to look into some new, tiresome matter of probate.''

"But why Bow Street?" Gwenyth did not dare look at Pamela.

Lady Cadogan was reluctant to elucidate, but after a small silence she said, "There is nothing in it, I daresay, and we will find it was an accident after all, but there has been some unpleasantness over it, so Lyford thought it best—"

"Aunt, please," Gwenyth begged, "what happened?"

"Lyford's steward died rather mysteriously, I'm afraid, and people hereabouts are spouting nonsense about a treasure they say he discovered shortly before his death. They think the poor man was murdered. Foolishness, of course, but Lyford decided it was best to confront the thing directly. In any event, it don't do to refine too much upon it, I daresay.''

When Pamela breathed an audible sigh of relief, Lady Cadogan's eyes narrowed suddenly and speculatively. Although she said nothing further, she shot Gwenyth a shrewd look that promised a private discussion in the not distant future.

It could not come at once, however, for they had to prepare

themselves for dinner. They did so in record time, and in the dining room, thirty minutes later, they met the countess at last, discovering to their surprise that she didn't look ancient at all. In fact, despite the cane she carried, she managed to hide her seventy-eight years very well, for her skin was still soft, and her slight plumpness was becoming, giving her a rounded, youthful appearance. She was much more interested in Sir Spenser Newton, however, than in the two young women; consequently, Gwenyth found it unnecessary to explain more than that they had traveled into Berkshire in order to make a change from the city.

Throughout the meal, Sir Spenser, an elderly gentleman of dandified habits, gazed approvingly upon Pamela, but upon Gwenyth with some disfavor, particularly when she accepted a second generous helping of tarragon chicken from the footman. Raising his quizzing glass then, the old gentleman peered nearsightedly through it as he said, "Forgive me, Lady Gwenyth, but one so naturally associates female softness and delicacy with a correspondent delicacy of constitution that it rather startles one when a young woman shows such extraordinary appetite."

"Nonsense, Newton," declared a new and much deeper voice from the shadows of the threshold, drawing everyone's attention to the tall broad-shouldered figure standing there. "Not all men recoil from healthy young females, I promise you."

With a squeal of horror and a resounding clatter of metal against china, Pamela dropped her fork and clasped her hands together at her bosom. "M-Marcus!"

3

Lady Lyford blinked myopic blue eyes at the newcomer. "You're back," she said flatly. "Set another place for his lordship, Frythorpe." Then she added in the same colorless tone, "Not only do you show your poor manners by contradicting Spenser, Marcus, but he is perfectly right. Though good health may well be one of the greatest blessings of life, one ought never to flaunt it, or make a boast of it, or discuss it at all, for that matter. One simply enjoys it in grateful ladylike silence."

Sir Spenser lowered his quizzing glass, nodded, and said with pontifical approval, "Very true, Almeria."

Lyford stepped forward from the shadow of the doorway, revealing himself more clearly as he said on a note of irony, "I will accept your superior knowledge of the subject, Grandmother."

Gwenyth stared, fascinated, for Lyford, like his grandmama, was nothing like what she had imagined. She had expected to find just another ordinary man, but he stood as tall as her brother-in-law Antony, who was very large indeed, and Lyford's shoulders were even wider than Tallyn's. His hair was so black it glinted with silver highlights in the glow cast by the chandelier above the table, and at first his eyes looked black too, until a gleam of light showed them to be a deep blue instead. He bore not the least hint of a man of fashion, for he wore riding dress, and his coat was cut so loosely as to seem at first that it must be someone else's. Even his buckskin breeches were loose-fitting, though not so much so that they hid the hard muscles in his thighs. Only his snow-white neckcloth and his boots, polished to perfection, showed any sign of particular care.

"Leave the man be, Almeria," Lady Cadogan interjected when the countess demanded to know why the earl had stayed away for so long. "He must be wanting his dinner."

Sir Spenser coughed delicately. "Wants to change his dress first, I expect."

Lyford glanced at him, his face expressionless. "I've ordered a tray sent to my library, I'm afraid, for I've a number of letters to write. I'd intended to return yesterday, but"—his glance, hardening noticeably, shifted to Pamela, who still watched him in wide-eyed shock—"other matters requiring my attention were drawn to my notice. Pamela, you will oblige me by coming to me when you have finished your meal."

Her eyes grew even wider, and she nibbled her lower lip. Then, as he turned to leave, she stammered, "M-Marcus, please, you must—" The sternness of his expression when he turned back stopped her mid-sentence. She gulped, visibly.

When he was certain that she would not continue, he said gently, "Do not be all night about it, if you please. I have a number of things I want to say to you."

"Lyford is her guardian, you see," Lady Cadogan explained in an audible aside to Sir Spenser.

"Good gracious," exclaimed Lady Lyford. "Of course—Beckley! Why did I not recall the name at once, I wonder? Marcus's mother was a Beckley, was she not?"

"She was my father's sister, ma'am," Pamela said, throwing another anxious glance at Lyford, who had not yet left the room.

"Then you are certainly the schoolgirl to whom Marcus stands guardian," declared Lady Lyford on a note of satisfaction, having at last made the final connection for herself. "But surely," she added before Pamela could speak, "you are too old for school, my gel. You look to be twenty at least."

"Only just nearing eighteen, ma'am, but"—sensing allies

at hand, she shot a defiant look at Lyford—"definitely too old to be kept in school."

"That remains to be seen," he said. "Don't dawdle. I will be waiting for you." He turned and left the room, at which point Pamela's bravado deserted her completely, and she looked quickly down at her plate.

Lady Lyford, turning to Sir Spenser, went on to describe in exact detail the relationship of Pamela to Lyford, and thus to herself and to her late husband. Under cover of that steady discourse, Gwenyth watched as Pamela struggled to regain her composure. When it looked like being a losing battle, she decided to take a hand, thinking it would not do to have the younger girl's behavior elicit more revealing questions from the countess or her gentleman friend.

"Pamela," she said gently at the first lull in Lady Lyford's monologue, "you have been fighting fatigue all day long, and now you look ready to drop. Perhaps you will forgive us, ma'am," she added, looking at the countess, "if I take Miss Beckley up to her bedchamber now and see her quietly settled."

Lady Lyford glanced at Pamela. "She does look interestingly pale, to be sure, but first you must take her to Marcus. He will be vastly displeased if she just slips off to bed, which will make everyone uncomfortable. But, Gwenyth, I trust you won't desert us too, for I'd hoped to take advantage of your presence, and Sir Spenser's, for a rubber of whist before I retire."

"I shall be happy to play, ma'am," Gwenyth said, "as soon as Pamela has spoken with her cousin and I see her tucked up in her bed." Glancing at her aunt and noting that the speculative gleam had returned to that lady's eyes, she stood up and laid her hand upon Pamela's arm. "Come, dear, you must get some rest."

Pamela stiffened, and it seemed for a moment that she would resist, but when Gwenyth's hand tightened, she sighed and said, "Very well, but this is not at all what I wished for, you know."

Before Lady Lyford or anyone else could demand to know

what Pamela meant by such a statement, Gwenyth whisked her out of the room. It was necessary to ask one of the footmen to show them the way to his lordship's bookroom in the east wing, but when the proper door was indicated, Gwenyth dismissed the man, assuring him that there was no need to announce them.

"Oh, Gwen," Pamela said, dissolving into tears, "I cannot go in there. I simply cannot. He will send you away, and then he will . . . Oh, gracious, I do not know what he will do. But he is so angry. You could see that much. Anyone could. And he is so big. I had forgotten how big! Oh, how did he know I was here? He will make me do what he wants me to do, and I shan't be able to stop him. I wish we hadn't come!"

"I will stop him," Gwenyth said tartly. "Now, no vapors, Pamela, and do not argue with me. He will hear you, and then matters will go precisely as you have predicted. If I can talk to him first, perhaps I can throw a rub in his way." Glancing swiftly around the hall in which they stood, she indicated a door across the way. "Do you go in there and wait for me."

"What is in there?"

"Well, how should I know, for pity's sake? Just go in there and wait. He can't eat me. Indeed, he has no authority over me, so even if he chooses to express his feelings, that is the most he can do, and I have learned to manage Joss, after all. Heaven knows he has a terrible temper and is perfectly capable of reacting violently when one least expects him to do so, but even Joss would not lay hands on a woman to whom he is unrelated, so I've nothing to fear from Lyford. Just leave him to me."

Pamela insisted that Gwenyth accompany her into the room, to be certain that it was empty and to light the lamps so that she would not be left sitting in the dark. Though Gwenyth did so gladly, once she returned to the hall, she found herself standing in some trepidation before the bookroom door, remembering his lordship's size and undoubted power. Assuring herself that what she was doing was not the least bit unusual or dangerous, that she was merely helping a friend in need, she squared her shoulders and opened the door.

Lyford looked up expectantly from the letter he was writing at the large lamp-lit leather-topped desk set at an angle to the fireplace, where a healthy fire crackled, sending flames leaping high, with an occasional noisy burst of sparks. When Gwenyth entered and shut the door behind her, the earl put down his pen and got to his feet with a frown.

"Where is my cousin, Lady Gwenyth?"

"You know my name?" she said, remembering that during his brief visit to the dining room, no introductions had been made.

"Miss Fletcher suggested that Pamela would go to you," he explained, "and it was a simple matter to learn from your butler that you had come here. I suppose I must thank you for restoring her to my care, but I had rather you had returned her to school."

"There was no point to that, sir," Gwenyth said steadily. "Your plan will not answer, you know. 'Twould cause a dreadful scandal, for too many people will know your purpose."

His eyebrows lifted in puzzlement. "Plan? Purpose?"

Gwenyth stepped lightly to a tapestry armchair near his desk and sat down. "Pray, sir, do not attempt to prevaricate. It does not become you. Moreover, Pamela has told me everything."

As he slowly took his seat, she looked directly into his eyes, challenging him, and when he did not attempt to look away, but steadily returned her gaze, her breath caught sharply in her throat. She had never seen eyes of so dark a blue, nor had she ever felt so strong a physical response from her body to a simple exchange of looks. Not only was it difficult to breathe, but her mouth was dry and her hands felt damp upon the mahogany arms of her chair. She wished he would speak, though she suddenly experienced a thrill of fear at what he might choose to say to her. Surreptitiously she moved her hands to her lap, attempting to pat them dry on her skirt.

For a moment Lyford looked as stunned as she felt, but he did not take his gaze from hers. Then his lips twitched a little, as though he might smile.

Gwenyth's attention was drawn by the tiny movement, and when she realized that she was staring at his mouth, thinking only how full his lower lip was and how soft it must be, her cheeks grew hot. What it must feel like when he . . . With a start, she said sharply, "Have you nothing to say for yourself, sir?"

His mouth twisted then into a wry grimace. "I can scarcely defend myself when I know not the charge, my lady. Perhaps you would care to speak more to the point. What is this 'everything' of which I stand accused?"

She spoke quickly—too quickly. "You have kept poor Pamela incarcerated at Miss Fletcher's for no purpose other than to suit your own convenience. Do you dare to deny the fact that she is a considerable heiress?"

"Not at all. 'Considerable' would be an apt description."

The calm reply steadied her, gave her confidence. "Do you dare deny that the estate you inherited is heavily encumbered?"

His expression changed then, dramatically, and Gwenyth shivered at both its harshness and the glint of steel in his eyes. He folded his hands on the desk, but she did not believe for a moment that the gesture was a casual one; it was as though each hand restrained the other in order to keep him from strangling her. She found that she could not look away from them; neither could she speak or swallow.

He said softly, "I do not believe that my affairs are any concern of yours, Lady Gwenyth, so we will not continue this discussion. It is of no use for you to champion Pamela, in any event. She has disobeyed me, and she will return to school because it is my considered opinion that it is the safest place for her to be until I can turn my attention from more important matters to provide for her future."

Goaded by the note of dismissal in his voice, Gwenyth said, "Until you can arrange to marry her yourself, you mean."

He stiffened. "Until what?"

Determined not to let him frighten her more than he already had, she said firmly, "You heard me, sir, and you need not think that I shall remain silent on the subject if you attempt such an odious stratagem. I move in the very best circles, as I am sure you must know, and I promise you that if you try to force that poor young woman to marry you, I will see your name trampled in the mud. I can do it, Lyford. She is not for the likes of you."

More than anything just then did she want to look away from him, to fix her eyes upon nothing more dangerous than the brass oil lamp aglow on his desk, but she would not give him that satisfaction. She forced herself to look directly at him, meeting the dark and angry glare, commanding her body to behave itself no matter how fierce he became.

To her astonishment, the hard line of his mouth softened and his eyes began to twinkle. "Pamela is scarcely the wife I would choose for myself," he said, his amusement audible in his voice. "I do not customarily dangle after self-centered schoolgirls, Lady Gwenyth. Indeed, you are much more the sort of woman I should look for to warm my bed and to care for me in my dotage."

She stood up swiftly, indignantly, and stamped her foot. "I should be much more likely to snatch your hair from your scalp, sir, than to warm your bed. Don't you dare to make mock of me!"

"Acquit me," he said, also rising, albeit with less haste, and stepping around his desk to confront her. "I should much rather make love to you than mock you."

"Stand where you are, my lord," Gwenyth said, white-faced with anger. "If you cannot discuss Pamela's situation with me without spouting nonsense, I shall take my leave of you."

He moved nearer, saying softly, "If I send Pamela back to school, will you have to go away too?"

"Well, of course . . ." The thought of leaving Molesford

Abbey was suddenly, despite her anger, a most unappealing one. Collecting herself, she repeated firmly, "Of course I would go. I only came with Pamela." Then, realizing that he was almost upon her, she swallowed her pride and said quickly, "Please, sir, stay where you are. You are beginning to frighten me."

He stopped at once, with a rueful grimace. "I confess, I meant to do so, but only a little. Whatever were you thinking of to come in here alone? You don't know me. Indeed, from the sound of it, you believe me to be some sort of villainous beast. Yet you traipse unchaperoned into my lair. Are you mad?"

Ignoring the strange feeling of disappointment that colored her relief when he stopped moving toward her, Gwenyth said, "Not mad, sir, only angry and concerned for Pamela. Think how you would have felt had your people left you to kick your heels at school once you were old enough to leave. Not that you would have stayed, of course." She sighed. "Everything is different for men."

"No," he agreed thoughtfully, "I would not have stayed. Fortunately, however, the thought of leaving me at Winchester never occurred to my uncle. He had other use for me."

"Your uncle? Not your father?"

"My father died when I was small. I scarcely knew him. My Uncle Henry raised me, along with his son, my cousin Jared, who was a year ahead of me at school."

"But your uncle did not become the earl, so you must be from the senior branch." She bit her lip, then looked up at him again with an apologetic smile. "Forgive my curiosity, sir, but you must know that I have lived nearly half my life hearing my aunt bemoan her fate. When my Uncle Cadogan died, the fact that he had predeceased his papa made her so furious that she never told us he had even one brother, let alone two of them. Somehow I grew up believing that only the old earl was left."

"Your uncle actually had four brothers and two sisters," Lyford said, smiling back at her. "My father was Grandfather's fourth son, so I never expected to inherit the title; but Cadogan had no children, Edward and his two sons died of the typhus two years ago, and my Uncle Stephen, who was a soldier, waited until he was nearly fifty to wed. Then, before producing an heir, he fell ill of a fever and died six months before Grandfather did. My father, James, was next, so when it was certain that Uncle Stephen's wife was not in a family way, everything came to me, which was a shock, since I scarcely knew this place. My cousin Jared spent more time at Molesford than I ever did. I didn't get on as well as he did with the old man, I'm afraid.''

"I'm sorry."

"Don't be. I didn't tell you all that in order to gain your sympathy." His expression hardened. "Where is Pamela? Despite her daring escape from Miss Fletcher, I doubt she will have had the temerity to defy me here in my own house.''

"No, of course she did not. She is in the room opposite to this one, probably quaking in her shoes.''

"As well she should be. She had no business to leave school without permission. If she was unhappy there, she had only to tell me so. She never did.''

"No doubt you frightened her so that she was unable to confide in you," Gwenyth told him, looking him in the eye again and then wishing she hadn't done so foolish a thing. How, she wondered, could a man's eyes express sternness and, at the same time, such audacious desire? Her skin glowed from the warmth of that look. This would never do. But she could not look away.

He said gently, "Do you honestly think I frightened her?"

"Yes, I do.'' She licked suddenly dry lips.

"Do I frighten you?" His voice was caressing now, and he took one last step toward her, his left hand moving to touch her shoulder. His touch was light, but the warmth of his fingers through the thin puffed sleeve of her dress stirred unfamiliar sensations throughout her body.

Gathering her wits, though not without effort, she forced herself to speak calmly and with dignity. "Of course you do not frighten me, Lyford, but I am Welsh, not English.''

Stepping beyond his reach, she turned abruptly toward the fireplace and so did not immediately see the twinkle that leapt to his eyes.

"Are Welshwomen so much more dauntless, then?" he asked, folding his arms across his chest as he turned to watch her.

Glancing over her shoulder, she again had the feeling that his posture was one of self-restraint. Coupled with the twinkle, however, instead of frightening her, that awareness gave her a sense of her own power. Lifting her chin, she said, "We Welsh are not trained to be so submissive as our English cousins."

He raised his eyebrows. "Indeed?"

"Certainly," Gwenyth said, shutting her eyes to an instant mental vision of her domineering elder brother. "North Wales is neither so civilized nor so tame as England, sir, and our women are not tamed easily either. My sister Meriel," she went on quickly as he unfolded his arms and took another step toward her, "traveled into France alone when she was little more than my age. We learned to look after ourselves in a most unforgiving environment, Lyford, so I have no reason to fear any mere man."

He was very close to her again, and her last words came out less confidently, sounding more as though she were trying to convince herself than him. Lyford smiled and looked down the length of himself, forcing her gaze to follow his. "I am not generally thought of as 'mere,' you know."

"N-no, sir," she agreed, refusing to look up at his face and hating herself for the stammer. He was not mere. "*Mere*" was a very poor word to describe him. The top of her head was not quite level with his shoulder, but it was not his height so much as his breadth that made her feel small next to him. If he were to put his arms around her, she told herself, she would feel swallowed up by his body. That thought, plus the awareness deep within that she would very much like to experience that feeling, brought a brilliant flush to her cheeks.

Lyford chuckled, low and deep in his throat. "Perhaps

if you were to look up, ma'am, you would be spared your blushes, though I promise you they are most becoming.''

Realizing where on his splendid anatomy she had allowed her gaze to linger, Gwenyth gasped and grew beet red, looking up so quickly that she thought it a wonder her neck didn't snap. It was no comfort to find him grinning broadly at her.

He said, chuckling, "I don't mind in the least, Lady Gwenyth. Look your fill.''

Anger replaced embarrassment. "You are unsufferable, sir. To speak in such a fashion to a gently nurtured female is both unmannerly and crude. You ought to think shame to yourself.''

"Ah, but you have just explained that you are not gently nurtured, so I thought you would not mind. However,'' he added quickly when her lips tightened in fury, "it would perhaps be as well if we were to find Pamela now.''

Recalled to her duty, Gwenyth replied through clenched teeth, "It is to be hoped that she has not expired from terror.''

"More likely she has fallen asleep,'' he said dryly.

As she swept past him, Gwenyth found herself hoping fervently that he would not prove to be right. Her tenuous composure would not withstand gloating, and she was certain Lyford was a man who, given the least cause, would gloat.

Fortunately, Pamela was awake when they entered. "Gwen! M-Marcus,'' she cried, scrambling up from her chair. Then, running to Gwenyth, she clutched at her arm, keeping Gwenyth's body between herself and the earl, who had stopped to regard her sternly from just inside the open door. Peeping past her protector at him, she said, "Oh, Gwen, what is he going to do?''

As Gwenyth gently detached herself from Pamela's clutches, she realized that she had no idea what Lyford meant to do. A swift echo of their conversation sped through her mind, and she saw at once that they had scarcely discussed Pamela at all after the first two moments. Not that she hadn't tried, but his attention, to that subject at least, had been emphemeral. Indeed, he had seemed quite unable to focus upon Pamela. Glancing back at him, she saw his warm but mocking smile and gritted her teeth.

"I don't know what he means to do," she said when he made no effort to answer for her, "but I do not think he will send you back to Miss Fletcher."

"He cannot!" Still standing close to her, as though to take strength from her presence, Pamela added defiantly, "I wouldn't go. I won't!" She glared at the earl. "You cannot make me!"

"Can I not?" he asked in the gentle tone that Gwenyth had already come to recognize as a danger signal.

Pamela evidently recognized it too, for her defiant air collapsed and she looked at him more coaxingly. "Please, Marcus, say you will not make me go. I can stay here, and truly I will be no trouble. I can help Gwen's aunt and your grandmama, and Gwen herself will stay to bear me company, so I shan't be bored, and I won't even plague you to take me to London—"

"Much good that would do you," he murmured.

"No," she agreed, "for Gwen told me that even the Italian opera has closed for the summer, so there would be nothing much to do there now. But perhaps, if Lady Cadogan will agree to sponsor me—and I am sure I cannot think why she would not—you will agree to let me take part in the Little Season, and—"

"I have not said I will not send you back," he reminded her. "You do not deserve to be rewarded for what you have done."

Gwenyth said sharply, "Do not tease her, sir. You know very well that you have decided to let her stay."

"Have I?" He quirked an eyebrow. "I have not said so."

She knew that he had decided. She did not know how she knew, but she knew, and she was not going to allow him to play games with them. "You have said little to the purpose at all," she said crisply, "but I believe that had you intended to insist upon her return to Miss Fletcher's, you'd have made your position adamantly clear long before now. That you have not done so can only mean that you intend to let her stay.''

''How well you seem to know me,'' he said with a mocking twist of his mouth, ''and on such short acquaintance, too.''

''Do you deny what I say, Lyford?''

He shrugged. ''I have denied nothing you have said tonight, nor shall I begin now. Despite what you or my grandmother may think of my manners, I was raised a gentleman and rarely contradict a lady's word. Pamela may stay as long as she behaves herself, enacts me no tragedies, and does not plague me with foolish demands.'' With that, he turned on his heel and left the room.

Pamela flung herself joyously into the astonished Gwenyth's arms. ''Oh, you did it! I didn't think you could, and I don't know how you did, but you did. Oh, how did you convince him, Gwen? I was certain he meant to send me back.'' Straightening, she clasped her hands to her bosom. ''I couldn't think how to stop him! I was persuaded there would be nothing for it but for me to run away again to someone else, somewhere where he could not find me so easily.''

Without realizing she meant to do such a thing, Gwenyth grabbed her by the shoulders and gave her a hard shake, saying furiously, ''Put that notion straight out of your head at once, Pamela Beckley. What you did in running away—and on a common coach, at that—was extremely foolish and dangerous! Anything might have happened. 'Tis only your excellent good fortune that nothing did. The truth of the matter is that you deserve to be soundly thrashed, and if your idiotish guardian were attending to his duty, that is precisely what he would do!''

Pamela stared at her in dismay, her eyes like saucers beneath their thick lashes. ''You w-want Marcus to b-beat me?''

With an impatient gesture Gwenyth snatched her hands from Pamela's shoulders and turned away, only to turn back again at once in remorse. ''No, I do not want him to beat you. I don't know what I was saying, Pamela, for there is naught to be gained now by taking you to task. I ought only to be pleased that he has seen the sense of allowing you to remain at Molesford."

"He did not say about the Little Season, though, did he?"

Taking a deep breath to ease her exasperation, Gwenyth let it out again before saying evenly, "No, he did not."

"Then we shall have to devise a scheme to convince him of its being a good thing," Pamela said with a musing frown.

Sternly repressing an urge to slap her, Gwenyth said in a tight voice, "I am persuaded that right now you ought to go to bed. It has been a long day for both of us."

"Oh, but I am not at all tired now," Pamela said sunnily. "Would you not prefer that I go back with you to the drawing room? You will recall that the countess expressed a desire for you to make a fourth at her whist table."

"You," Gwenyth said, turning her by the shoulders and giving her a push toward the door, "are going to bed because I told the countess you were, and if you go back into the drawing room now, she and Sir Spenser will want to know the reason for your sudden burst of energy. Since I have no desire to be party to that conversation or any like it, you will do precisely as I tell you, or, by heaven, I will return to London first thing tomorrow."

Looking back as she was propelled across the threshold into the hall, Pamela said in astonishment, "Goodness, Gwen, I had forgotten that you can be so fierce."

"Then it would behoove you to remember it, my girl, for I am rapidly losing all patience with you."

"Oh, please don't be angry," Pamela begged, turning to face her. "I'll be good, I promise. Say you aren't angry with me anymore and that you won't go to London. Please, Gwen."

She looked like a puppy who had been scolded, and Gwenyth, no match for the look, shook her head in defeat. "Very well, but no more tricks."

"Oh," Pamela said earnestly, "I wouldn't!" Obedient

now, she let Gwenyth take her to her bedchamber and ring for the chambermaid assigned to assist her.

Free at last to return to the drawing room, Gwenyth did so with the aid of a friendly footman; but, once there, she was not at all disappointed to discover that the countess, seated at the central table opposite Sir Spenser, had lost interest in whist.

Smiling at Gwenyth, she said, "You were such a time that we decided to play piquet instead. Perhaps you will like to read or attend to your needlework, as Wynnefreda is forever doing."

Lady Cadogan, unable to miss the note of censure in the countess's voice, looked over the tambour frame set before her and said calmly, "I do it to keep my fingers limber, Almeria, as you know perfectly well. My poor hands would soon be useless if I did not keep them occupied."

"So you are forever telling me." The countess held her own plump hands up and added complacently, "Fortunately, I do not suffer from rheumatism, so I do not know." Then, noticing that Gwenyth had not moved, she said, "Don't stand there, gel. Ring for someone to fetch your workbasket."

"I fear I have left my needlework in London," Gwenyth said, seeing no point in confessing her loathing for the ladylike task.

Her aunt patted the armless straight-backed chair beside her own and said with a knowing smile, "Never mind, my dear, you may sit here and entertain me with town gossip instead." Her tambour was not the small one on which she had been working earlier, but a larger frame that stood on the floor before her chair. Noting her niece's interest in the woodland-nymph scene coming to colorful life on the canvas, she said, " 'Tis a cover for one of the dining-room chairs. I found the pattern with some stuff in a chest in my bed-chamber, and we believe it to be one in which the chairs were worked before Cromwell imposed himself on the country and the Hawtrey ancestor allowed the abbey to fall to ruins. Now," she added in an undertone, peering closely at Gwenyth, "how did it go for your friend Pamela?"

"She is staying," Gwenyth said.

"I think you have more to tell me than that." She spoke in a low voice, but Gwenyth could not miss the undertone of determination and knew her aunt meant to have the whole tale.

"Do you know, ma'am," she said wistfully, "I well remember a time, and not so long ago at that, when Eliza and Davy and I were able to intimidate you and not turnabout, when you were content to leave well enough alone."

Lady Cadogan chuckled. "I remember. I recall, too, how abruptly that state of affairs ended when Tallyn returned from America and took the three of you in hand. Ah, but his first day back in London was a day to remember. Astley's, I believe, is where you and Davy had slipped off to that morning."

Gwenyth grimaced, remembering only too well. "Our lives certainly changed," she said. "Meriel had been both mother and father to us for nearly three years by then, but she was in France and you were busy launching Eliza into society, so Davy and I had been left pretty much to our own devices."

"You had a tutor," Lady Cadogan reminded her.

"Yes, and we very soon got a new one once Joss discovered the mischief we'd been up to," Gwenyth said ruefully. "Soon after that he packed me off to Miss Fletcher's."

"And Miss Beckley was a schoolmate there, you say?" Lady Cadogan's eyebrows lifted in a gentle query.

Gwenyth sighed, recognizing her intent. "I cannot tell you the whole tale here and now, Auntie Wynne, believe me."

"Then," said her ladyship placidly, "you must excuse yourself to the countess and seek your bedchamber, for I mean to know what's what before this night is done." She glanced at the card players, adding dryly, "I suppose we may leave them alone. Sir Spenser's honor is safe enough so long as he continues to enjoy good health."

Choking back a gurgle of laughter, Gwenyth rose obediently to bid her hostess good night.

4

Fifteen minutes later, in Gwenyth's bedchamber, Lady Cadogan settled herself into an armchair near the single tall window and demanded to know what mischief was afoot. "For if the pair of you was disappointed to learn of Lyford's absence or pleased by his return, you fooled me, and that's a fact."

Gwenyth shot an oblique glance at Annie Gray, who had been waiting to put her to bed. Annie's eyes twinkled and her lips were pressed tightly together, so Gwenyth was not surprised to see her turn quickly away to pull back the covers on the bed.

"Why have you brought that Beckley girl here?" Lady Cadogan demanded, ignoring Annie. "If all she wanted was to speak with her guardian, she might easily have written to him."

Gwenyth, turning to her abigail, said, "Help me into my nightdress, Annie, and then you may go."

Although Lady Cadogan was clearly on the verge of demanding instant elucidation, she sighed and drew aside the heavy blue velvet curtain to look out the window. "This room overlooks the river, I see. I hope your friend is as well-situated."

"She is, though her bedchamber looks onto the courtyard."

Lady Cadogan chuckled. "Then, for her sake, we will pray for temperate weather. The stable block forms the south-western corner of that courtyard."

Gwenyth smiled but said nothing, for her head was buried

just then in the folds of her lawn nightdress. Annie would not leave before brushing out her hair and loosely plaiting it for the night, but she departed at last, and Gwenyth saw at once that her aunt would brook no further delay. Accordingly, she explained the situation as quickly and clearly as she was able.

"Very odd," Lady Cadogan observed when she had finished. "Despite Lyford's position and his clear duty to secure the succession, I must say he has shown no inclination to marry or even to make himself particularly agreeable to his neighbors, several of whom have eligible daughters. But why he should have chosen to leave Miss Beckley at school when she might as easily have been kept here under his eye, I am sure I cannot tell you."

"Has he said nothing at all about her, ma'am?"

Lady Cadogan shrugged. "He don't say much about anything. He dines with us when he's home, but Almeria looks down her nose at him one minute and nags at him the next to provide her with money. They don't get on well."

"Then he does have money problems?"

"Everyone does," said Lady Cadogan tartly. "Good gracious, child, we have been at war for years, and prices just keep going up. To keep body and soul together is the most anyone can hope to do, and the old earl was not one to guard his pennies, so I doubt that Lyford inherited much more than debts."

"Then Pamela may be right," Gwenyth mused. "He may be either misusing her fortune or planning to force her to marry him so that he can gain complete control over it."

"It is possible," Lady Cadogan said doubtfully, "though he has not appeared to me to be that sort of man. And whatever the provocation, Pamela ought never to have run away from school. He cannot have liked that, nor will Almeria if she should learn of it. Like as not, she'll take a pet at hearing no more than that Lyford has been put out of temper, for she wants to turn him up sweet just now, before he receives any more of her bills."

Gwenyth lifted one eyebrow. "Turn him up sweet, ma'am?"

Lady Cadogan laughed. "I had a letter from Davy in this morning's post. He and his friend Mr. Webster mean to pay us a visit. He didn't see fit to say when, but he did say he meant to turn *me* up sweet, so I daresay we may look to see him any day."

"He wants money, then." She knew her brother.

Her ladyship's thin shoulders lifted in a casual shrug. "Nothing new in that. He will have it that Tallyn keeps him too short by half, desiring him to learn methods of economy."

"Well, that will never happen," Gwenyth said, sitting on her bed and drawing her knees up so that she might tuck her chilly toes under her bedclothes. "Davy doesn't try, of course, but Joss believes one ought to live as cheaply in London or at Oxford as in the backwoods of America. Unless," she added wryly, "one has one's position as the twelfth Earl of Tallyn to uphold."

Lady Cadogan thoughtfully examined the fingernails on her left hand. "He would sympathize with Lyford, I believe."

"But Pamela is not expensive, ma'am," Gwenyth protested. "Even if she now wishes to cut a dash—"

"I was speaking not of Miss Beckley but of the ancient dowager." Her hazel eyes danced mischievously. "I know I ought not to call her so, but I do admire Mr. Coleridge's poetry, and somehow the phrase popped to mind one day."

Gwenyth chuckled. "I expected her to look a great deal more decrepit than she does."

"Oh, she is not decrepit in the least. Uses that cane more to emphasize what she says—bangs it on the floor, you know—than to help her walk. On the other hand, it is not difficult to think of her as something of an albatross around poor Lyford's neck."

"Oh." Gwenyth thought about that for a moment. "Is she really on the lookout for a new husband?"

"She is. Since she cannot wind Lyford round her thumb and will not be able to live in the style she likes if he removes her to the dower house, as he is certain to do if he ever does marry, she says she must." Lady Cadogan grimaced. "I must say, the old earl did not leave her well to pass. She expected at least to receive her own dower money, but when he died, it was found that he had wasted most of it, gaming and whatever."

Gwenyth knew better than to ask what her aunt meant by "whatever," so she observed tactfully instead that she supposed the old earl had been very ill in his last days and might not have used the best judgment in managing his affairs.

Lady Cadogan stared at her. "Ill! He was no more ill than I am. He was still going just as strong the day he died as he ever had, the lecherous old goat."

"But the newspaper reported that he died in bed here at—"

"He died in the Covent Garden fire," Lady Cadogan snapped, "and . . ." But here, although it was clear that she had nearly said more, she folded her lips tightly and looked away.

"Oh, no you don't," Gwenyth said, swinging her feet over the side of the bed and leaning toward her. "You don't end the tale like that, ma'am, not with me. I know perfectly well that the fire at Covent Garden Theater began in the middle of the night, long after the evening performance had ended. If the earl died in that fire, he was not in the theater, and if he was neither there nor safe in bed as the *Times* reported, then where was he?"

"Oh, he was in bed," the viscountess said grimly, "but the bed was in Hart Street, in a house across from the theater."

Gwenyth's brow wrinkled in concentration. "Some of those houses were scorched, I know, but I thought they saved them all."

Lady Cadogan snorted. " 'Twould have been a deal better for all of us, I promise you, if Number Three had burnt flat to the ground without a trace of its inhabitants."

"Aunt!" Gwenyth stared at her in shock, but when Lady Cadogan returned her gaze without a blink, the truth struck her with some force. "Goodness," she breathed, "a mistress?"

"And more shame to him! Eighty-six years old, he was, and still as much a rake as he'd been at twenty. One of his mistresses was even older than he was!"

Gwenyth couldn't help it; she burst into laughter. "*One* of his mistresses? How many did he have?"

But Lady Cadogan stiffened indignantly. "I am sure I have no idea. One was more than enough, I believe, however beholden Almeria may be to the woman for managing to get him home without anyone else's being the wiser. That cannot have been easy."

"What happened?"

"They were awakened by all the noise of the fire wagons and the shouting, and I suspect, in his guilt, old Lyford thought the Day of Judgment had arrived. In any event, his mistress said he was so startled that he leapt straight out of bed and collapsed. By the time she reached him, he had breathed his last."

"And she?" Gwenyth tried to think how to put the matter delicately. "She won't . . . that is, she must realize that Lady Lyford would pay for her silence. Won't she—?"

"We needn't fear that," Lady Cadogan said crisply. "She is no flighty girl, but a sensible woman in her fifties, for which we may be thankful, because she quite understood the necessity for discretion and refused all offers other than to pay the expenses of her journey. Said she'd had all she wanted from his lordship while he lived." She grimaced. "Generous to a fault, I daresay, and probably with Almeria's money, for he was not so generous to her. It is as well that the woman did not ask for anything else, for although Almeria didn't know the state of her own affairs at that time, I've no doubt but what she would have handed the old earl's corpse right back and told her to bury him herself."

"But then she might have taken her tale to Lyford."

Gwenyth's imagination boggled as she tried to visualize a scene between the late earl's mistress and his heir.

After a small silence Lady Cadogan said carefully, "That would have been something to see. I trust you won't cross him, my dear. I have seen him out of temper, and it will not do."

Remembering that she, too, had seen Lyford out of temper, Gwenyth did not contradict her, and their conversation moved to safer topics until Lady Cadogan bade her good night and left her to her own confused reflections. It was not long, however, before fatigue overcame her and she drifted into dreamless sleep.

She was awakened the following morning by the sound of curtain rings rattling against the rod as her bedchamber was flooded with sunlight. Opening her eyes, she beheld Annie's plump form silhouetted against the window, one arm still raised as she paused to look out.

"Good morning," Gwenyth said sleepily.

"It is that," Annie replied, letting her hand fall and moving away from the window. She was smiling. "The sunlight sparkles on that river like . . . well, I don't rightly know what, m'lady, but 'tis a beautiful sight, and no mistake."

Gwenyth sat up and bunched her pillows behind her. "Have you taken to doing the chambermaid's tasks, or is the abbey short of servants?"

Annie clicked her tongue against her teeth as she picked up a tray from a nearby table. "Just wanted to see your chocolate was hot and that that no-account lass didn't forget you like your toast crisp." She settled the tray across Gwenyth's lap.

Gwenyth surveyed its contents and smiled with approval. "It looks fine. What kind of jam is that?"

Annie peered at the dark mixture. "Some sort of berry. Shall I send for marmalade?"

"No. Is Pamela awake yet?"

"The only person I've seen is his lordship. He was up with the birds and left for the stables nigh onto an hour ago. He don't appear to be one for letting the day get on without him.''

Gwenyth turned her attention to applying jam to toast, but a few moments later, when she saw Annie taking a sprigged muslin round gown from the wardrobe, she said quickly, ''I think I'll wear my blue habit, Annie. If the morning is as lovely as you say, I believe I'd enjoy a ride along the river.''

''You didn't bring your mare,'' the abigail said, giving her a sharp look but exchanging the round gown for the habit.

''I daresay his lordship will have a horse suitable for a lady to ride,'' Gwenyth replied airily.

''And a groom, miss,'' Annie said grimly, still watching her.

Gwenyth sighed. ''Yes, Annie. Even I am not so foolish as to ride over unknown countryside without a knowledgeable groom.''

Twenty minutes later she left the house by way of the courtyard and, remembering her aunt's comment the night before, found her way to the southwest corner without trouble. When she stepped through the narrow door in the wall, the stable appeared to be deserted. Except for the stirring of hooves on straw and an occasional whicker, there was no other sound.

''Hallo!'' she called.

The only response was a second rustle of straw and another, louder whicker, coming from a stall twenty feet away, near the stableyard entrance. A noble chestnut head appeared over the gate, and alert brown eyes gazed curiously at her.

Gwenyth chuckled and moved toward him. ''I didn't bring you any sugar,'' she said, ''but perhaps you won't mind. My, you are a handsome fellow, aren't you?'' She held her hand out to him.

The stallion tossed his head playfully, then pushed his nose against her hand. Finding it empty, he snorted and turned away.

''Oh, so you mean to sulk, do you?'' She looked around,

but there was still no one else to be seen. A bridle hung temptingly from a hook near the stall gate. She took it down, and at the sound, he regarded her hopefully again. "Yes," she told him, "I'll take you out, but just for a walk, mind. I don't think I ought to try putting a saddle on you without asking someone."

As she lifted the latch, there was a sudden, sharper rustle from inside and the stallion shied. Then, before she realized what was happening, he whinnied nervously and reared, his front hooves crashing against the opening gate, knocking her off-balance. With a cry, she stumbled, catching herself on the heavy gate and clinging to it as it continued to swing open.

There was a shout from behind her, but Gwenyth had suddenly seen what was causing the stallion's distress and, terrified, managed to collect her wits enough to straighten, throw the gate wide, and leap aside. The stallion plunged past her.

Seconds later Lyford had her by the shoulders and had spun her about to face him. "What the devil do you think you are doing?" he bellowed, shaking her roughly.

"I . . ." She couldn't speak, but he had already seen what she had seen, and releasing her abruptly, he strode past her to glare into the stall.

"Come out of there at once," he snapped.

After a long, silent moment, there was more rustling and a skinny little red-headed, freckle-faced boy, no more than eight or nine years old, emerged from the stall, pulling straw from various openings in his neatly patched plaid shirt as he kept his light blue eyes focused warily upon the earl's angry face.

"What were you doing in there?" Lyford demanded.

Swallowing carefully, the boy said, "Brung Cyrano a carrot."

"You needn't go into his stall to give him a carrot."

Flushing, the youngster looked down at the ground and said, "Warn't no one about, so I thought I'd give him a brush. The currycomb's in there," he added, pointing. "I dropped it when the lady come in and hallooed."

"You'd no business to be in that stall at all, my lad," the earl said sternly, "and you certainly ought to know better than to leave the gate open."

"I never!" The thin face turned up sharply, eyes blazing indignantly. "I shut it, I did. Then the lady come inside, and I knowed I warn't s'posed ter be there, so I went ter ground, hopin' she wouldn't see me. But I never opened yon gate. I wouldn't! She done it."

"I did," Gwenyth said quietly. There was a noise behind them, and looking over her shoulder, she saw that a groom had captured the stallion and was bringing him back. "He is so beautiful," she said, "that I wanted to see him in the sunlight. He seemed gentle enough, and the bridle was right there. I never expected him to go crazy when I opened the gate."

Lyford, too, was aware of the groom, now standing patiently, awaiting orders, just behind him. "You and I," he told Gwenyth quietly but ominously enough to send a thrill racing up her spine, "will discuss your part in this shortly." He turned back to the boy. "Did you startle him, Joey?"

Looking down again, Joey scuffed the dirt with the toe of one shoe. "Aye, I rightly 'spect I did. Startled me, she did, when she opened yon gate. Knew she'd see me, like as not, and I 'spect I hit Cyrano's hind leg when I jumped. Made him step on yon currycomb too," he added with an air of confessing the worst. He looked up from under his sandy lashes, biting his lower lip at the sight of Lyford's forbidding expression. "I won't do it again," he muttered pleadingly.

Gwenyth's heart was wrung. "Please, sir," she said, "he's only a little boy, and it was my fault that the horse got loose."

Lyford looked at her for a long moment, then looked back down at the culprit. "This is not the first time I have caught you in my stable without permission, is it?"

Sighing wretchedly, the boy shook his head.

The earl's lips twitched, but his voice remained stern. "You like my horses, don't you, Joey?"

"Aye." His eyes lit with enthusiasm. "Me dad says I'm

ter be a scufflehunter like hisself, but me, I wants ter be a groom, mebbe stablemaster when I'm growed."

"A groom needs to learn obedience," Lyford said gently.

Joey chewed his lip again; then, recognizing that a response was expected, he said, "Aye, that's true, I 'spect."

Lyford nodded, satisfied. "I'll tell you what, Joey. When your father gets home tonight, you tell him what you did—"

"But, he'll . . ." The boy's freckles stood out vividly on his chalk-white face, and he seemed momentarily to have lost his voice. Then, when Lyford remained silent, he took a deep breath and regarded him searchingly, his expression slowly turning to one of calculation. "You won't tell him yerself, then?"

Gwenyth, watching the earl almost as closely as Joey did, wasn't surprised to see his lips twitch again, but he said in the soft tone she had come to respect, "No, but I will know if you don't tell him, and I won't have anyone working in my stables who doesn't do as he is told or who is too much of a coward to accept the consequences of his deeds."

Joey's expressive face reddened painfully at the word "coward," but his eyes were sparkling by the time Lyford had finished speaking. "In yer stables? You would take me fer a groom? Kin I tell me dad as much?"

"You may tell him that if he agrees, I will take you on as a stableboy," Lyford replied. "You'll muck out a lot of stalls, my lad, and you'll grow at least six inches before you ever become a groom of mine."

"I'll grow fast," Joey promised. "Kin I start now?"

The earl shook his head. "First, you talk to your father."

The brightness faded from the boy's face, making Gwenyth yearn to hug him and tell him everything would be all right. He moved past them, feet dragging, and left the stable without so much as glancing at the stallion or the waiting, silent groom.

Lyford, who had turned to watch him, turned back now, and Gwenyth, unnerved by the look on his face and her anticipation of what he meant to say, said quickly, "What's a scufflehunter?"

His eyes glinted appreciatively, but all he said was, "Put him away, Ned." Then, taking hold of Gwenyth's arm, he moved her gently out of the way, saying nothing more until the groom had put the stallion in his stall, latched the gate, and with a brief nod of his head taken his leave of them. Once he was gone, Lyford said, "Now, then, perhaps you will be so—"

"You didn't tell me what it means," Gwenyth protested.

He looked sternly down at her. "What what means?"

"S-scufflehunter." She licked her lips and tried to step away from him, but he had retained his hold on her arm and he did not let go.

"Scufflehunters are what people hereabouts call the gangs of men who tow the barges upriver," he said. "Now, perhaps—"

"Then Joey's father must be very strong," Gwenyth said, looking at him in distress. "Won't he . . . ? Oh, Lyford, you ought not to have . . . Oh, dear, the poor little boy!"

He shook his head, the expression in his eyes softening. "Big Joe Ferguson is about as fierce as a woolly spring lamb."

She looked more hopeful. "Then he won't—"

"Oh, he'll dust the lad's jacket for him, and he'll do a thorough job of it, but Joey deserves no less. What he did was both forbidden and dangerous, and I'd have punished him myself had I not known Joe would see to it. As for you—"

"I know," she said swiftly, seeking to disarm him, "I ought never to have opened that gate, and I apologize, sir."

But he was not so easily pacified. "You deserve everything that Joey deserves, and more," he said grimly, still holding her arm and looking directly into her eyes. His expression made her wish that she were far, far away.

"I said I was sorry," she muttered, wondering how it was that he could make her feel so guilty and ashamed of herself when all her brother's scolds ever did was arouse her resentment.

He wasn't through with her. " 'Sorry' doesn't pay the

piper, Gwen," he said. "Cyrano is not a woolly lamb, but a stallion grown and utterly unpredictable. He might have killed you."

She scarcely noticed that his voice trembled on the last words, for they had conjured up in her mind a sudden dreadful vision of the stallion rearing, his steel-clad hooves slashing the air above the crouching, frightened boy. Her stomach clenched with a fear greater even than she had felt while it was happening. "H-he might have killed Joey," she whispered, tears springing to her eyes. "All because I was such fool as to open that gate and startle them both." As she stared at him in dismay, the tears spilled over.

"Here, now, none of that. Come here."

Without protest or thought she went into his arms, letting him hold her tightly against his broad chest, sobbing gently as the hot tears coursed down her cheeks.

He said nothing, just held her, his strength and size fully as comforting as she had expected they would be. That thought stopped her weeping as though a tap had been turned, and she moved to free herself. Briefly his arms tightened, but then he released her and withdrew a large white handkerchief from his jacket pocket. Silently he handed it to her, and she mopped her cheeks without looking at him, sniffing childishly when her nose threatened to run. She blew it, then wadded up the handkerchief and held it in her fist, clenched against her habit skirt.

"You won't want it back," she said.

"No." There was amusement in his voice now, and she looked up to see laughter in his eyes. Then he said gently, "Did you think to unman me with your hardy Welshwoman's tears?"

"How dare you laugh!" she snapped indignantly. But she knew his accusation was not entirely unwarranted, and her gaze fell when he continued to regard her with mocking amusement.

"There is little that I will not dare in a good cause," he said in that same gentle tone, "and since you have once again invaded my territory unchaperoned, it occurs to me that I know exactly how to punish you. 'Tis what I have wanted to do since last night, which you do not want me to do, and thus 'tis a most suitable penalty.'' His hands came to her shoulders, and as she stared up at him in wide-eyed shock, he drew her slowly toward him, his eyes still alight with silent laughter.

Gwenyth's mouth was dry, but the only fear she felt was dismay at her own response to his clear intent to kiss her. She ought to slap him, she told herself. At the very least, she ought to resist. Any halfway respectable female would stomp his shiny boots for him or kick him where it would do some good. No true lady would just stand there mesmerized, waiting, her blood racing through her in a way that made her body hum with exhilaration. At the same time, oddly, she felt limp, much too limp to defend herself against what was coming. She had stopped breathing, and at any moment now, she knew, if he didn't get on with it, she would swoon at his feet in the manner of the very best Gothic heroines.

His lips touched hers, gently, searchingly, his kiss no more than a feather-light whisper of breath upon her skin. With a moan, she pressed upward, rising on her toes, putting her hands at his waist to steady herself as she urged him to get on with it, to stop tormenting her. If he was going to punish her, then let him do so now, at once.

Lyford's hands moved from her shoulders, caressingly, to the back of her neck and her waist, and his kiss grew more demanding, more possessive. His tongue now pressed gently against her lips, craving admittance. When she didn't respond as he wished, he moved one finger lightly across the back of her neck, so lightly that it tickled the fine hairs there, chilling her and drawing a gasp of surprise that parted her lips for him.

As he pressed his advantage, an unfamiliar masculine voice spoke from behind him. ''I say, Marcus, I didn't expect to find you tumbling a maid in the stable at this hour. But don't let me interrupt,'' the slim, handsome stranger went on as Gwenyth, in embarrassed dismay, sprang away from the earl.

"Truly, I don't mind waiting my turn. Though I believe," he added, raising a gold-rimmed quizzing glass to one blue eye, "that I have mistaken the matter. She don't appear to be a maidservant after all."

"Your manners don't improve much, coz," the earl said, glancing ruefully at Gwenyth. "You insult my guest, the Lady Gwenyth Traherne. Lady Gwenyth, much though I regret his arrival just now, may I present my cousin Jared Hawtrey."

"At your service, ma'am." The newcomer's eyes gleamed with amusement as he swept his hat from his coffee-colored curls and made his bow. He, too, wore riding dress, but his appearance was much more fashionable than Lyford's, and Gwenyth had no difficulty in identifying him as a town beau. He continued smoothly, "In view of his own manners, I refuse to allow Marcus to condemn mine. Shall I call him out for you?"

"That won't be necessary, Mr. Hawtrey," she said.

"Ah, then do I detect a romance?"

"Indeed not, sir!"

Lyford said easily, "You were nearer the mark the first time, Jared. I owe Lady Gwenyth an apology for taking unfair advantage of her. What are you doing here at such an hour?"

"Couldn't sleep for all the racket on the river," Hawtrey retorted. "Worse than the city, because it ain't a steady drone, don't you know. More like fits and starts, and I don't know but what the silences in between ain't worst of all."

"Then you arrived last night?"

"Aye, had a breakdown outside Reading. Decided to push on, though, rather than rack up there for the night."

"Squeezed again, coz?"

Hawtrey shrugged. "Nothing beyond the ordinary. Just don't care to waste my blunt. Thought you'd approve."

Lyford looked at him for a long moment, then said casually, "I was just going to invite Lady Gwenyth to take a ride along the riverbank. Care to join us?"

Hawtrey smiled at Gwenyth, letting his gaze drift from

the top of her head to the hem of her habit before he said with a drawl, "Don't mind if I do, at that. And don't be thinking I'll be neglecting my duties either, Marcus. My man Powell's looked after things while I was away. Traherne, did you say? Would you be related to the Earl of Tallyn, ma'am?"

"My brother," Gwenyth said. "Lady Cadogan is my aunt."

"Then I have heard a good deal about you," Hawtrey said, grinning. "You must tell me how much of it I may believe."

5

As they made their way to the hard-beaten ride along the river, Lyford told Gwenyth that the abbey and its gardens had been sketched in watercolors and immortalized in oil by nearly every famous landscape artist of the past and present day, and she saw at once why that was so. To the east, osier bogs and green meadows gave way to low hills that sloped upward until they joined the beautiful Chilterns. To the west, more abruptly, the steep, grassy sides of the Berkshire chalk downs emerged above the thick forest of trees that covered the vast abbey grounds, framing gardens and house from the river's edge to the road and beyond, providing any artist with a magnificent background.

When they reached the riverbank, Lyford turned Cyrano south, toward Pangbourne. "We'll ride to Streatley another day," he said. "This way is quite pleasant, and you will see the ruins."

"Ruins?" Gwenyth looked about curiously.

"The remains of the old abbey," Jared said. " 'Tis naught but a pile of rocks now, with a few old monks' cells beneath. Rather boring, but fashionably picturesque, I believe." He gestured toward a heavily laden barge being poled downstream, accompanied by a number of interested swans, swimming alongside like guardsmen escorting a royal coach. "More interesting, I think, to watch the Molesford lock in operation. Have you ever seen a flash lock before, ma'am?"

"Not up close," Gwenyth admitted, turning her head and noting that the barge he indicated was not the only traffic on the river. "Why are the men on that smaller barge poling so hard?" she asked.

Both men chuckled, and Lyford said, "They don't want to get caught behind the slower-moving vessel. They can be miles on their way before the big one clears the gates if they can pass it and slip through first." He urged Cyrano to a trot, and Gwenyth followed on the roan gelding named Prince Joseph that he had given her to ride. Jared followed them on his black.

They passed the ruins first. Gwenyth's first thought when Lyford had mentioned them had been of something Gothic, possibly even haunted, so she was disappointed to see that, as Jared had warned, they weren't much more than a picturesque pile of stones in a clearing just before a wide bend in the river. The lock, located fifty yards beyond the bend, was far more interesting.

When the two barges came around the bend, she saw what her companions had meant about the difference between them. The lockkeeper, a wiry little man wearing a bright red cap, had been warned of their coming and had already opened the lock, and as the smaller barge neared the opening and was caught in the surge of water, it picked up momentum. Gwenyth saw the tillerman straining against the drag of his huge wooden rudder, while the other crewmen worked feverishly to keep a straight course with their long poles. Then with a rush and an outburst of cheering they were over the weir into white water, riding the flow.

"Now they pray," Jared said with a laugh.

"Goodness, why?" Gwenyth demanded.

Lyford said, "It's deep right below the gate, but there are shallows beyond, where gravel is thrown up by the back current. The flash will carry them over, though, if they keep to their proper course. Watch the big one, now. Its progress must be more carefully controlled, but a heavy barge can't move too slowly or it might go aground above the lock when the water level drops."

She saw that several towlines had been thrown from the

stern of the larger craft to men some distance upriver on the towpath along the opposite bank. The lines were wound around a capstan, or large winch, and six men controlled it, letting the heavily laden barge slowly down through the opening, where little white water showed now that the river had begun to even out.

"They'll tow the upstream traffic through now," Lyford said, "and then the gates will be closed and the water level will rise again. There are mills upriver at both Streatley and Goring that depend upon the level remaining somewhat constant, so the lockkeepers tend to let traffic back up during the middle of the day. Barges can be kept waiting hours for the water level to rise before they can move to the next section of the river."

"One doesn't do much swimming in the river, then," Gwenyth said on a note of disappointment.

Lyford grinned at her. "So Welshwomen swim, do they?"

She lifted her chin. "Many of them do, sir. My father insisted that my sisters and I learn along with my brothers. There are two wild rivers near our home, and he desired us to learn what to do should we ever fall into one."

Jared was astounded. "You learned to swim in a wild river?"

She smiled at him. "We learned in a pond where a portion of the gentler of the two had been dammed. Perhaps you have something similar here." She looked questioningly at Lyford.

He shook his head. "There are any number of backwaters and streams that feed into the river hereabouts," he said, "but none of them is really very suitable for damming. If you are a good swimmer, however, there is no reason you cannot do so if you pick your time carefully. At this time of the year, when the river is not in spate, the waters between locks are fairly calm so long as the locks remain closed. There is still a strong current, of course, but it is not dangerous unless someone opens the gates."

Shooting her a challenging look, Jared said, "We often swim from the riverbank below the gardens in the evening or on Sundays. Perhaps if you were to join us then, we could look after you while you dip your toes.''

"Thank you, sir, but I should like to dip more than my toes, so I believe I will require at least a modicum of privacy.'' She didn't think it necessary to mention that for her to observe gentlemen engaged in that particular sport would be most improper. Jared was clearly trying to bait her, but he would soon discover she was no fish to rise at such a paltry fly.

Lyford had been thinking. Now he said, "I don't think it would be wise for you to swim alone, ma'am, but I can show you at least one spot that might suit you, not far from here, where a backwater joins the main flow. It won't afford you complete privacy, of course, but you will have more there than swimming from the open riverbank. I can have someone rig a rope to one of the trees. If you promise always to take someone with you and to tie the rope securely round your waist, I would have no objection to your bathing as and when you like.''

She looked at him in surprise. "Why, thank you, sir. I would enjoy that. Perhaps Miss Beckley will agree to join me, but if she will not, my own maid will attend me.''

"A woman swimming seems dashed unnatural to me,'' muttered Jared. "Unsafe too. You sure you know what you're about, to permit it, Marcus? Wouldn't do to let the pretty lady drown.''

Lyford smiled at Gwenyth. "She won't drown,'' he said. There was warmth in his eyes again, and Gwenyth glanced quickly at Jared, hoping he would not comment upon that look.

But his thoughts had traveled in a new direction. "Who is Miss Beckley?'' he demanded.

"My ward,'' Lyford said calmly.

"That's it!'' Jared said, snapping his fingers. "Knew I'd heard the name. Your mama's niece, ain't she?'' When Lyford nodded, he went on, "Thought you said she was fixed at school.''

"She was," Lyford said with a rueful look at Gwenyth,, "but she decided to leave."

"Dashed right, too," Jared said. "I say, ain't she an heiress or something?"

"Something," Lyford agreed, "but don't attempt to attach her affections, coz. It won't answer."

Grimacing, Jared afforded his cousin a measuring look. What he saw in the other man's face did not appear to comfort him. "Like that, is it? Daresay you want her yourself. You haven't ever been one to miss the main chance, have you?"

There was bitterness in his tone, and Gwenyth looked at him sharply, but when he caught her look, he shook his head and shrugged, and when Lyford did not comment, she decided she had been imagining things. She rather liked Mr. Hawtrey. In some ways, although he had more polish, he reminded her of her brother Davy, and she wondered why she had never met him in town. After three Seasons, she thought she had met everyone.

They rode only as far as the abbey's southern boundary, and when they turned back, Lyford apologized for the shortness of the outing. "I've a number of things to see to this morning," he said, "and I daresay your aunt will be wondering where you've got to. She's an early riser herself, you know, unlike Grandmother."

"Lord, Marcus, can't you call her the countess?" demanded Jared. "You know she turns blue every time you remind her she's a grandmama. I should never do so tactless a thing."

"She is my grandmother," Lyford said calmly. "She has never attempted to engage my affection, or stirred in me any desire to please her. I see no reason to change my ways now to suit her."

"You'll sing a new tune when she cuts you out of her will," Jared said, chuckling.

"You're welcome to what little she has, coz."

"Ah, but she will have more before she goes aloft, you know, and then you'll be the one to look blue. That woman means to die wealthy, and I'll wager she does as she says she will."

"Well, you're the lad who'll get whatever there is to get," Lyford said. "She won't leave it to your father, and she won't leave it to me, whatever I choose to call her. She likes you."

Jared preened himself and grinned at Gwenyth. "Likes a man who cuts a dash, does the countess."

Gwenyth grinned back, then glanced at Lyford. He was not amused. If anything, she thought he looked a little sad.

When they reached the stableyard, an older, grizzled man whom Gwenyth had not seen before waved to Lyford and shouted for grooms to attend the horses. Jared waited until one held his mount's bridle before dismounting, but Lyford slid from his saddle at once, dropping the stallion's reins to the ground when he turned to assist Gwenyth.

"I thought you said Cyrano was unpredictable," she said mockingly as she lifted her right leg from its rest and swiveled on her sidesaddle to face him, steadying herself with a hand on the gelding's rump. "Do you truly trust him to stand there, even for a moment?"

"He knows better than to defy me," Lyford said, returning her look. He placed his hands firmly at her waist and lifted her effortlessly from her saddle without taking his gaze from hers. But before she could decide whether there had been undue stress on the first word in his sentence, he set her on the ground and turned away to tell the stablemaster that he would want the stallion later to visit some of his tenant farms.

"I'll go inside with you," Jared said, offering Gwenyth his arm as she drew the reins over the gelding's head and handed them to a waiting groom. "I've not yet had my breakfast."

Glancing at Lyford, she saw that he was listening intently to something his stablemaster was saying to him, so she scooped up her train with her left hand, rested the fingers of her right lightly upon Jared's forearm, and murmured dulcetly, "You are very kind, sir."

He chuckled. "I have heard it said, ma'am, that you are not so easily charmed as all that."

"Have you, indeed, sir? Do you know me, then? I daresay that we have met in town, but I fear that I do not remember you."

"I have not had the pleasure of a proper introduction, but I daresay we have acquaintances in common." He mentioned several people she knew, but his artless conversation did not deceive her, and she was disappointed in him, for he spoke like a coxcomb, puffing off acquaintance with persons who, had they known him as well as he wanted her to believe they did, would certainly have introduced him to her.

By the time they reached the breakfast parlor, a sunny chamber on the second floor with an excellent view of the river, she had begun to wonder why an earl's grandson who appeared to have money to spend had *not* been introduced to her as an eligible acquaintance, if not as a suitable aspirant to her hand. While Jared moved to pull the bell to order his breakfast, Gwenyth removed her hat and gloves, set them on a nearby chair, and greeted Lady Cadogan, who was still seated at the breakfast table, enjoying a cup of tea as she read her morning post.

She looked up and smiled. "What a pretty habit, my dear. The color matches your eyes exactly."

"Thank you. I ought to have changed, I suppose."

"Nonsense, not on my account. Have you broken your fast?"

"I had toast with my chocolate when I awoke," Gwenyth said, bending to kiss her cheek, "but I wouldn't refuse something more substantial now. Is there tea in that pot?"

"There is, newly hot, and extra cups on the sideboard there," Lady Cadogan said with a gesture.

Gwenyth moved to help herself. "Tea, Mr. Hawtrey?"

"I'll have coffee," he said, repeating himself a moment later for the footman who responded to his ring. "They will bring the food quickly," he added when the man had gone. "Seems they were expecting our arrival."

"I sent the dishes from the sideboard back to the kitchen half an hour ago," Lady Cadogan said. "Thought no one else meant to appear. Miss Beckley must intend to sleep the day away, and I didn't know you were here, Jared."

"Arrived in the dead of night," he said. "I've my own key to the east wing, you know, so there was no need to rouse anyone to let me in."

Conversation drifted casually from topic to topic while they ate, and afterward Jared said he wanted to visit some friends in the neighborhood. Gwenyth half-expected him to invite her to join him, and was unaccountably relieved when he did not. When he had gone, she said, "Why have I never met him in town, ma'am?"

"He don't frequent the sort of parties you like, I expect," her ladyship said, glancing up at her. "Why do you ask?"

Gwenyth shrugged. "He seems very charming. I just thought I ought to have remembered him. Is he perhaps a fortune hunter?" she asked, remembering his quick interest in Pamela.

"All men are fortune hunters," Lady Cadogan said bluntly. "Any man who says he ain't interested in marrying a girl with a large fortune is a liar. Don't matter a particle what his own worth might be. As for Jared, his father is well enough to pass, and the lad will inherit what there is one day. Still and all, knowing Henry, I doubt he's overgenerous, so I daresay Jared wouldn't whistle an heiress down the wind." She paused, reflecting, then added, "He does live better than one might expect. Always travels post, rides fine horses, dines at the best inns, patronizes the best tailors and bootmakers, but I daresay he makes and scrapes where it don't show to make up the difference. Either that or he simply don't pay his creditors. Very fashionable, that is, for a man to pay his gaming debts but cheat the people who do for him. Always thought that was an odd way to go about things. Daresay that's why the good Lord didn't see fit to make me a gentleman."

Gwenyth laughed. Then another thought struck her, knitting her brow with perplexity. "But if Jared's father, who is the youngest son, is plump in the pockets, then Lyford must have inherited money from his father too, did he not?"

"Not," replied her ladyship. "James never had a feather

to fly with. Scapegrace, that's what he was. Charming fellow—I liked him best of them all, except Cadogan, of course," she added loyally, "but James didn't leave Marcus anything but a run-down manor house. Henry sold it at once, I believe, to pay for Marcus's schooling."

"So he was completely dependent upon his uncle's generosity," Gwenyth felt a tug of sympathy for the earl.

"Oh, Henry looked after him well enough. Were you thinking him the poor relation, always serving and being ill-used?" She chuckled. "I daresay he was ill-used more than once at Winchester, where Henry sent him to school, for they tell me boys generally are, but he got his education. Oxford too. And Henry saw to it the lad traveled. India, Barbados, even the Continent, or the safer portions of it, in any event."

"Goodness. Then perhaps that is why I have never met Mr. Hawtrey before, for surely if his papa sent Lyford abroad, he did as much for his own son."

"Oh, no, for I daresay Henry found Marcus useful, you know, and Jared had no interest then in traveling or, for that matter, in his father's affairs. Not that Henry didn't try. Put the lad in charge of the Bristol end some time ago, if I remember right, and now, of course, he's supposed to be doing it all. I doubt he does more now than before, though, only enough to keep Lyford from noticing and calling him to account. Jared's attitude toward that sort of thing is as starched-up as the dowager's."

"What sort of thing?"

Lady Cadogan lowered her voice. "Henry owns ships, a vast number of them. In point of fact, he is in trade, my dear, and we mustn't speak of it, for Almeria don't like the connection. Well," she added fairly, "no one would. 'Tis as well Lyford's out of it now. Of course, while he was no more than Marcus Hawtrey, a man of no title or expectations, working for his uncle was a way for him to make an adequate living, but he don't talk about it now either, which is perfectly understandable."

"Yes," Gwenyth agreed. "I don't suppose he would if

he wishes to be received. And that explains better than anything else, I daresay, why I have never met Mr. Hawtrey
in town. Even if he ignores the connection, it would quickly
be discovered if he were to attempt to push his way into the
higher circles."

"Yes, and although Jared despises the source, and the
work, he don't despise the income, and Henry won't
begrudge it to him, for he understands as well as anyone
could. Lives in India himself, you know. But while he don't
object to his son's living like a gentleman on the profits, his
nephew was a different matter. At one point, I believe
Marcus hoped for a military career, but Henry refused to
purchase his colors. Said it was best for him to learn to make
his own way, not to depend on others to look after him."
She grimaced. "Marcus learned his lessons well, I must say.
He's determined to increase his estate and to make this place
support itself again, whatever it takes."

"Well, one cannot blame him for that, ma'am."

"You won't say that after you've heard Almeria expound
on the subject," Lady Cadogan retorted tartly. Then her
expression and tone changed to polite cordiality as she said,
"Good morning, Miss Beckley. I trust you slept well."

Gwenyth turned to see Pamela poised upon the threshold,
her eyes sparkling, her lips parted in a breathless smile. "Oh,
yes, thank you, ma'am." Her gaze swept the room, coming
to rest upon the covered dishes on the sideboard. "Oh, good,
I was afraid everyone here would rise early. I have heard
that persons living in the country often do so. How very
pleasant that you do not."

"In point of fact, we generally do," Lady Cadogan told
her. "However, Gwenyth and Mr. Hawtrey went for an early
ride." She paused, looking at Gwenyth. "I declare, my dear,
I do trust you took a groom with you. It won't serve, you
know, to be out riding with only Mr. Hawtrey to accompany
you."

"Well, we didn't take a groom," Gwenyth confessed,
twinkling, "but we did take the earl. I daresay no one would
cavil at my having two gentleman escorts."

"No, if Marcus went along, that's all to the good."

"Who is Mr. Hawtrey?" Pamela asked, helping herself from the selection of dishes on the sideboard.

Gwenyth explained, while Lady Cadogan turned her attention back to her letter.

Pamela sat down across from Gwenyth. "Is he handsome?"

"Why, I suppose he is," Gwenyth replied, smiling. "He is of medium height and slender, with dark brown hair, blue eyes, and a pleasant countenance."

"Sky-blue eyes? I fancy gentlemen with sky-blue eyes, like your brother Tallyn has."

"Well, you'd best not fancy this gentleman," Gwenyth told her. "Lyford has already said the connection will not answer."

Pamela raised her eyebrows. "Has he? But then, I do not think Marcus will have everything all his own way, do you?"

Remembering the way the earl had looked at her the night before and again that morning, Gwenyth wasn't so sure. He was clearly a man accustomed to having things his own way. She could handle him, of course, but Pamela didn't have three London Seasons to her credit. And as her guardian, Lyford had a great deal to say about what Pamela would or would not do.

Her reflections were interrupted by the countess, who made her appearance before Pamela had finished eating. Upon being informed of Mr. Hawtrey's arrival, Lady Lyford expressed herself well-pleased. "For you said that young Davy and his friend will arrive soon too, Wynnefreda, did you not? We must plan a dinner party, I believe. Will they arrive by the end of next week, do you think? Saturday is always a good night for a party. We must make a list of eligible gentlemen to invite. Some young ones too, girls, if you like," she added as an obvious afterthought.

"Almeria, you are still in mourning for another month," Lady Cadogan reminded her.

"That's true," Pamela said, turning sympathetically to the countess. "A dinner party would be delightful, ma'am, but we would not wish you to compromise your principles merely for our pleasure. While you remain in mourning, I suppose it would not be at all the proper thing.''

"Fiddle faddle," retorted Lady Lyford, looking down her nose. "At my age, young woman, a body don't have time to waste on such fustian. In point of fact, I've waited longer than I ought to have done, for if you think my late departed husband would have mourned my passing for longer than a fortnight, you much mistake the matter. He would have consoled himself with another woman at once, for he was a thoroughly selfish man; whereas, I have mourned him, more or less, for eleven months, so no one can blame me if I decide to be sensible now.''

Lady Cadogan said quietly, "Marcus might well have something to say about dinner parties, Almeria.''

"Then I shall show him his error," the countess said tartly, "for I am still mistress in this house. That idiotish man would have me live within my income, which any fool can tell him cannot be done. 'Tis no more than a simple fact of life that anyone who would live properly must live above his income.''

"Goodness, ma'am," Pamela said, staring at her, "I should think that always to live beyond one's income would be most uncomfortable.''

"Fiddle faddle. I certainly cannot live on the pittance my late husband left me. I daresay he left it only because he overlooked it or didn't live long enough to spend it himself. But the fact remains that since Marcus stupidly forbids my punting on tick, as dearest Jared would call it, he gives me no choice in the matter.''

Pamela said, "No choice but what, ma'am?''

"I must find a suitable husband as quickly as may be," the countess informed her flatly.

"But . . ." Pamela glanced at the others. "I know Lady Cadogan said you were looking for a husband, ma'am, but I simply could not credit it. Why, at your advanced age . . ." A look of outrage from the countess made her blink, but then she went on with a determined air, "Well, you are not precisely in the first blush of . . . that is to say . . ." She looked at the others again, discomfited at last by the heavy silence.

"How very fortunate you are, my dear," Lady Lyford said icily, "to have been born an only child and the last of your family. Since you lack sense, 'tis well you enjoy that condition most likely to enhance a lady's reputation and prospects."

"You are probably right, Countess," Jared said from the doorway, where he stood with Lyford on the point of entering the room, "but a trifle outspoken, don't you agree? Miss Beckley will think you are out of charity with her, and surely you do not wish to distress so pretty a child." He crossed the room in long strides then and bent to kiss his grandmother's forehead.

She put her hand to his cheek. "Dear boy, how delightful to have you back with us so soon."

Lady Cadogan, watching this affecting display, said, "I thought you had gone a-visiting, Jared."

He gestured toward Lyford, who still stood in the doorway, his warm gaze resting upon Gwenyth. "Marcus is going out later," he said, "and he suggested I accompany him then. Perhaps"—he smiled at Pamela—"Miss Beckley and Lady Gwenyth would care to accompany us, to see some Berkshire countryside?"

"Perhaps," Lyford said dryly, watching Gwenyth steadily enough now to make her wonder if she had a spot forming, "you might introduce yourself properly, coz, before issuing your invitations to my ward."

Jared shrugged, laughter lighting his eyes. "I daresay she has heard of me by now and knows precisely who I am. Oh, very well," he added when his grandmother made a gesture of amused protest, "I am Jared Hawtrey, at your service, Miss Beckley, and I shall be honored if you will ride with us this afternoon. Marcus will have his mind on the improvements he must make to the land, of course, but I can promise my head will be full of compliments for your riding, your lovely appearance, your—"

"Enough," declared the countess. "You will turn the chit's head without paying her so much as one proper compliment. And just when I have given her a well-deserved set-down, too."

Pamela blushed. "Oh, ma'am, but—"

"You need not apologize," Lady Lyford told her with an imperious gesture. "You spoke thoughtlessly, but you are young. I do not begrudge my brothers and sisters their existence, of course, for to do so would be uncharitable, but one cannot deny that my lot at present would be far more comfortable had I been privileged to be born a great heiress like yourself. Your lot too, dear boy," she added, speaking kindly to Jared, "for I promise that I should have been most generous to you in my will. And to Marcus too, of course," she went on with a speculative look in that direction, "though he don't deserve my generosity in the face of his present nipcheese behavior. Still, I daresay he would be more open-handed now if he thought he stood to gain by it in the future."

Lyford regarded her with a glint of amusement in his eyes. "Content yourself, madam, with the knowledge that greater wealth in your purse would dispose of the necessity for you to beg another penny from mine."

"Humph," snorted the countess. "Just as one might expect. Cheeseparing, that's what you are, Marcus, and no mistake about it. Common, nipfarthing notions, that's what you've got."

Lady Cadogan chuckled. "Careful, Almeria, unless you want to stand all the nonsense for your dinner party yourself."

"What dinner party?" Lyford looked from one older woman to the other.

"I say," Jared said at the same time, "what an excellent notion that is! We've not entertained here in a twelve-month."

Lady Cadogan regarded him sternly. "There is good and sufficient reason for that, young man."

"Oh, I beg your pardon, ma'am, but you needn't take a fellow up so," Jared said, regarding her anxiously. "I meant no harm. Surely my grandfather would be the last to begrudge one a dinner party, and the poor countess is moped to death. What about it, Marcus? You won't deny the ladies a treat, I'll wager."

Lady Cadogan shifted her gaze to the earl, but he ignored the ironic look in her eyes, as well as the hopeful one in three other pairs of eyes, and kept his gaze fixed upon Gwenyth. "What think you, ma'am? Should we set all the tabbies a-twitter?"

"Birds twitter, my lord," Gwenyth replied, smiling at him.

"Ah, so they do, which don't necessarily mean the tabbies won't, however. Nevertheless," he went on with a nod to his grandmother, "I daresay I can indulge you, madam, if you will be so good as to avoid outrunning my purse."

"Fat chance of that, or of your letting her," Jared said scornfully. "You could be a deal more generous if you would but open those pockets of yours. At least a dinner party will show the folks hereabouts that we ain't paupers, after all."

"That is scarcely my intent," Lyford said.

The countess sniffed. "No need to tell us that, young man, but 'tis an excellent notion, nonetheless. One must keep up appearances. Who one is is well enough, but living well is essential if one does not wish to offend one's neighbors. We have a position to maintain, after all. People expect us to live a certain way, and it is unthinkable that we should let others see how things really are with us."

"You tell him, Countess."

"Yes, coz," Lyford said with a grim look at Jared, "well enough for you to foster such notions, being the sort yourself who ignores his duties out of a false sense of worth, borrows to pay off his debts, and orders more coats when he cannot pay his tailor. I'll thank you not to encourage her."

Jared shrugged. "Spoke out of turn. Bad habit, that. But you'll allow the party despite my faults?"

"I have said that I will."

"Then that is that." Clearly desiring a change of subject, he turned brightly to Gwenyth. "Will you ladies join us for our outing this afternoon?"

She saw that Lyford's attention had again returned to her, and she felt warmth creeping into her cheeks, but she said evenly enough, "I would enjoy another ride, thank you."

The earl smiled at her. "At two, then. You coming along now, Jared? There are matters we ought to discuss."

"No, thanks. Powell can tell you all you want to know. I must tell my man to be certain I have the appropriate attire for a country dinner party."

Lyford did not press him, and when they had gone, the countess turned her attention to preparing a list of guests for her party. "Let me see, now," she said to no one in particular, "there is Sir Spenser, of course, and Mr. Harold Ponsonby. I believe he is worth a a tidy sum. Do you know him, Wynnefreda?"

"Well, of course I do. He was a friend of Cadogan's and is, I might remind you, young enough to be your son."

"Very true, but his health is not good. Gout since he was forty, I'm told. I don't admire a man for drinking a great deal, you know, but it does have its advantages. Now, what think you of Lord Margate? Nearly ninety, I believe, but he still hunts. Not a good sign. Here, Miss Beckley—oh, nonsense, I shall call you Pamela, of course—fetch me a pen and paper!"

"I'll ring, ma'am," Gwenyth said, standing and suiting action to words, before Pamela, who was staring at the countess in awe, had so much as moved a muscle in response.

6

Gwenyth had changed to a morning frock, so it was necessary to don her habit again before she and Pamela joined the two gentlemen for their ride. The day remained a fine one, but the air was cool enough so that she was glad of her jacket. She was looking well, she thought, but she could not be surprised when both gentlemen fixed approving gazes upon Pamela.

The younger girl's habit had originally been intended for a wealthy tradesman's daughter, but when Lady Gwenyth's modiste had realized it would fit her favorite customer's young protégée perfectly, she had parted with it gladly. A brilliant pink, it was trimmed with gold braid, and had military epauletes on the shoulders and gold buttons down the front of its close-fitting jacket. The hat, an elegant confection ornamented with pheasant feathers and silk rosebuds, was tied beneath Pamela's chin with a neat pink bow, the color emphasizing the roses in her lips and cheeks and making her eyes look more like violets than ever. Gwenyth stifled a sigh of envy, knowing the outfit could not possibly have become its intended owner as well as it did Pamela.

Their mounts were ready, and they were soon off, turning this time along the drive to the road and across it, following a gravel trail up onto the chalk downs. There was room for only two to ride abreast, and for a time the two young women rode ahead, with the gentlemen following behind.

"Heard you went to London," Gwenyth heard Jared say

to the earl after they had been riding for a short time. "More trouble over the will?"

"No, just business."

Gwenyth glanced at Pamela, but the girl appeared to be paying no heed to the conversation behind them.

"Devilish dull stuff, business," Jared said. "Thought you'd given up the daily details, or were you checking up on me?"

"As a matter of fact," Lyford said, "I went to Bow Street."

"Good Lord, what for?"

Pamela looked over her shoulder then and proved that she had been listening after all. "Lady Cadogan told us you had done so, Marcus, but I confess I had forgotten all about it. I was so relieved when she said she was persuaded you had no intention of hiring Runners to find me that I quite forgot why you wanted them. It was your steward, was it not?"

Lyford said to Jared, "You must have heard that Silas Ferguson died the day after you left for Somerset. There have been some odd rumors. I want them quashed."

"I heard, of course, but his death was an accident! Drowned in the river, I thought. Happens all the time."

"His head was broken, however, and that doesn't happen so often. Where he was found, the riverbed is mostly silt."

"Then whatever he hit his head on drifted away with the current, or he floated some distance himself. Folks are only trying to make more of it than there is. You know how they are."

"No doubt you are right," Lyford said calmly.

Pamela said, "Did you bring any Runners home with you, Marcus? I have never seen one."

"No," he replied. "I talked with the chief magistrate at Bow Street, but after he explained what would be necessary, I changed my mind."

Jared chuckled. "Too expensive to suit you, coz? I know they require that all their expenses be paid, plus their fees."

"I would not count cost if I thought they would learn

much," Lyford said, "but there is no reason to waste my blunt when we don't even know that a crime took place. I decided my own people will learn more than a stranger would."

"Well," Pamela said with a disappointed sigh, "I should have liked to see a Runner. It seems a pity you went all the way to London without bringing even one back with you."

"As it happened, I had other business too," Lyford said.

Blushing, she turned away, but Jared said, "Business?"

"There was a shipload of wheat due from India," Lyford told him in a rather grim tone. "Your father, thinking perhaps that you would be too busy to attend to it, wrote ahead to ask me to see it safely landed. When I arrived, I found our Bristol agent there and in a dither about some mix-up or other with the London people over a number of the bills of lading for drawback—"

"Have mercy!" cried his cousin, laughing. "You don't mean to bore on about such stuff as that. Devil take it, man, you're a lord now and ought to act accordingly. You must trust Powell and his people to look after everything. I do. He was our agent in Bristol, you know, before I dragooned him to be my man of affairs. I say, Marcus, I've just had a notion. Powell would make an excellent replacement for Silas Ferguson."

"I think not."

"Well, you must decide, of course, but I think he would make an excellent steward. In any event, these ladies don't wish to hear about bills of lading or customs difficulties. I say, Miss Beckley," he went on, "wouldn't you like to work the fidgets out of that nag? You've an excellent seat for a lady, and I'll wager you're tired of this plodding pace. I'll race you to the top of that hill yonder if you like."

"Done!" she cried, lashing her mount's flank with her little whip before anyone could stop her. They were off and gone, leaving Gwenyth to turn ruefully to the earl as he brought Cyrano up alongside her gelding.

"Perhaps we ought to catch them up, sir."

He shrugged. "They won't go far. Talk to me instead. Are you enjoying your stay at Molesford?"

"Oh, yes, for I have seen little of my aunt this year, you know. She was in London for a time during the Season, but when my sister Meriel discovered she was in the family way, Auntie Wynne removed to Maidenhead until your grandmama insisted that she return to the abbey. By then, I daresay the truth was that she'd had a surfeit of small children, for she left at once. Did you say your steward's name was Ferguson, sir?"

He glanced at her sharply, taken aback by the abrupt change of subject. "Yes, Silas Ferguson. Why?"

"Well, Joey—"

"Oh, yes, of course. He was Joey's uncle."

She nodded. "Do you often look after business for your uncle, sir?"

He looked at her for a long moment, then said casually, "Since he is fixed in India, he occasionally requests my assistance when he wishes to know a matter will be properly attended to, and I oblige him."

"Oh your cousin's behalf, I collect. He does not seem to be particularly interested in his father's business."

"He wasn't raised to be. Though my uncle would like to see Jared take over my late duties, I do not think it will answer."

"I see. What is a bill of lading?"

He chuckled. "I doubt that it would interest you."

"You wrong me, sir. I am interested in many things." Besides, she told herself, if he talked about such boring stuff as that, perhaps she would not continue to feel so overwhelmed by his nearness. Cyrano was so close to Prince Joseph that Lyford's body nearly touched hers. Bills of lading might help defuse the tension rapidly building within her.

Lyford looked at her narrowly, but when she returned his look with one of limpid innocence, he shrugged. "Very well, then, a bill of lading is a list of the items in a ship's cargo."

"That's all?" That would never do. Jared and Pamela had

disappeared over the hill, so she had time to fill. She remembered something else that had aroused her curiosity. "Tell me again why your Bristol agent went to London. For that matter, why do some vessels land at Bristol and others in London?"

"Enough!" He grimaced. "If you are really interested, I will explain. Our ships from Barbados land at Bristol because the cargo, which is primarily rum and tobacco, is not meant only for England but for other places too. It would be a waste of valuable time to sail all the way to London."

"But why come to England at all? I should think it would be more efficient to sail directly to the port of intent."

He grunted. "The law says they must. One cannot export goods from Barbados to other countries without first bringing them here to register them with customs. Foolishness, but many laws are foolish. The reason the agent went to London is more difficult to explain. Duty must be paid on all goods coming into England, you see, even if they will go somewhere else."

"But that is not fair," Gwenyth said, becoming interested despite herself.

"The unfair part is that some goods, including tobacco and rum, have to pay both duty and the excise tax. However, anything that is then exported is eligible for what they call a drawback. That means the money is repaid once the goods leave the country. Since some of our tobacco and rum stays here in England and the rest goes elsewhere, there are sometimes hitches in the proceedings. Generally, the paperwork is handled in Bristol, but in this case there was a question of a bad count, either before they left Barbados, or when they landed, or after the London goods reached London. The Bristol agent had dealt with the situation with his customary competence, but since his London counterpart questioned some of the details, they wanted to discuss the matter with me, that's all."

"I see." She didn't, but they had reached the top of the hill, and she could not see the other two riders ahead. "Where are they, do you suppose?"

"The other side of the grove of trees, I imagine," he replied, clearly unconcerned. "Are you looking forward to my grandmother's dinner party?"

She looked at him, smiling, perfectly willing to accept the change of subject. "Will you think ill of me if I confess that I am? I find your grandmother vastly entertaining."

"From which statement I deduce that she has a plan to entice as many eligible bachelors to her table as possible."

"Yes, but you must not be thinking she means to play matchmaker for Pamela or me," Gwenyth said, grinning.

"I don't. Indeed, I wish her luck in her pursuit."

Gwenyth chuckled and said without thinking, "Truly, I think she would be well-advised to place an advertisement on the first page of the *Times*." Then, hearing herself, she bit her lip and said, "I beg your pardon. What a thing to say!"

"Not at all," he replied blandly. "I know just the style of thing you mean. Very tasteful. Let me see . . ." He gazed upward, thinking, while Gwenyth watched him in astonishment. Then, just as she decided that he had thought better of it, he said musingly, " 'Attractive widow in reduced circumstances requires wealthy—' No, that won't do. How about . . . ?" He pondered as they entered the shade of the wood, then continued in a satisfied tone, "Ah, yes. 'Recently widowed lady of title, wishing to avoid the discomfort of existence in reduced circumstances, desires to wed wealthy gentleman—' "

" 'Wealthy gentleman in poor health, preferably unencumbered by heirs,' " Gwenyth put in, gurgling with laughter. "Oh, sir, we mustn't. How very dreadful we are to make fun of her!"

"Nonsense, she invites it," he said, smiling at her.

Gwenyth returned his look, wondering not for the first time just what manner of man he was. Her brother Tallyn would have taken her immediately to task for the remark she had made. He would certainly never have expanded upon it or encouraged her to do so. But this was not the first time Lyford had surprised her. He had handled the boy, Joey, with deftness, and he had not only not objected to her unfeminine desire to swim but also promised to arrange it for her. He was not a conforming sort of man at all, which was rather disconcerting at times. Indeed, he was precisely the sort of man who made the ladies of the *beau monde* frown and shake their heads. But how pleasant it was to speak one's mind to a man without fear of censure or consequence.

"There they are," he said, looking away at last as they emerged into the sunlight again.

Gwenyth gave herself a shake and noted that Jared and Pamela had dismounted some distance ahead, where the road disappeared into a second grove of trees. "What is wrong, do you think?"

"Looks like Pamela's mount picked up a stone in its shoe."

They soon discovered that that was precisely what had happened, but when they joined the other two, Gwenyth saw immediately that Pamela's cheeks were flushed, and when Jared lifted her to her saddle again, she avoided Gwenyth's gaze but made no protest when he fell in beside her, leaving Lyford and Gwenyth to follow along behind.

A quarter of an hour later, they reached a small tenant farm, and Gwenyth stayed with Jared and Pamela when Lyford dismounted, grounded his reins, and strode into the barn.

He returned in minutes. "All's well here. Lacy's a capable fellow." He mounted and led the way from the yard.

"Barn's got a new roof, I see," Jared noted.

"Put it up himself."

"So you're refitting the farms, are you?" Jared observed, raising his eyebrows.

"I'm providing materials for those who wish to do the work."

"Grandpapa said that trying to put this place in trim again would be a waste of good blunt," Jared said provocatively.

"And so it would be if I just hired men to do the work without demanding a return for it. This way the tenants take pride in what they accomplish, and when they feel a sense of pride, they do their work better and their production

increases. Lacy tells me he's already harvested his crop and
cleared two fields for the new one. Crop wasn't much this
year, because his seed was bad and there wasn't much
incentive to grow a great deal of corn or barley with the prices
forced so low. But I've promised to find a market for all
he can grow next year.''

"Fine words.''

Lyford looked at him. "I'll do it. The market is there, as
we've discovered with the Indian wheat. The mills are
working again, and we can export the surplus. Prices will
go up too, as the demand for fairness in home trade increases.''

"You ought to take your seat in the Lords,'' Jared said.
"You'd make a fine speechmaker.''

Lyford laughed. "I may do it, coz, and then you'll look
no-account.''

Pamela had been looking around her. "I don't understand
why you don't whitewash these buildings and refurbish the
fences, at least. You could get a great deal done more quickly
if you just hired it done, I should think. That is what Papa
always did.''

"Yes,'' Gwenyth agreed. "Why, I should order the grass
scythed and new fields put to hay for the farm animals, and
then I should encourage people to grow their own vegetables
and fruit and''—she lifted her chin in response to his mocking
smile—"and then I'd see to their cottages . . . and . . .''

When her voice trailed into silence, he said, "You are very
extravagant, ma'am. I have allowed Beckley's steward to
carry on as he has in the past, trusting him to know his men,
but I have no steward of my own at the moment, if you recall,
so my tenants will have improvements only if the improvements pay for themselves and the tenants do the work.''

Jared said, "I'll wager they aren't all so happy as Lacy.''

"There's been some grumbling,'' Lyford admitted, "but
they'll learn. There's naught to be gained by giving a new
cottage to a wastrel, and until I know my people better, they'll
have to prove themselves by hard work.''

They visited other farms, and Gwenyth saw that while

some showed signs of refurbishing, others showed no improvement at all. Though she understood the earl's reasoning, she thought it a pity he was unwilling or unable to spend more. Remembering the methods her sister Meriel had used to get the most out of Tallyn tenants after their parents had died and before Joss had come home to tend to his duties, she was certain the earl's penny-pinching ways would hinder the progress he so clearly desired.

When they returned to the abbey, Pamela, who had remained quiet and withdrawn, hurriedly excused herself and rushed upstairs to her bedchamber, so wrapped in her own thoughts that Gwenyth, having promptly followed her without so much as a word to their companions, nearly had the door slammed in her face.

She caught it, stepped inside, and shut it quietly behind her, though not so quietly as to avoid startling the other girl.

Pamela whirled, gasping. "What? Oh, it's you. I didn't hear you behind me. Did I hurt you?"

"Never mind that. Whatever is the matter?"

"Matter?" Pamela pulled the elegant hat from her dark curls. "I cannot think what you mean."

"Gently, my dear," Gwenyth said. "You look as guilty and distressed as a cat at an empty cream pot. Just the way you looked when Lyford and I caught up with you and Mr. Hawtrey. What possessed you to go flying off with him like that? It is not the thing, for all he is as much your cousin as Lyford is."

"Well, of course he is my cousin, and there can be nothing at all amiss in my riding out with him, even if I should choose to do so without any other company," Pamela said defiantly. "You make a piece of work about nothing, Gwen. You are not related to me, after all." Her chin was high, and her nose was up.

Gwenyth stifled a laugh. "Would you prefer that I go back to London and leave you to your relations, then, my dear?"

To her dismay, Pamela burst into tears.

"Good gracious, my dear, what is it?"

"Don't leave me!"

"Well, of course I shan't leave you. I was only trying to make you see how idiotish you were being. You will quickly bring Lyford's wrath down about your ears if you do anything so foolish as to encourage Mr. Hawtrey's interest."

"Oh, I don't care about Marcus," Pamela wailed, dashing tears from her eyes with a childish fist. "He only wants to keep me for himself. Jared thinks I'm beautiful, but, oh, Gwen, I am not by any means certain I want him to flirt with me, even if he does think that, and I don't want him to touch me!"

Gwenyth said quietly, "What happened on the road, Pamela, before we rode up to you?"

"He kissed me!"

"I thought so. Did you try to stop him?"

Pamela's eyes rounded. "No, of course not. I wanted to see how he kissed. He is very handsome, after all, is he not?"

"After a fashion," she agreed. "He is well-enough-made, and his taste in dress is unexceptionable. But for all that, he is rather childish, and there is something—"

"I stomped his foot for him," Pamela said with satisfaction.

"What? After you had encouraged him? That was not well done of you at all."

"Well, I found I didn't like kissing him, and he would not stop." She grimaced expressively. "He began moving his hands over my body, and I can tell you, I did not like that at all."

"Oh." Gwenyth looked at her for a long moment, then asked in an offhand manner, "Why did you wish to know how he kissed?"

"Have you never kissed a man, for goodness' sake?"

Remembering Lyford's kiss with a surge of warmth through her entire body, Gwenyth said brusquely, "Of course I have been kissed. I just wondered why you would invite his. I have never stomped any man's foot, Pamela."

"He made me angry because he would not let me go," Pamela said. "His hands were all over me, as though I were a mare he was testing for good lines, and if you must know,

I wanted to be far away the minute he touched me. That is always how I feel. Fanny Melcher—you wouldn't know her, for she came to Miss Fletcher's after you left—she said kissing made her knees go weak, but that is never so with me. Rather, it makes me feel a little sick. I keep hoping it will be different—with a new gentleman, you know."

"Good gracious, Pamela, do you go about experimenting with each new gentleman you meet?"

Pamela thought before she said, "Well, not every one, of course, but they all wish to kiss me, you know, except perhaps for Marcus, so it does seem a pity—"

"Don't say any more! If Lyford were to hear you talk like this, he would lock you up until he finds you a proper husband, and you would have no say in the matter at all."

"He does not intend for me to have any say. But you will not tell him Jared kissed me, will you? In all likelihood, Marcus will blame me for it, rather than him."

Gwenyth no longer thought Lyford had the slightest intention of marrying Pamela, but she was certain that her conviction would carry no weight with her friend. It was more likely, she knew from past experience, that Pamela was enjoying her little drama. On the other hand, Gwenyth could not with honesty give her the reassurance she sought regarding the incident with Jared.

"I believe that Lyford guessed what had happened as easily as I did," she said. "If he does blame you, you will hear about it soon enough."

Pamela bit her lower lip but recovered quickly, tossing her head. "I shan't let him scold me. It was not my fault."

"You had better change your dress for supper," Gwenyth said dryly, "and I had better do the same."

At the table an hour later, Lady Lyford bent a critical eye upon Pamela and said, "My dear, is that not the same dress you wore last evening?"

"Yes, ma'am," Pamela said, glancing from Lyford to Jared and back before she looked again at the countess. "I left school in rather a hurry, you see, and had only an afternoon's shopping in London, so I brought very little with me. I was fortunate enough to purchase a riding habit, but we could get only two dresses suitable to wear in the evening. I thought I had better save the second one for your dinner party."

The countess nodded. "I see. Well, that will not do at all. We must go shopping."

Pamela's eyes brightened and she carefully avoided looking at her guardian. "Oh, may we, ma'am? My papa said the only shops worth patronizing were in London, so I daresay—"

"There are some excellent shops in Oxford," said her ladyship crushingly, "but it will not be necessary even to go so far as that, for we shall find all we need in Streatley. We will make an expedition tomorrow. I've a taste for some more colorful garb, myself." She looked directly at Lyford. "There can be no objection to that plan, I trust?"

The earl gazed back at her. "There are persons, madam, who would make every objection. You have more than a month yet—"

"Of mourning? Don't be daft, Marcus. I have done more than your grandfather deserved I should do, and I have been hiding my light under gray and purple long enough. My woman has let out my pomona-green evening dress for Saturday night, and I mean to have several new gowns made up at once. I can see to Miss Beckley's needs at the same time."

"Her needs can scarcely be very great," he said dampingly. "She is not out to cut a dash, as you are, Grandmother."

Lady Lyford winced at the appellation. "We may no longer take the *Times*, Marcus, but we are not altogether out of the world, and we know perfectly well that the *beau monde* is already beginning to return to town for the king's Jubilee celebration. I don't mean to be left out of everything, I assure you, nor does Wynnefreda. Imagine a fifty-year reign. 'Tis an historical event, young man, and you'll not deny us our share of it with your fusty notions of propriety. Pamela is not in mourning, and it is your duty to see her properly fired off.''

Lyford frowned. ''It will do her credit little good to be fired off, as you call it, ma'am, by two ladies who ought to be observing those fusty proprieties to the letter. Persons of the *beau monde* set great store by such stuff, and Pamela is not old enough or of high enough rank to flout rules of proper conduct.''

''Well, I am,'' said the countess fiercely.

Pamela had been watching her in awe and unblinking hope, and Gwenyth, who had been watching them both, found it difficult to control her increasing amusement. Glancing at her aunt, she immediately wished she had not done so, for Lady Cadogan was looking straight at her, her own awareness of absurdity vying with her sense of what was right. Gwenyth knew the viscountess was tired of the restrictions of mourning, that, given the least excuse to do so, she would go back to London in a twinkling. What, she wondered, would Lyford do in the face of all-out rebellion from the females under his roof?

He continued to gaze steadily at his grandmother. ''You must do as you please, madam,'' he said with a chill in his voice, ''but I will remind you that I am responsible for Miss Beckley. She will obey me or she will return to school.''

''Pooh,'' said the old lady, undaunted. ''Miss Fletcher won't take her back. Why should she? Pamela is no longer a child, in case you haven't noted the fact. She is a young lady who ought to be looking about her for a husband.'' She smiled pointedly at Jared, who winked at her.

Lyford growled, and with a tingle racing up her spine as she waited to hear what he would say, Gwenyth thanked whatever fates had kept Lady Lyford from inviting another of her potential swains to sup with them that evening. At last, controlling his temper with visible effort, the earl said, ''Do not push me too far, madam. You may enjoy your shopping expedition, though I trust that for once you will keep a rein on your extravagance. But do not think to flout my authority over Pamela. And you," he added, turning the full force of his inflexible gaze upon his ward, "will be well-advised to behave yourself."

There was a wealth of meaning in his voice, and Gwenyth glanced immediately from the red-faced Pamela to Jared, who was also looking self-conscious. In a twinkling she knew that the earl had already spoken to Jared, at least, about what had taken place during their ride that afternoon.

Jared looked up just then and caught her gaze upon him. His mouth twisted into a wry grimace, and he rolled his eyes toward the ceiling. Not wishing to encourage him in such behavior, she looked away, only to find her gaze clashing with Lyford's.

His expression was unmistakable. He was angry, and his anger had spilled over to include her.

She looked back steadily, even defiantly. The fault was not hers, and she had no intention of allowing him to cow her with his stern looks. Her eyes flashed fire as her temper flared.

His expression softened then, but he said nothing, merely holding her gaze for a long, disconcerting moment before returning his attention to his plate. Still, it was enough. She felt as though she had won a small victory over him at last.

7

Gwenyth's first view of the fashionable little village of Streatley, with its new white bridge, shady backwaters, lively weir, and busy mills, all set before an artistic backdrop of woods and hills, filled her with pleasure. She realized at once that Streatley did not owe its reputation to one distinguishing attraction, but to many, not the least of which was its neighbor across the Thames, the Oxfordshire village of Goring.

"Does one never go to Goring?" Pamela asked Lady Lyford when that village was identified to her. "You didn't even mention its existence before."

"One doesn't mention it," the countess replied, gazing out across the river, seen clearly from their vantage point upon the cobbled roadway running alongside it. "One merely says Streatley, the name doing duty for both villages. Perhaps we will drive across the bridge once we have seen my seamstress. 'Tis an irritation, of course, that one must pay a toll for the privilege of doing so, but even Marcus can scarcely cavil at the expense when you have never been here before."

Gwenyth saw that the two communities possessed certain characteristics in common. To each was allotted a mill, but she saw at once that the mill across the river was a busier, more modern affair than the one on the near bank. The latter was by far the more picturesque, however, a fact that had inspired a number of artists to set up their easels nearby.

Lady Lyford's carriage passed the inn, the boat-builders and timberyard, and a number of pretty waterside cottages set in gardens with gay flowerbeds and ornamental walks, before turning up the main street of the village, which extended in a straggling fashion uphill from the bridge toward the base of the downs. Many people were afoot, ranging from fashionably attired ladies to sundry shoppers and the rather more startlingly attired artists, some sitting with their easels, others carrying palettes and easels as though they had been no more than reticules or parasols beneath their arms.

Lady Cadogan, though she had been knitting steadily throughout their journey, had no need to look at her work and was watching the busy street as they passed along it. Without turning her head, she said casually, ''The higher land commands the best views of the river and adjacent countryside, I believe.''

Lady Lyford said, ''We have not come this distance to bother about the view, Wynnefreda.'' Looking out and about as the carriage came to a gentle halt beside the narrow flagway, she added, ''There is a superior-looking gentleman yonder whom I have not seen before. I wonder if he is married. No, no, Wynnefreda, do not sneer. One must always be on the lookout if one is to succeed in one's endeavors. But come, we have arrived.''

Lady Cadogan stowed her knitting in the voluminous bag she carried with her for the purpose, while the footman opened the door and let down the steps, holding out his hand to assist Pamela. The others followed, with the countess descending last. She banged her silver-tipped ebony cane on the cobbles, much, Gwenyth thought, as though to shake from it the dust of their journey. Then, moving without its assistance and with the briskness that always surprised those who knew her true age, the little old lady led the way up the flagway the few yards to Madame Mathilde's establishment, and her companions soon found themselves comfortably seated upon velvet chairs exclaiming over styles, patterns, fabrics, and furbelows.

Gwenyth had not intended to make any purchases for herself, for her own woman in London was already at work on a number of rigs for the Jubilee celebration and the Little Season; however, she found herself unable to resist a Grecian frock of fine French cambric with a border of shaded purple embroidery. Its full long sleeves with their turned-up cuffs of lace, fastened with gold studs, were a particular novelty that pleased her very much.

The two older ladies also ordered gowns, Lady Lyford ordering several cut from colorful, rich materials and demanding that they all be edged with yards of lace. "I look well in lace," she said simply when Lady Cadogan mentioned the fact that lace was still ruinously expensive because of the duty that had to be paid. "Moreover," the old lady added with an oblique glance at her dressmaker, "I daresay Mathilde has methods of coping with that problem. Gentlemen like a lady to wear lace."

Gwenyth noticed that the countess did not insist upon lace to trim Pamela's outfits, but when the number of these was totted up at the end, she winced, deciding that it would be as well to be far from Molesford when the earl received the bills.

When they had finished their shopping, Lady Lyford commanded her coachman to drive them to Goring, and as soon as he pulled his horses to a stop in the center of the bridge to pay their toll, she shouted to her footman to open the door. "Get down, gels. I make no doubt you'll want to see the wondrous view."

Fortunately there was no traffic at the moment, and the toll keeper made no effort to move them along, so both Gwenyth and Pamela descended obediently, and Gwenyth saw at once why so many artists inhabited the two villages. The main lock and weir were just above them on the Goring side, but because the river branched below into two arms around a tree-shrouded island, there were actually two weirs and corresponding backwaters, the latter alive with waterfowl, including a number of the ubiquitous white swans for which the Thames was famous.

" 'Tis so beautiful," Pamela said. "The river branches are so much narrower below the bridge that it makes all those shady recesses and streams look like brooks in an enchanted forest."

The Goring lock was opened just then to allow the passage of a loaded barge, and the spewing water poured beneath the bridge in a tumble of white water, fighting, dancing, surging beneath their feet with a roar of noise that startled them both.

"Good gracious!" Gwenyth exclaimed, watching as one quiet backwater after another turned to roiling foam before their very eyes. Water birds, including the graceful swans, instantly took wing before the flash, their raucous cries barely audible over the roar of the water. Moments later, the barge passed below them, narrowly missing the bridge pilings on either side of it as it slipped between them. One of the bargemen, Gwenyth noted, was so tall he had to duck to avoid hitting his head on the bridge.

The nearness of the barge and the awesome power of the water made it seem for a moment or two as though the bridge would be swept away with them on it, but within a minute or two the river had returned to normal. Gwenyth drew a long, steadying breath and turned to look back at the lock as it was swung back into place. Sighting a string of laden pack mules moving onto the bridge from the Berkshire side, she realized that their driver would wish to cross to the other side in order to continue his journey, for the Berkshire-side towpath ended at the bridge, so she touched Pamela's arm, and they returned to the carriage.

In Goring there was little of interest to be seen other than the ancient church near the river, with its square gray tower and round-headed windows. As the carriage passed it, Lady Lyford explained that the church dated from the days of Henry II and Thomas à Becket.

Pamela sighed audibly.

"Yes," agreed the countess at once, "fusty stuff. But I thought you would like to look across from here. If you look downriver a bit to that point just before the bend—"

"Why, what a lovely house!" Pamela exclaimed.

Gwenyth, too, caught her breath in pleasure, for half-hidden in the foliage was a magnificent manor house ringed by beeches, elms, oaks, and chestnuts. Colorful flower gardens spilled from the symmetrical entrance nearly all the way to the riverbank.

Lady Lyford nodded, folding her hands neatly on the head of her cane. "It does present a tolerable appearance from here," she said. "Not so grand as the abbey, of course, but tolerable."

Lady Cadogan chuckled, her needles clicking rapidly. "One mustn't mention that the abbey, having been added to over a pair of centuries, looks like it was put together by guess and by happenstance, while Newton Park looks as though it was planned from start to finish, as indeed it was. I think it a most beautiful place."

"Newton Park?" Gwenyth raised her eyebrows. "Sir Spenser Newton's home?"

"The same," her aunt replied.

"Well," said Pamela, eyeing the manor house enviously, "I think it is a very beautiful house. He must be proud of it."

Lady Lyford shot her a sharp look. "You needn't think you'll ever live there, gel. He ain't a marryin' man, Sir Spenser ain't. He's avoided the parson's mousetrap these fifty years and more, and I can tell you it has been set for him by sharper wits than yours. He ain't about to be snared by a sugar-candy morsel like you."

Pamela's mouth dropped open. "Goodness, ma'am, I shouldn't think so for a moment. I am persuaded that he is the finest of gentlemen, but he's old enough to be my grandpapa, is he not?"

"Fiddle faddle!" snapped the countess.

A long silence fell, lasting until the carriage had crossed the bridge again to the other side, when Lady Cadogan broke it by commenting upon the difference in foliage from one side to the other, with vast fields of osier on the one side and thick forests on the other. With this harmless topic to encourage them, they soon passed on to a discussion of the superiority of Berkshire over Oxfordshire, and the rest of the journey passed without incident. Nonetheless, Gwenyth was glad to return and to leave the others behind when she went to her bedchamber to change out of her carriage gown.

Annie was in the room when she entered, in the process of selecting Gwenyth's dress for dinner. "Wasn't certain this one had been pressed proper, m'lady," she said, holding up a pale blue muslin trimmed with a border of floral embroidery.

Gwenyth chuckled. "Why don't you just admit you don't trust the Molesford servants to do their jobs properly and have done with it, Annie? Do you honestly think his lordship is the sort of man who would accept less than perfection from his people?"

"As far as he knows what perfection is," Annie replied vaguely, her mind still occupied with her search for non-existent wrinkles. She did not notice her mistress's silence.

After a long moment Gwenyth said quietly, "Do you question his lordship's qualifications, Annie?"

There was another silence, and the air grew heavy between them. Annie's cheeks flushed with dark color. She stood a little straighter and looked at her mistress, instantly chastened. "I spoke out of turn, m'lady. I beg your pardon."

"As well you might," Gwenyth said sternly. But her curiosity proved too great to allow her to drop the matter. "What did you mean by such a statement?"

"Please, Miss Gwenyth," Annie said, reverting to the way she had addressed Gwenyth in her childhood, "I've said I was sorry."

"Tell me."

"He ain't lived in England, that's all," Annie said with a hasty, dismissing gesture. "God knows where, but some heathen place, not civilized. How would he know?"

"He visited in India for a time, I believe, with his uncle, but Henry Hawtrey is a gentleman born, Annie."

"In trade," Annie said, looking down her nose.

"Perhaps, but he is an earl's son, all the same. And Lyford went to Winchester and to Oxford. He knows his position, Annie. This household lacks for nothing."

Annie pressed her lips together tightly, thus informing her mistress that she had a good deal more to say, but Gwenyth did not encourage her. Indeed, she wondered why, in the face of the countess's disapproval and Annie's—which certainly came from gossiping with the Molesford servants—she was so quick to defend the earl. She didn't doubt his capabilities, or even his ability to defend himself, for that matter, but she could scarcely say he was like any other nobleman she knew. He didn't even dress like a London gentleman, his casual attitude toward dress going beyond that of even the most determined Corinthian. Even Tallyn, for all his casual ways, dressed with much more of an eye to what was due his position than did the Earl of Lyford. And Lyford's attitude toward money was unusual too. Tallyn might balk at spending the unnecessary penny on what he considered to be unimportant details, but he never stinted himself or even his sister, despite certain complaints she had made from time to time. Her appearance, after all, reflected on him.

Thinking of Lyford put her in mind of something else. "I want my riding habit, Annie, but with the heavier cotton shirt, please, not the cambric."

Annie, in full possession of herself again, regarded her suspiciously. "It be too hot for that heavy shirt."

Gwenyth grinned at her. "But if I get it wet, it will not show so much, and I am not by any means certain that I shall find a private place for what I have in mind."

Annie sniffed. "Swimming! You're going swimming. I know you, Miss Gwenyth, and it won't do. Why, 'tis broad daylight outside, and that riverbank's just bound t' be teeming with anglers and mule drivers and heaven knows what else!"

"The mule drivers are on the public towpath, clear across the river, and if I see an angler in the vicinity, I shan't disrobe, but Lyford told me there is a place where I can swim, and I mean to find it. I shall take Miss Pamela with me, and you may come along as well, if you like, to keep a lookout and to protect my virtue."

"What, ride a horse? Me?"

Gwenyth laughed. "Don't put on airs with me, Annie Gray. I know you ride well enough when you wish to do so."

"Well, I don't wish to do so. Perhaps you might walk."

"I prefer to ride, but you needn't come. Pamela will, and we can swim turn by turn if she wishes to do so."

But Pamela had no wish to swim. Indeed, as she told Gwenyth when she was asked, she thought swimming was a masculine sport and not one in which ladies ought to engage. "Besides," she added with a shrug, "I don't know how."

"I can teach you, if you like," Gwenyth said, "but right now I need someone to accompany me. I promised Lyford I'd not go alone."

Pamela agreed willingly and went up to change into her habit. Once she was ready, Gwenyth led her through the courtyard to the stables. If Pamela wondered why she had not ordered their mounts brought around to the front instead, she said nothing.

Gwenyth had hoped to find Lyford there, for she had not seen him all day, but disappointedly he was not. Though he had pointed out the swimming place when they passed it the day before, she was not by any means certain she would remember which of several streams it had been. It was a simple enough thing to ask the stablemaster, however, and not until he told her that several of the grooms would know the spot did she realize it had never occurred to her to doubt that Lyford had kept his promise.

"I'll send one of the lads along ter show ye, m'lady," the man said. "Bright young fella, Ned be, and not one who would think ter disturb yer privacy. He'll keep a sharp lookout on the river, so as to warn ye if the locks be opened."

She nodded, agreeing at once, for neither she nor Pamela was experienced enough yet to know when a warning was necessary, and she remembered with some trepidation the force of the water pouring beneath the Streately bridge. While they waited for their horses, she looked around the stable, not really realizing what she was looking for until she espied young Joey Ferguson cleaning out one of the stalls. He looked up just then and grinned at her, looking none the worse for whatever confrontation he had had with his father.

"You have a new job, I see," she said.

He grinned. "Aye, mum, though me dad ain't best pleased."

"He didn't want you to work here?"

"He means me ter be a scufflehunter," Joey said, stopping his work to lean on his rake.

"Ah, yes, one of the men who tow the barges," Gwenyth said, puffing off her knowledge. "You're a bit small for that, I should think."

"I'll grow," he said indignantly. "Ben Forbes—that's 'is lordship's stablemaster—'e lets me curry the 'orses already, and I mean ter get 'im ter let me saddle 'em up and put traces on the carriage 'orses next. But 'e says I've got ter learn ter polish tack first," he added with a disconsolate air. "I like doing the 'orses best."

"Here, Joey," snapped the stablemaster from behind Gwenyth, "what're you about there, lad? Get back to yer work."

Hastily the boy did as he was bid, and Ben Forbes approached Gwenyth, his eyes atwinkle.

She smiled back. "He is very proud of his new job."

"Aye, ma'am, he is that, and a promising lad, at that. Your mounts be ready, and I've told young Ned ter go along wi' ye."

Half an hour later found them at a shady backwater where a pretty little stream fed into the Thames. The chalk downs rose steeply behind the surrounding forest. They were below the ruins and the Molesford lock, just above a wooden footbridge, a much less distinguished cousin of the toll bridge at Streatley.

They had paused to watch the lockkeeper open the flash lock, and Gwenyth saw that the operation was a simple one. Standing on a catwalk above the gate, he removed a series of paddles and the posts between them, then opened a latch, allowing the catwalk that had held them all to swing back on a pivot-post set into the bank, the man riding it as it swung. When the barge had passed, he easily poled the catwalk back into place, replacing the paddles and beams when he had the walk in position again.

When asked what kept them in place, Ned explained, "There be a sill at the bottom, and the current keeps 'em pressed against it. Harder the current, stronger they hold. Be safe a while now fer swimming, m'lady. There be a pound lock at Pangbourne, ye see—a sort o' channel to one side o' the river, closed both ends—so the current don't change so much as wi' the flash locks. If'n ye keep t' the near side o' yonder point, should be safe enough, I'm thinkin'."

Gwenyth nodded, remembering the activity they had watched on the river at Pangbourne and realizing that the river had not been blocked all the way across but only on the Oxfordshire side, where a channel had been constructed with gates at either end. The greatest danger would come from upriver.

They soon came to the backwater, and it was all she had expected it to be and more. A strong rope had been tied round the trunk of a sturdy tree, and there was a noose already tied in the free end that she could slip over her head and around her waist. The area Ned indicated as being safe was not large, but she could certainly immerse herself and swim a short distance in near-seclusion, for the branches of several large willow trees dipped low over the opening where the stream met the river, providing a screen from the river traffic.

"This is delicious," she said to Pamela when Ned had left them alone and ridden back to a point along the riverbank from which he could watch the Molesford lock.

The younger girl shook her head and bent to test the ground beneath the trees. " 'Tis damp, Gwen. I make no doubt the river runs right up onto the shore here when the lock is opened."

Gwenyth looked closely. "Oh, I don't think so. There are no puddles, and the bank is steep. Don't sit on my towel, goose. There is a blanket tied to my cantle that you may use."

Pamela helped her out of her habit, and Gwenyth removed her shirt, deciding that the area was secluded enough for her to swim in her shift. The water was chilly, but its chill was welcome, for the ride had been a warm one; however, knowing that Annie would have a fit if she returned with her hair in a wet tangle, she kept her head above water as she paddled back and forth.

She could feel the current from both stream and river. If not for the rope around her middle, she mused, and if she were to let herself just float, she would be carried right out into the middle of the Thames, past Pangbourne, no doubt all the way to London and the sea. The thought was a pleasant one. Just to drift on the current without any cares or concerns. She let herself go, but it was only a moment or two before the rope caught. Swimming back toward the bank required more powerful strokes, but it was not difficult. The place would do nicely, she decided.

On the way back, to her surprise and pleasure, they met Jared and the earl riding along the riverbank. Lyford raised his brows in silent query.

"The pool is perfect," Gwenyth told him. "I enjoyed my swim very much. Thank you, sir."

He grinned. "And you, Pamela, did you enjoy yourself?"

"There were bugs," she said flatly, as though no further comment were necessary.

Jared laughed. "I like the whirligig beetles and damselflies best, don't you?"

She wrinkled her nose at him, making him laugh all the more.

Lyford said, "Did you like Streatley?"

"The village is charming," Pamela said. "I was surprised to find an establishment like Madame Mathilde's so far from London, but I quite understand why she should prefer Streatley, and your grandmama tells me that she finds plenty of customers there."

Gwenyth held her breath, refusing to look at the earl, but he only grunted noncommittally, and she breathed easily again until Jared said, "I've heard of Madame. Dashed costly, her bits of silk and lace. Hope you didn't outrun the constable, Pamela. Lyford won't like that, you may be sure."

Gwenyth glared at him, but Pamela said only, "One must have clothes, Jared. Even Gwenyth ordered a new gown, although she had not intended to do so."

Lyford grimaced. "I am certain the urge to be extravagant overcame her just as it did the rest of you. I have noted that that is the natural way with women, and with many young men, for that matter," he added with a speaking look at Jared.

Pamela was still concerned with her own thoughts. "But one must dress, Marcus, and it is my money I spend, not yours, and since your grandmama intends for us all to go to London for the king's Jubilee celebration—"

Lyford cut into her artless prattle without ceremony. "We have already discussed that, Pamela. Until matters here have been sorted out to my satisfaction, I cannot afford to dally in town, and until I can remain there with you, you will not go, Jubilee or no Jubilee."

"But—"

"That is my final word on the subject," he said, turning abruptly to Gwenyth. "Do you choose to return to London for the celebration, ma'am? I've naught to say about what you do, of course." His concern, however, as well as the wish that he did have the power to stop her, was evident in his expression.

Gwenyth smiled at him. "I fear you are saddled with me until my brother returns from Wales, sir, which may be some time yet, though he said he would be no longer than a fortnight. He has forbidden me to stay alone at Tallyn London House."

Pamela looked at her, and Gwenyth knew she was remembering her threat to return to London if she did not behave. There was nothing to say to that, however, so Gwenyth ignored the look, keeping her gaze fixed upon the earl.

He returned her smile, his own showing visible relief and a touch of amusement as well. "I agree that you ought not to stay alone, ma'am, and my cousin will be grateful for your company."

"This cousin will, certainly," Jared said with a flirtatious wink. "But will you not regret missing the excitement in town, Lady Gwenyth?"

Deciding it was best to ignore his manner, Gwenyth replied calmly, "I shall no doubt find activities here to occupy my time, sir. I am not dependent upon balls or soirees to entertain me."

"Balls and soirees," said Pamela dreamily, rousing at once from her sulks. "I have never been to a real ball."

"That is scarcely surprising," Lyford said, "but you will no doubt go to many when you are a little older."

Gwenyth, hoping to avoid an argument between the two, said quickly, "Once you are properly out, Pamela, you will soon find yourself so busy that you will scarcely have time to think. At the height of the Season, it is not unknown for a lady to visit as many as five parties in a single night."

Pamela's eyes lit up. "I daresay I shall never have to stay quietly at home."

"To be sure," Lyford said, "but for now you will have to be satisfied with my grandmother's dinner party."

She glared at him, but a look from Gwenyth was, for once, enough to prevent her from testing his patience any further.

Nothing of interest occurred in the days that followed, for apart from Sunday, when they attended services in Streatley, Gwenyth and Pamela spent their mornings in ladylike occupation in the morning room and their afternoons helping the older ladies entertain callers. Despite a steady stream of these, however, they provided little by way of stimulating entertainment, for they were all elderly and, for the most part, rather decrepit.

Most were gentlemen, for like the Berry sisters of London, Lady Lyford soon tired of the company of women. And Gwenyth soon tired of the elderly gentlemen. Apart from having her bottom pinched by two of the livelier ones, she found little in their company to amuse or interest her. Not, as she freely admitted, that they tried to divert her. They were much more interested in exchanging flirtatious repartee with their hostess, while Lady Cadogan tended to her knitting or to her tambour frame and Pamela or Gwenyth invited them to take sweet biscuits or wine.

By the following Wednesday, Gwenyth had had enough. She had seen little of Lyford or Jared except at the dinner table, and she had had a surfeit of women and old men. Above all, she wanted time and space to herself. More than once she had seen the earl or his cousin go down to the river after sunset and had assumed from the towels they carried that they went swimming, but despite the envy she felt for their activity, she had not returned to her backwater. Pamela's reaction upon being asked to accompany her a second time having been a decided negative, she had not asked again, doing her best instead to stifle her growing frustration. However, at the sound of the front bell's ringing for what must have been the twentieth time Wednesday afternoon, she suddenly stood up.

"I hope you will excuse me, ma'am," she said to Lady Lyford. "I have just remembered something I must attend to."

The countess, her mind on a tale the gray-haired gentleman at her side had been telling, merely waved a hand at her, but Lady Cdogan said, "What is it, my dear?"

Gwenyth looked at her helplessly. "I . . . I believe I am getting a headache, Aunt."

"But you never . . . Oh." Lady Cadogan looked around at the company and nodded. "I see. Perhaps some fresh air would help."

Gwenyth nodded.

Pamela, seated beside Sir Spenser Newton on a claw-footed settee, said, "Do you wish me to go with you, Gwen?"

Sir Spenser took the opportunity to shoot a glare at the old gentleman beside the countess, and Gwenyth, seeing the look, hid a smile. "If you wish to do so, you may, certainly," she said, "but it is not at all necessary."

"Then I will stay here," Pamela said cheerfully. "Sir Spenser is just telling me the most fascinating story about when Cromwell's men took over Newton Park. They rode their horses right into that glorious house, Gwen, and burned volumes and volumes of precious books and papers! Can you credit it?''

Gwenyth shook her head, not wishing to be drawn into the discussion, and she was grateful when her understanding aunt made a surreptitious little gesture of dismissal. Heeding it, she fled to her bedchamber, ringing for Annie to fetch out her riding habit. When she was dressed, she slipped out and across the courtyard to the doorway leading into the stable wing.

The stables were quiet at the moment, so she walked quickly through them, sure she would find the grooms in the outer yard. Not until she saw Joey feeding a carrot to the young roan gelding she generally rode did she realize what she really wanted to do.

"Joey," she said quickly, "can you saddle Prince Joseph if I help you?"

"Kin do it m'self," the boy said scornfully, coming toward her, "but there b'ain't no need. The others be just outside. Ben's beginning ter train a young colt 'is lordship brung home. I'd a gorn ter watch 'im too, but 'e said I was ter muck out stalls instead. Don't matter 'ow much a feller mucks, either," he added dolefully. "There's allus more muck ter muck."

She chuckled. "You fetch the gear, and I'll go ask Ben if you can come along as my groom. The practice will do you good."

The boy's eyes lit up enthusiastically, making her hope she could convince the stablemaster to let her take him.

8

Gwenyth found Ben Forbes in the yard, as Joey had said she would. Neither Lyford nor Jared—fortunately, from her point of view at the moment—was anywhere to be seen. She knew Jared had intended to visit friends that afternoon, and assumed that the earl was once again doing the rounds of his tenant farms or attending to other estate business. She approached the group of stableboys and grooms watching Ben with the colt.

The stablemaster saw her and handed the lead rein to one of his minions. "D'ye need a mount, m'lady?"

"Yes, I do, but I've a favor to ask, Ben." She explained that she wanted to take Joey with her.

"His lordship wouldn't like it, ma'am. Ought ter have a proper groom, you ought."

"I mean just to ride to the backwater where I swim, Ben, no further, and I promise we shan't be gone above two hours. The thing is, you see, that Miss Beckley does not wish to go, and I want someone who will talk to me. You know how it is when one takes a groom. He is nervous of talking to a lady. But Joey interests me, and he will tell me things about the river and the nearby countryside."

"That he will," the head groom agreed with a grin. "He'll chatter right willingly, but like as not I'd best send another along wi' ye, ter be safe."

"No, you mustn't, for that would silence Joey as well. He would take his tone from the older groom."

She had to exert herself to convince him, but at last Ben agreed, sending Ned only to oversee the saddling of Prince

Joseph. By then, however, Joey had managed the task on his own and was standing with a smug look on his face beside the gentle gelding. A second horse, also saddled and bridled, stood nearby.

Ned looked at the boy sternly. "This b'ain't yer task, lad. Like as not, ye've mucked it up."

"No, I ain't," the boy said. "Even the cinches be tight. I waited till Prince Joseph stopped puffing 'is belly out, just like you do, and then I yanked 'er tight. I'm stronger nor what I look ter be, Ned."

Checking girth, cinch, stirrup, and bridle, Ned nodded. "Looks good enough, I reckon, but ye'd best not let harm come to her ladyship, lest ye've a wish for a talk with the lord."

Gwenyth didn't think for a moment that Ned referred to the Almighty, although from his point of view, it might well, as she knew, amount to the same thing. She grinned at Joey. "He'll take excellent care of me." Then she nearly ruined it by adding, "We're only riding along the river path, after all."

Joey's face fell, but he recovered quickly. "There be bad men on the river," he said stoutly. "Me dad said so. But I'll look atter you, I will."

"I'm sure you will," she said.

They rode in silence until they reached the grassy path along the river. Then Gwenyth said, "What sort of bad men did you mean back there, Joey?"

He slanted her a look without turning his head. "Just men," he muttered. "Me dad said."

Realizing that more direct methods were called for, she said bluntly, "I know that Silas Ferguson was your uncle. Do you think someone killed him?"

He turned his head and looked straight at her, replying with equal bluntness, "Aye, they did."

"But his death might just as well have been an accident," she pointed out.

"Warn't," he retorted, turning his gaze back to the path. "Uncle Silas died o' a clout on the 'ead. Me dad said so.

Said it come o' talkin'out o' turn and that a body mustn't.''
He looked stricken for a moment, then glanced guiltily at
Gwenyth. "I oughtn't ter talk neither, I reckon.''

"Well, if you are afraid to do so,'' she replied thoughtfully, "then of course you must not. But I am only a woman,
you know, not a villain. And furthermore, I will engage to
say nothing to anyone of what you tell me. It is a trifle
worrisome, you know, thinking there might be murderers
about.''

"I ain't afraid,'' Joey said, straightening in his saddle.
"Nor ter talk and not o' them. ''They'll be looking fer yon
treasure, like or not.''

"Treasure! My goodness, what treasure?''

"Uncle Silas said there be a treasure hid. That was afore
he was kilt, o' course. Said it were as good as the 'Oly Grail,
whatever that be. Uncle could read, so like as not 'e found
it in a book. O' course, others might already 'ave found it—
the treasure, I mean. Me dad did say as 'ow someone opened
the lock the night Uncle Silas were clouted.''

"How could he know that? Did the lockkeeper tell him?''

"No, Nat Philps were fit ter bust, 'e were, 'cause they
didn't get 'is paddles back in straight. Two of 'is new ones
got split on account o' not bein' fit proper against yon sill.''

"Can anyone open a lock, then?''

"Aye, but they be s'posed ter put it back proper.''

"I see. Tell me what your uncle said about the treasure,
Joey. What kind of treasure is it?''

He shrugged. "Don't know no more 'bout it. Uncle Silas
said 'e seen what 'e seen. Me, I think it musta been near
the river somewheres, 'cause 'e took a boat the night afore
'e died ter visit a lady 'e knowed 'cross the river. Come back
late then, 'e did. I looked, though,'' the boy added, frowning.
"Couldn't find nothing. Even looked under the ruins—there
be some old monks' cells there—and in them storage sheds
in the garden and by the lock. Warn't nothin' nowheres 'cept
some great piles o' barley husks and such like muck in the
cells.''

A chill raced up and down her spine as she realized he

had been snooping into the same sort of thing that had probably got his uncle killed. There was no doubt in her mind that Silas Ferguson had been murdered. "Joey," she said gently, "you must promise me you won't talk to anyone else about any of this. 'Tis best if you don't mention the treasure or even your uncle."

"That's what me dad said," the boy replied, furrowing his brow. "Said 'e'd skelp me an I did." He looked at her, taking her measure yet again. "You won't tell, will you? Don't need another skelpin' yet a while, if'n it's all the same ter you."

She grinned at him. "I won't tell."

He nodded, and they fell silent for a time, until they reached the backwater. Then, thinking he might prove to be an acceptable lookout for her swimming, Gwenyth set him to watching the lock for her, making certain he understood the importance of watching carefully before she guided Prince Joseph to the shady place she and Pamela had visited before.

It was lonely there, and quiet. She had not noticed before how quiet. Even the river noises were muffled. Then, a moment later, a single swan glided past, and soon afterward the noises of the woods began again, giving her to understand that her own presence had silenced them. Even so, her desire to swim had vanished. She felt vulnerable, and she realized she would have difficulty getting in and out of her habit without help and that she didn't really trust Joey to keep his eyes on the river. Sooner or later he was likely to get bored and come to see what was keeping her. Thus, she removed only her boots and stockings to paddle her feet in the cool water, but even that was refreshing. A half-hour later, pulling on her boots again and leading Prince Joseph, she went to find the boy.

They spoke little on the way back, Joey merely pointing out the wiry figure of Nat Philps for her as they passed the lock and, a few moments later, pointing to his father in a gang of men across the river by the capstan.

"He be the biggest," the boy said proudly.

"I see him," Gwenyth said. She had seen someone else as well. "His lordship is coming, Joey. See, there, on the path ahead near the bend."

"Aye." The boy glanced uncertainly at her, and she realized that he thought Lyford might disapprove of his absence from the stable and had doubts of her ability to protect him against the earl's possible displeasure.

Lyford was indeed frowning when they joined him, but he said no more than, "I will attend her ladyship now, Joey. You ride on ahead and help Ned and the others with the feedbags."

With visible relief, the boy urged his mount to a canter and soon left them behind.

Gwenyth said calmly, "He serves as my groom, sir. You ought not to have dismissed him so cavalierly."

Giving her a straight look, he said, "He is not only not your groom, but he cannot provide sufficient protection for you either while you ride or while you swim. Indeed, if you should dare to tell me that you did swim with only that brat for company, I shall have a good deal more to say to you than you will like to hear."

She returned look for look. "Indeed, sir? You have not that right, I believe."

"You would be wiser not to put me to the test, Lady Gwenyth." The stern look on his face as he said the words was similar to one she had seen on Tallyn's face more than once. Biting her tongue, she decided not to press the issue.

He was riding on her left, and just then the two horses moved nearer one another and Gwenyth's skirt brushed against his leg. He took a firmer grip of the stallion's rein and widened the distance again, but the touch had made her singularly conscious of the fact that she was alone with him. She saw a tightness in his jaw that she had not noted before and wondered if he had worried about her safety.

When she still had not spoken a moment later, he said, "Well, must I ask?"

"Ask?" She looked at him, puzzled, but only briefly. "I didn't swim, sir. I thought about it but decided . . . that is,

I was afraid that . . ." She blushed, not wanting to tell him she had feared that the boy would watch her. "Well, I didn't, that's all."

To her surprise, he chuckled. "Joey has a stronger sense of integrity than one might think. I doubt that he would invade your privacy if you made it clear to him that you trusted him not to do so. However," he added, serious again, "when I asked you not to swim alone, I meant that you should take an adult with you, not a child, and not only a groom to watch for the flash but a woman as well, to sit nearby. You could drown before your lookout ever realized you were in trouble."

"I swim well, Lyford," she said.

"There are weeds and the current to reckon with," he retorted. "We won't argue about it."

She looked at him for a moment, then smiled. "No," she said, "we won't. I trust you won't blame Joey or Ben for any of this. It was entirely my fault. I fled your grandmama's drawing room out of boredom and decided I wanted company on my ride."

"Yes, Ben explained that much to me," he replied, looking straight ahead.

"Oh, dear," she said, conscience-stricken. "You were angry with him. I hope you were not too harsh, sir."

His lips pressed together for a brief moment before he said abruptly, "What did you want to talk to the boy about?"

Gwenyth's breath caught in her throat, and she looked away, unable to think what to say to him. Not for a moment did she believe he would think kindly of her attempt to learn more about Silas Ferguson's death. "I . . . I merely wanted to talk, sir, about various matters—the river, Berkshire, the chalk, scufflehunters . . ." She glanced at him, only to look quickly away again when she found him regarding her more sternly than ever.

"I expected honesty from you at least, Gwen," he said, very gently indeed.

Flushing, she forced herself to look at him again. "I beg your pardon, sir. That was uncommonly cowardly of me,

I know, but I am persuaded you won't like the truth.''

"No doubt you are right," he replied, "but suppose you tell me anyway.''

With a sigh she said bluntly, "You told me that Silas Ferguson was Joey's uncle. I wanted to know more about him, that's all, about his death.''

"I thought that might be it.'' He sounded grim rather than satisfied, however, and she knew he was displeased, but there was nothing she could say in her own defense, so she remained silent. After a long moment he said, "Do you fancy yourself in the role of first female Bow Street Runner, Lady Gwenyth? If you mean to play the part seriously, you must order yourself a small black occurrence book to carry in your reticule.''

She wasn't certain whether he had meant to hurt her or not, nor could she have explained why the lump rose in her throat, making it hard for her to swallow. She did know, however, that a scolding would have been easier to bear than his gentle mockery. Glancing at him again, she saw that he was watching her closely, measuringly, as though he would guess how his words had affected her. The look stirred her temper, making her eyes flash.

"You need not mock me, sir. I have seen little by way of extraordinary investigation into the matter of Mr. Ferguson's death, although more than one person has suggested foul play. I am a guest here, as is my aunt. I believe I have every right to question whether we are safe in your house.''

"Certainly," he agreed, "but you would have done better to question me, you know, rather than Joey. I should then have assured you that I have the matter well in hand, that there is no cause for you or Lady Cadogan to be alarmed.''

"Would you have admitted that Mr. Ferguson was most likely murdered?" she asked. "Or would you have insisted, as Mr. Hawtrey did, that his death was an accident? As I recall, when the subject arose before, you allowed Mr. Hawtrey's comments to pass unchallenged.''

He did not answer immediately, again surprising her, for

she had been certain he would tell her it was no concern of hers, that she ought to trust him to protect her. It was what her brother would have said in a like circumstance.

"I don't know what I would have told you," he said at last. "I suppose much would have depended upon what, precisely, you happened to ask me."

"Was he murdered?"

"Yes, I'm nearly certain of it, but I should prefer that that information not be bruited about as a proven fact."

"Is there a treasure?"

His eyebrows rose. "Young Joey has been busy."

"Well, is there?"

He shook his head, but more in resignation than as a negative response. "I shouldn't suppose there is anything hereabouts that would count as a real treasure. It is my belief that Ferguson discovered something, but I don't know what it could possibly have been. Perhaps he then made certain unwise demands in the wrong quarter."

"Money for silence about what he had found?"

"It would not be the first time a man was killed for such a reason," he said. Then, looking directly at her, he said harshly, "Look here, my girl, you keep out of all this."

"And if I don't?" She returned his look, challenging him.

He groaned. "Why hasn't your brother married you off to a strict, overbearing husband who could keep you out of mischief? Tell me that, for I should like very much to know."

She pretended to consider the matter. "I do not think I should like one who was overbearing, you know. In fact, I am persuaded that I shouldn't like having one at all." When she saw the surprise in his face, she said with a smile, "Tallyn doesn't force me, sir. That is the one great advantage to have come out of his years in America, that he does not constrain me, or indeed any of us, to march to his piping. Oh, he was strict when I was young, and still can be so if one of us behaves badly, for he takes his duties as head of the family seriously. But when I told him I had no wish to marry, that was the end of it."

His surprise was clearer than ever now. They had reached

the abbey, but he made no move to turn from the river path, and she could not take the lead while he rode where he did. Realizing that she had no wish to end this particular conversation anyway, she held her peace, allowing him to guide her past the front gardens to the tree-shaded riverbank beyond.

Finally, watching her closely, he said, "You truly have no wish to marry? Ever?"

She shrugged. "I cannot imagine why any female of sense would wish to do so, unless of course, like your grandmama, she requires financial support."

"My grandmother," he said grimly, "has no such need while she remains beneath my roof."

Seeing that she had offended him, she was quick to apologize. "I was not criticizing you or your grandmama, sir. Truly, I was not. But you must see that while you control the purse strings—as indeed you do, for she cannot live as she is accustomed to living without your leave to do so—she lives under your thumb. Auntie Wynne has a great deal more independence."

"Your aunt is no spendthrift."

"Do you think not? You ought to see her during the Season, my lord, before you make such a judgment. The point is, however, that she has control over her own life and fortune. I do not, and your grandmama does not, though she would have had it, had your grandfather done properly by her and not wasted her fortune on himself. A woman must be married and her husband must die before she has any right to look after herself. Then she can live well only if she has been provided for in his will or if he has left her dower money untouched. And men, in my experience, rarely concern themselves with their wives' needs. There, that is plain speaking indeed, but you provoked it."

He was silent again for a moment before he said, "From what you say, I must suppose that you also are on the lookout for an elderly, decrepit husband."

"Goodness, no!" She laughed. "Whatever would make you suppose such a thing as that, sir?"

"Under circumstances as you present them, getting through the marriage itself as quickly as possible seems to be the smart thing for any sensible woman to do. You did say that she must marry and be widowed before she can control her life."

"The law says that; I didn't. 'Tis as foolish a law as the one that says goods must be shipped to England before they can go elsewhere. As you must know, sir, until a woman marries, she is by law a child and therefore somewhat protected. If her husband dies, she is by law a widow with certain rights. But while a woman is married, she has no position under the law, but belongs to her husband entirely, to use as caprice moves him to use her, just as he may use whatever wealth she brings to the marriage."

"I would perhaps be foolish to suggest that men are rather better trained than women to handle money," he said dulcetly.

"But that is a weakness in the upbringing of women, not in the women themselves," Gwenyth told him, keeping her temper in check. "My brother explained the whole to me one day when I was in a passion with him over some triviality or other. The truth came as a shock to me, for I must tell you that I had expected better things of life."

"Yes," he said, "tell me."

She looked at him curiously, put out of countenance once again by the fact that he seemed genuinely interested. She had a sudden fleeting image of the two of them in London at Almack's Assembly Rooms, discussing such matters over cups of orgeat while members of the fashionable *beau monde* whirled about the dance floor behind them. The thought brought a twinkle to her eye, and she saw his expression sharpen, as though he would see into her mind. She had a sudden feeling that he would laugh if she shared the image with him, but although she could not bring herself to do that, she had no qualms about otherwise explaining.

"I had seen my sister Meriel as an independent lady," she said. "For a time while we were growing up, she took charge of everything. She ran Plas Tallyn for three years after my father died, before Joss came home again from America, and everyone did her bidding. I also saw a good deal of my aunt during that time, and she was clearly independent, so I thought one had only to age to achieve such status. I made the mistake of telling Joss he would have nothing to say about what I did once I grew up, so you will comprehend my dismay when he informed me, rather brutally, that I should then have to answer to a husband.''

"But did you not think of marriage before then?''

"Oh, perhaps, I suppose, in a romantical sort of way. Every young girl does that. But I was not entirely conformable as a child—don't snort like that, you will do harm to yourself.'' She paused expectantly, but he made no further comment, so she said, "I fear it never occurred to me that marriage would mean letting someone else choose my friends for me, restrict my spending money, order my coming and going—even tell me what to think!''

He was silent for a moment. Then he said thoughtfully, "I expect a good many husbands do that sort of thing.''

"All gentlemen are accustomed to ordering matters as they choose,'' she said. "You are.'' She had not meant to speak the last two words aloud, but now that they were out, she watched him closely to see how he would react.

He smiled, catching her gaze and holding it, making her wonder again how it was that he did so so easily. "I have grown accustomed to telling others what to do and having them obey me,'' he said, "but I did not grow up believing I should have control over everyone around me, as I have now, without doing anything more to earn it other than to have been born. My Uncle Edward had that attitude after Cadogan died, as did Edward's eldest son, because they each expected to inherit Molesford. I didn't. My father left me to Uncle Henry, and I was raised to believe I would have to control my own destiny by hard work.''

She made a sound of sympathy, only to have him shake his head at her.

"I don't regret my past. My uncle taught me things that are worth knowing, and he provided me with an excellent education. I made my own way, and I think I am better prepared for the position I now hold than many are who grow up knowing what they will have. I only hope that someday I will find myself a wife who won't hold my connection with trade against me.''

"Good gracious, Lyford," she said, stunned, "you are an earl with a vast estate, however impoverished it may be. You will find any number of ladies of quality who would willingly overlook much worse things than a youthful connection with trade, now left safely behind, to share all that with you!"

She sensed his immediate withdrawal and his voice was tight when he said, "Does that include you, Lady Gwenyth? If I put my past behind me, would you marry me for my title and estate—if I were to ask you to do so, that is?" he added hastily.

Gwenyth felt an unexplainable thrill race through her as he spoke, but his last words recalled her to her senses. With careful dignity she said, "I have already explained, my lord, that I do not intend ever to marry. If I were ever to change my mind, however, I can safely assure you that no title or estate, however impressive, would influence my decision."

He looked at her for a long moment, then appeared to realize how far they had ridden. "Look here," he said suddenly, "they will be wondering what's become of us." He wheeled Cyrano, waited only until she had turned Prince Joseph, then urged the stallion to an easy, ground-covering lope.

Following him, Gwenyth wondered whether they would be able to continue their interesting conversation when they got back, for she wanted to know more. But when they rode into the stableyard, the sight of two young men striding toward them out of the stable banished all other subjects from her mind.

"Davy!" she shrieked, practically flinging herself from her saddle into the taller young man's upstretched arms. Hugging him tightly, she said, "Oh, how good it is to see you! How was the Lake District? Did you enjoy your tour?

Oh, and this is Lyford, Davy. Sir, this is my brother—''

"Davy," he finished for her, grinning. "I collected as much. How do you do?"

"Very well, thank you, sir," the fair-haired young man said, offering his hand. "I hope you won't think us unmannerly for descending upon you like this. This is my friend, Alex Webster."

The earl greeted the other young man, who was dark-haired and endowed with a round cherubic face and a pair of twinkling hazel eyes. He was an inch or so shorter than Davy Traherne and several stone heavier. He grinned, showing even white teeth. "Pleasure, sir," he said.

"Webster . . . you Salton's son?"

"I have that honor."

Lyford nodded. "You'll be right welcome then, lad. Your late grandfather was one of my grandmother's beaux. She will be delighted to meet you."

Lady Lyford was indeed glad to welcome both young gentlemen when they were presented to her in her drawing room and at once informed them of the dinner party she had planned in their honor.

"Dinner party!" Davy looked aghast. "Thought you was in mourning, ma'am."

"Fiddle faddle," the countess said. "One don't wish to molder on the vine merely through following outdated fashions."

Lady Cadogan spoke with amused reproach. "Almeria, what will these young men think of you?"

Lady Lyford waved the protest aside. "Tend to your knitting, Wynnefreda. For you to be telling me how to behave after you took yourself off to London for the Season is the outside of enough. For all you cared, I might as well have been rooted in my garden, for I could not leave Molesford."

"You stayed here," Lady Cadogan said calmly, "because you knew perfectly well that you would dislike being in London without being able to do anything of interest there."

Davy and Mr. Webster were looking distinctly uncomfortable, and Gwenyth could not blame them. Nor did she think she ought to leave them alone with the two women while she went up to change out of her riding habit. Lyford had not accompanied them to the drawing room, nor had Jared returned from wherever he had gone. She was wondering if she might suggest that they allow a servant to show them to their rooms, where they could tidy themselves before dinner, when the door opened and Pamela entered.

She was wearing one of her new gowns, a delicious white muslin embroidered at the hem and over the bodice with tiny violets entwined with greenery. A narrow green sash encircled her ribs just below her magnificent breasts, and her hair had been piled in an artful tumble of curls atop her shapely head. Her eyes sparkled at the sight of the two young men.

"Oh," she said, halting just past the threshold. "I did not know you were entertaining, ma'am."

"Come in, gel, come in," commanded the countess. "These two handsome young gentlemen have come to stay a spell. The tall, fair one is David Traherne, Gwenyth's brother. The other is his friend Alexander Webster, who is the son of Viscount Salton." She smiled reminiscently. "I remember the viscount's grandpapa very well. Very well, indeed. Impudent fellow."

Pamela stared at her, but when Davy and Alex got quickly to their feet, she collected herself to acknowledge their greetings. Lowering her eyelashes, she smiled demurely. "You have been in the Lake District, Gwen tells me."

"We were," Davy said, staring at her in awe. His friend was no less stricken. Indeed, Mr. Webster seemed to have lost his tongue altogether. Only when Davy jabbed him with his elbow after Pamela had taken her seat near the countess did he realize he was still standing and scramble hastily back to his chair.

Hiding a smile, Gwenyth said politely that she wished to change her habit for a dinner gown. As she turned to leave the room, however, a footman stepped through the open doorway to announce the arrival of Sir Antony Davies.

"Antony?" Gwenyth looked in surprise at Lady Cadogan. "Were you expecting Antony, ma'am?"

She shook her head, but the countess said sharply to the footman, "Show him up, for goodness' sake, and tell the housekeeper to prepare a room for him. He will stay for our dinner party. Can't ever have too many gentlemen."

9

When Sir Antony Davies entered the drawing room several moments later, the Earl of Lyford accompanied him, and the pair, both tall and broad-shouldered, made an imposing sight.

Like Lyford, Sir Antony wore riding dress, but despite his journey, he was precise to a pin, not a thread or hair out of place, his boots polished to a mirror gloss, his breeches stainless, his coat fitting without wrinkle or crease. Lyford, on the other hand, looked like a man who had been working all day. Both gentlemen appeared to be relaxed, but beneath the earl's surface composure one sensed suppressed but simmering energy, while Sir Antony merely looked a trifle sleepy.

He made his bow to the countess and Lady Cadogan, then turned that sleepy gaze upon Gwenyth. "Well, little sister?"

She grinned at him. "Very well, thank you, sir, but how come you here to us? What a surprise it is to see you!"

"My lamentable manners," he said glibly, stepping forward to bow, to her great delight, over Gwenyth's hand. "I received a letter from my wife, informing me of your presence here," he went on, his eyes twinkling as he straightened and looked down at her. "She commanded me to present myself forthwith to . . . ah, that is . . . to discover if all was well with you."

Lady Cadogan regarded him shrewdly. "To see that Gwenyth had not got into mischief yet is more likely what Meriel commanded, but if her letter took well nigh a fortnight to reach you, our post hereabouts must be lacking indeed. She told us you were in Oxfordshire, you know. Only across the river, no doubt.''

"Did she tell you that?" The sleepy gaze turned full upon her. "Then she will also have told you that I had business there, ma'am. It has kept me fully occupied, no doubt due to my unworthiness for my position."

"Your unworthiness is naught but air in your head," Lady Cadogan retorted tartly, looking him directly in the eye, "but your business, if I may be so bold, sir, is not in Oxford-shire, but at home with your wife. I do not like what tale I hear of her from Gwenyth, and that I tell you to your face."

The sleepiness disappeared at once, and Gwenyth thought the large gentleman grew even larger before her very eyes, till he seemed to fill the room and to dwarf even the earl, still standing silently beside him. "What's this?" he demanded. "Is something amiss with Meriel? Tell me!"

Before Lady Cadogan could speak, Gwenyth said quickly, "She is perfectly stout, sir, only a little tired. She promised that it is nothing out of the ordinary and assured me that she is being obedient to your command to take care."

If he looked more suspicious than ever, she could scarcely blame him, for her sister Meriel was not known for her sub-missive nature, but he relaxed visibly when she was able to meet his gaze steadily without looking away.

Lady Cadogan turned back to her knitting, her needles clicking with their customary rapid rhythm, but Lady Lyford snorted and said, "Left commands, did he? Typical man. Home only long enough to set her to breeding, I daresay, then off again, leaving no more than orders behind to comfort her. I know the way. How many brats is she saddled with now? Three, is it not? Well, Sir Antony," she demanded when no one else responded, "puff off your progeny for us. Ain't it three of 'em?"

Sir Antony smiled at her, his lazy manner settling back into place like an old familiar cloak. "It is, madam. Three strong, healthy children, and another of the same, I hope, on the way." He shot Gwenyth an oblique look. "Just how tired is she?"

But Lady Lyford did not give Gwenyth a chance to reassure him. Cracking her cane against the floor, she snapped, "is it any wonder if she is tired? Confinements tire most women and very likely would kill a member of the true weaker sex, which is why the good Lord don't see fit to inflict them upon you."

Looking up from her work without missing a click, Lady Cadogan said with a rueful smile, "I did not intend to frighten you, Antony, dear. I was but voicing what must be every woman's wish when she is with child, to have her husband near. In any case, I daresay you mean to see Meriel soon enough."

He frowned. "I meant to remain here until Monday to visit with you and Gwen, and"—he glanced at the younger men, deep in conversation with Pamela across the room—"and Davy too, now I see he's here. Then I'd intended to pass two or three nights at home on the way to London, where important matters require my attention, but perhaps I'd best ride on tomorrow instead."

"Fiddle faddle," the countess said sharply, changing her tune without a blink. "Meriel is perfectly stout, as Gwenyth has just told you, and has a houseful of servants to look after her if she requires them. Moreover, she's proved three times already that she breeds easily enough—"

"Almeria, please!" protested Lady Cadogan.

"What?" demanded the countess. "Would you prefer that I say she's in a family way, expects to be confined, or some other modern mealymouthed twaddle? 'Breeding' is a perfectly good word. Says just what I want to say. Furthermore, it describes a perfectly natural event that most sensible women manage without fuss. Certainly, I did—seven times, though two were female. So you let the man be. He will remain for my dinner party to make up a proper number of persons at table."

Pamela's attention was diverted from her swains at last. "Have you invited more ladies, then, ma'am?" she inquired innocently. "You told us before, when we were drawing up your guest list, that we didn't have need of any more ladies, although we'd already got more gentlemen than we need.''

Lady Lyford cast her a look of profound dislike. "The *number* of guests is uneven, gel. That's all I meant. Serving is much easier with an even number of persons at the table.''

Gwenyth hid a smile and instinctively avoided meeting either the earl's gaze or Sir Antony's. Knowing the latter for a man with a well-developed sense of the absurd and an even livelier curiosity, she knew that now, barring bad news from home, there was little likelihood of his departing before the countess's dinner party.

The two younger men, both clearly besotted with Miss Beckley, likewise made no further objection to lending their presence to the occasion, going so far as to be among the first to present themselves, late the following afternoon, in the Chinese drawing room, where the guests began to gather before the meal. Lyford and Jared entered twenty minutes later, and Gwenyth, who had been watching for one of them, at least, smiled approvingly when she noted that Lyford, like his cousin, was precise to a pin in knee breeches, white stockings, and a dark coat.

Jared moved to greet his grandmother, but Lyford walked up to Gwenyth, fingering the single gold fob on his ribbon, and said without preamble, "I like that dress.''

"Do you, sir?" she replied demurely, smoothing one embroidered cuff. ''Then perhaps you will be so kind now as to forgive my extravagance.''

He looked bewildered. ''I have nothing to say about how much money you spend, ma'am.''

''Have you not? But the amount appeared to distress you most severely the day I ordered this gown,'' she reminded him with enough wide-eyed innocence to compete with Pamela.

His expression cleared. ''That is the Streatley gown?''

She nodded, adding provocatively, ''I wanted it for tonight, you see, and by being just a trifle more extravagant, was able to induce Madame Mathilde to accommodate me.''

There was a brief silence before he leaned nearer and said softly, "A properly overbearing husband would know how to deal with impertinence in his wife, I believe."

She grinned at him. "You provide me with yet another excellent reason for pursuing a permanent, independent spinsterhood, my lord." Then, before he could gather himself to reply in kind, or at all for that matter, she patted his arm gently and stepped past him to greet Sir Antony, who had that moment appeared on the threshold and, being among the last to arrive, was looking father stunned as he surveyed the assembly through his quizzing glass.

At her approach, he collected himself with visible effort, but his gaze flicked past her again before coming back to rest upon her face. "I say, m'dear," he drawled, "do you know that Lyford's standing where you left him with his mouth agape. Not the thing. Not the thing at all. Looks like a fish out of water. And who the devil are all these old men? Do you know, I had the most awful fear, standing here, that if I were to take another step into the room, I should promptly age by forty years."

She laughed. "Never mind Lyford. He is only beginning to learn that all women are not cut from one bolt of cloth. And do, if you please, show a proper respect when you speak of the countess's beaux."

"What? Not all of them!"

Chuckling, she entwined her arm with his, drawing him farther into the room. "There are only five or six tonight, and"—she sighed dramatically, fluttering her lashes at him—"not one of them in a Bath chair, more's the pity."

"A Bath chair!" He looked across the room to where the countess was holding four of her gentlemen in thrall, but his brow knitted for only an instant before he turned back to Gwenyth, his eyes atwinkle, his lips quivering with suppressed amusement. "I see."

"I knew you would," she said, satisfied. "Whatever else unkind persons may say about you, sir, they cannot complain of your being a slowtop."

"Are there complaints?" he inquired, raising an eyebrow.

But Gwenyth only grinned at him. The butler announcing just then that dinner was served, Lady Lyford bounced up from her seat and approached the two of them, her retinue following close behind her.

"Sir Antony," she said briskly, without heed for the probability of being overheard by her followers, or anyone else, "you may give me your arm in to table. 'Twill do this lot good to see me with a younger man. And you, Gwenyth, will go in with Sir Spenser. That idiotish Beckley chit has been casting sheep's eyes at the poor man since he arrived, hanging on his lips and begging him to tell her more stories about his dratted house. I won't have him put off his feed by her nonsense. Jared can take her in. She will do nicely for him, I believe."

Nearly everyone in the room must have overheard her, but other than Pamela, who colored up to the roots of her hair, no one paid her much heed. But if Mr. Hawtrey had hoped to follow his grandmother's command, he soon found he was too late, for Davy Traherne and his friend Mr. Webster leapt to escort Miss Beckley to the table. Jared was left to attend to an elderly neighbor who had accompanied her son and daughter to the party, while Lyford, making no effort to discover the female guest of highest rank, offered his arm to Lady Cadogan, who accepted with a smile. The other guests trailed in after them.

Dinner was not so much of an ordeal as Gwenyth had expected it to be, for she enjoyed conversing with Sir Spenser, and the fact that the gentleman on her left was totally deaf relieved her from taxing her conversational ingenuity in that quarter. She was disappointed, however, when the gentlemen rejoined the ladies in the Chinese drawing room soon after they had left the table, because Lyford and Sir Antony moved apart from the others to play piquet at a table in the window embrasure. Their conversation, she noticed, appeared to interest them even more than the cards did, and no one attempted to interrupt them.

The young people set up a game of jackstraws, while Lady Lyford, Sir Spenser, and a number of the older guests made up several tables for whist. When two gentlemen were left over, they promptly asked Gwenyth and Lady Cadogan to make up one more. Gwenyth abhorred whist, but there was no graceful way to decline, and there was thus nothing she could do a half-hour later to prevent her brother-in-law and Lyford from leaving the room together, still deep in conversation. They did not return, and she was unable to escape until after the tea tray had been brought in. The guests who were not staying overnight departed soon afterward, and she was able at last to make her weary way to bed, thinking that as dinner parties went it had been neither the best nor the worst of her experience.

She did not run her brother-in-law to earth until the following morning after the ladies and those few remaining guests who wished to accompany them had returned from church, when she found him in the stable talking to Davy. The sky was overcast, and there was a damp chill in the air.

Hugging her shawl around her shoulders, she greeted them, adding, "Davy, I never asked how long you and Mr. Webster intend to stay with us. I hope you will not rush off too soon."

"Depends," he replied, grinning. "Web and I mean to be in town for the opening of the new theater at Covent Garden and the Jubilee festivities, but we've no reason to go down any sooner, and every reason to put up here for a bit."

"Burnt to the socket?" Sir Antony suggested amiably.

"No, only a trifle down pin." Davy's grin widened. "When does Joss return, Gwen?"

"I have no idea. It was idiotish of him to think to make a trip into Wales and back in a fortnight. Matters at home always take longer than he expects them to. Why? Did you wish to see him particularly?"

"On the contrary," he replied. "I shall do much better without him. He wouldn't give me a sou."

Sir Antony regarded him lazily. "Hope you don't think to apply to me."

"Good Lord, no," Davy said, thunderstruck. "I'd never expect you to frank me, sir."

"No reason you shouldn't expect it, but fortunate you don't," Sir Antony said. "I've a strong notion I'd do better to save my blunt for the future. That young sprout of mine looks like being the sort who will prove to be expensive."

"And his sisters?" Gwenyth reminded him sweetly.

"Hmmm? Oh, yes, of course, and the new one too. Daresay they'll run me off my legs, the lot of them."

Davy stared at him for a moment as though he wondered whether to believe him, but when Gwenyth chuckled, he laughed. "You must think us a pair of gulls for the catching, to spin that lot to us, sir." He looked at his sister. "He was looking for Jared, Gwen. Have you seen him?"

She shook her head, looking curiously at Sir Antony. "I didn't know you knew him, sir."

"I don't. That is, I was introduced, of course, but didn't know him before. Lyford suggested I speak with him about some trifling matters we discussed last evening."

"Perhaps I might help," she suggested, hoping by her casual tone to conceal her avid curiosity.

He smiled. "Not unless you know details of the shipping trade," he said. "I've a wish to learn something about it."

"Jared will most likely refer you to his man of affairs," Gwenyth said, laughing. "His name is Powell, and I believe he resides somewhere hereabouts, but for all I have seen of him, he may be entirely apocryphal. Jared prefers to ignore the fact that he himself has anything to do with his father's business."

"Perhaps," Sir Antony agreed, "but he knows about the Bristol-to-London routes, and I am curious to learn some details about them."

"Don't they just put the goods on a ship?" Davy asked.

"No, they use the Severn and the Thames rivers. A canal connects the two, and the goods are moved on barges. They must come right past this house, actually. I'm told that Hawtrey . . . Ah, there he is now. I'll just ask him myself."

He strode away from them to meet Jared, who had entered the stableyard from the garden.

Davy looked at Gwenyth. "Mysteries?"

She shook her head. "I don't know, precisely, but I daresay Antony is merely curious. He cannot help being, you know. 'Tis his nature. No doubt Lyford spoke of the business last evening while they played piquet, and Antony wants to know more. 'Tis odd, though, that he could not discover all he wanted to know from Lyford himself."

"He sounded as though he knows quite a lot, actually," Davy said, watching the two men as they walked toward the river together. "Wonder what he thinks the hook can tell him."

"Hook?"

He reddened. "Shouldn't have said that, Gwen. I apologize. Just don't like the fellow much, is all."

"But what does it mean?"

"Oh, nothing, really." When she did not respond, he looked away, unable to meet her gaze. "It ain't something I should have to explain to a female, if you must know. Just school slang, and I ain't going to tell you more than that, 'cause knowing you, you'll use it yourself, and then we'll both be in the suds."

"You are just annoyed with Jared because Pamela likes him," Gwenyth said, getting to the heart of the matter.

"No, she don't," he retorted. "Told me so herself. Thinks he's something of a cabbage seller."

"She never said that!"

"Well, no," he admitted, "but the way she talks about him, it wouldn't surprise me if he is one."

"Mr. Hawtrey does not sell cabbages!"

"Very true," agreed Lyford, coming up behind them in time to hear her exclamation. "Much more likely to have got his fag to sell them, you know. Not one to do a job himself when he can get someone else to do it for him." When Gwenyth only stared at him, then looked at her brother and back again, Lyford smiled at her. "A cabbage seller is one who sells crib notes," he said.

She continued to look steadily at him.

"It means he helped others to cheat and probably did so himself as well," he said, adding, "Not so sure about that. Jared would have been afraid to get caught."

She turned back to her brother, shocked. "You ought never to say such a thing about someone you scarcely know."

Davy shifted his feet, watching Lyford rather than Gwenyth. "I know. I told you, I don't care for the fellow, but I ought never to have said such stuff to you."

"Why not?" Lyford asked curiously. "If it is what you believe, you certainly have no reason not to say so."

Davy stared at him, but Gwenyth found herself smiling. "What's a hook, Lyford?"

His lips twitched, but he answered evenly, "A questionable sort of person, perhaps even a liar or thief. In any event, that's the meaning at my old school. I believe the term originally referred to a pickpocket. Why do you ask?"

"I wanted to know," she said, shooting a murderous glance at her brother before she added in an even tone, "Do you join us for supper today, sir? The countess has announced that we return to country hours at once."

The earl nodded, smiling back at her in his usual way and thus warming her to her toes despite the chill in the yard. "I've some errands to attend to first," he said, "but I'll be back by then. Would you like to ride with me?"

She shook her head in disappointment. "I promised Auntie Wynne I'd help shoo the few remaining guests away before supper. The countess keeps encouraging them to stay. Sir Spenser returned with us from church this morning and means to linger till suppertime, but although Auntie Wynne doesn't mind him, she says watching the other old gentlemen writhing in the countess's clutches gives her a pain. I think she wants them gone because Sir Spenser doesn't like them here, if you want my opinion."

Lyford nodded. "Newton thinks Grandmother's making a cake of herself. Daresay he's right, but if it makes her happy . . ." He shrugged, then turned to Davy. "Like to come along?"

"No, thanks," Davy said. Then, evidently thinking some excuse was necessary, he added quickly, "Web'll be up and about any moment now. Daresay he'd wonder where I'd gone."

Lyford nodded, but the moment he disappeared into the stable, Gwenyth said, "You know perfectly well that someone would tell Mr. Webster where you had gone. You don't live in his pocket, Davy, so why did you not go with Lyford?"

"A pretty fool I'd be to give my head to him so easily for washing," her brother said scornfully.

"What are you talking about?"

"Good Lord, Gwen, don't be such a tipping noddy. He walks bang into us when I'm as good as calling his cousin a name I've no business using, and then you demand to know the definition of a word you had to have heard from me, a word I ought not to have used in the presence of a lady, even if I didn't mean it so strongly as he thought. At Oxford a hook is just someone one don't like much, someone who pushes, encroaches—you know the sort of thing! Still and all, while Lyford may have brushed it all aside then, you can bet your best gown he'd have something to say to me privately if I were such a fool as to give him the opportunity to do so. No, thank you, ma'am."

She turned back toward the house, and he fell in beside her. "You are wrong, you know," she said. "He says precisely what he means, and encourages others to do likewise. Moreover, if he had thought you deserved censure, he would not have spared you just because of my being here."

"Perhaps," Davy said musingly, "he thought he did not have the right to censure me at all."

"No," she said, grinning at him. "I doubt he thought that. Nor would it have weighed much with him if he did."

"You sound as though you like him," Davy said.

"Well, of course I like him. Why should I not?"

"That isn't what I meant, precisely. I meant you really

like him." He regarded her narrowly. "Not falling toward the parson's mousetrap at last, are you, Gwen?"

"Don't be nonsensical," she snapped. "If I were so foolish as to marry any man, I can promise you I should never choose one like Lyford."

"Why not?"

She struggled to think why not, wishing her mind had not chosen that moment to present her with delightful fantasy visions of what married life with him might be like. "I . . . I cannot think why you need ask, Davy. The man . . . the man is like all men. Yes, that's right. Just like them."

"He ain't like Joss or he'd have taken me up straightaway about my language and the things I said," Davy pointed out.

"Well, he's just as likely as Joss is to take you up over your heedless extravagance," she said without thinking.

"Aha," he said, unabashed. "So Lyford don't like you tipping over the ready, is that it?"

"Don't be silly. He has nothing to say about what I spend."

"Well, he has nothing to say about what I spend either. Which reminds me, I must have a chat with Auntie Wynne."

They had reached the entrance hall, and he left her at once. She didn't see him again until suppertime, when he disconcerted her by openly studying the earl as though to learn as much as possible about him before departing with Mr. Webster for London. That they had decided to leave much sooner than he had led her to believe became clear before the end of the meal.

"Ooh," Pamela said in response to something Mr. Webster, sitting next to her, had said, "to be leaving Tuesday. How lucky you are, sir! I want more than anything to visit London and enjoy all the Jubilee festivities."

"Come with us," said Mr. Webster amiably.

"Oh, how I wish I could!" Turning her best smile on the earl, she said, "I know I said I would not plague you, Marcus—"

"And you would be very wise not to do so now," he said gently.

She fluttered her lashes. "But I want to go."

"Well, you cannot, so don't dwell upon the matter if you wish to avoid my displeasure."

Hoping to divert Pamela so that she would not make the mistake of teasing him, Gwenyth said, "Do you go so soon as Tuesday, then, Davy? I thought—"

"First night is a week from tomorrow, you know," her brother said glibly. "Wouldn't want to miss it, but they say tickets are going quickly, so I daresay we must get to Hookham's as soon as we can in order to buy ours before they are gone. Need some togs, as well," he added cheerfully, giving her to understand that his mission with their aunt had been even more successful than he had hoped.

Sir Antony said, "Why don't the pair of you ride with me tomorrow, lad? You can spend the night at the manor and visit Meriel. Lyford was going to travel with me, but he has decided to go to Bristol first. I'd be glad of your company."

Dismayed, Gwenyth turned sharply to the earl and, without giving her brother a chance to reply, said, "You're leaving?"

He nodded. "I'm afraid I must. I will return as quickly as I can, but you may be gone before I do." He spoke to her alone, as though no one else were present, but they were not alone. She could not demand that he explain himself, though she wanted very much to do so.

Pamela's outraged voice broke the brief spell. "You were going to go to London without us?"

He looked at her. "I was to have gone on business, Pamela, a brief visit only. My visit to Bristol will, I trust, also be brief. In any case, where I go has nothing to do with you."

She said angrily, "I think it is beastly that you did not even think of taking me with you. If you had business in London, we might all have gone. Indeed, it is monstrous unfair that we are not allowed to go, whatever you choose to do."

He sighed. "We have already discussed this subject."

"But I wish to go! You are most unfair."

"That will do." He still did not raise his voice.

She looked at him, then shifted her gaze to take in the presence of Jared, Davy, Sir Antony, Mr. Webster, and Sir

Spenser. Her eyes filled with tears. "You are unkind, Marcus." Blinking back the tears and smiling bravely, she turned her gaze full upon him. "I do not know why you wish to deny me pleasure, when I have had so little of it since Papa died, but surely—"

"Leave the table, Pamela."

"What?" Her tears dried instantly, leaving no trace of their presence, but before Gwenyth could do more than wonder how Pamela managed such a trick, she said indignantly, "You cannot order me from the table like a child! I won't go."

Lyford stood up. "We will go together. And," he added when she looked mutinously up at him, "if you are thinking that I won't pick you up and carry you if you continue to behave in this childish manner, you had better think again."

Looking scared now, Pamela glanced around the table, but no one spoke up in her defense. Indeed, except for Gwenyth, the others had returned studious attention to their meals. Gulping audibly, Pamela got up and left the room with the earl.

When the door had shut behind them, the countess sniffed and said, "Hope he burns that chit's ears good and proper. Too much to hope he'd burn her backside for her instead."

"Now, Almeria," Sir Spenser said, looking at her with noticeable affection, "Miss Beckley's very young and perhaps a bit spoiled, but I daresay—"

"You be quiet," snapped the countess. "I might have known you'd take up the cudgels in her defense."

"Yes," he said, his eyes twinkling at her now, "you might. You know me better than anyone else does. And I know you. And I know you don't begrudge that lovely child her desire for a crack at town life. You'd use her in a minute as your own excuse to go, if Lyford would only allow it."

"I don't need an excuse," she told him. "Indeed, had I realized that Covent Garden was to open so soon, I'd have made my plans already. Perhaps we ought to take the *Times* again. It was a mistake to cancel my subscription." She looked at Davy. "You come see me before you leave for town, young man. I shall want you to execute some small commissions on my behalf, if you will.''

Davy nodded at once, but Lady Cadogan, sounding slightly scandalized, said, "Not opening night, Almeria!"

"No, I suppose not," the countess agreed with a sigh, "but do not tell me I mustn't see something I enjoy, for I'll do as I please, thank you very much." She glared at Lady Cadogan as though daring her to speak. When she did not, the countess reached for her cane and stood up. "Good, then let us adjourn to the drawing room, ladies, and leave these gentlemen at their leisure to swill more port than is good for them."

10

By the time Gwenyth awoke on Monday morning, all the gentlemen except Jared had departed. She knew when she wakened that the others were gone, and the knowledge sat like a stone in her consciousness. Not the sight of the sun streaming through her windows when Annie opened the curtains, or the sound of the birds singing in the garden, or the smell of freshly baked buns with her morning chocolate had power enough to cheer her.

She told herself that her mood stemmed from the sudden lack of company at the abbey, from the fact that there was now no one to talk to. But there was still Pamela, though she had not seen her since her departure from the dining room with the earl the previous evening. Her aunt and the countess were still there too. And no doubt they would see more of Sir Spenser, since it was unlikely that the countess would really make good her threat to leave them for London. Certainly she had said nothing more about it the previous evening when the gentlemen had rejoined them in the drawing room. Of course, that might have been because Lyford had come in shortly after the others.

He had still been out of temper, but Gwenyth did not think that any of the others had noticed the fact. Indeed, he had seemed perfectly calm, and if she had <u>had</u> to explain how it was that she knew he was angry, she would have been hard-pressed to give a sensible answer. But she knew.

"Play for us, Gwen," Sir Antony had said, gesturing toward the pianoforte in the corner of the room, its gaily embroidered drapery as bright and busy as the rest of the room's decor.

Seeing the interest stir in the earl's eyes, she had agreed at once, knowing precisely what to play for him. That she was playing the gentle, soothing sonata for him and for no one else did not occur to her until she saw him begin to relax and realized that she had been watching him closely. Feeling sudden warmth in her cheeks, she had looked away at once, only to glance back at him again within moments.

He had winked at her.

Remembering his wink that morning was painful, and she tried to push the memory aside, calling herself a child, and foolish besides. Her mind disobeyed her. She seemed to think only of him. He cared for her; she knew it, again without knowing how it was that she could be so certain. And she cared for him. Being certain of that fact was easier, for he stirred feelings in her that had never stirred before. Not only had she more than once found herself watching a doorway in impatient anticipation of his entrance, but a mere glance from him was enough to send the blood surging through her body like river water through a flash lock. Why, she wondered, had no one ever warned her that such feelings existed? Only a dolt would continue to deny them.

Pushing the last thought firmly aside with the others, she drank her chocolate and ate the buns without further ado, all the while chattering determinedly to Annie, who was sorting out her clothes for the day. When she had finished her repast, she dressed in her habit and went to the stables, where she called out to Ned to saddle Prince Joseph and his own nag, determined to ride the fidgets out of her brain and body. After a long, hard ride across the downs, she returned, feeling only a little better, changed her clothes, and sought out Pamela.

She had fully intended to seek her out the evening before, but when she had finished playing and closed the instrument, Lyford, rising to help her put away her music, had asked her in a blunt undertone to leave Pamela to her own thoughts for a time.

"I hope you were not too harsh with her," she had said.

"No more than I had to be," he replied. "I don't like coming the guardian over her, you know, but she invites it."

Gwenyth sighed. "I know she does."

"She is my responsibility. I'm a poor choice for the position, I'll grant you, for I don't know anything about young females. Do you think I've treated her harshly before now?"

"I don't think you ought to have left her at school."

She would have said more to him, but he had not even had time to respond before they had been interrupted by the countess, who demanded to know if Lyford would take a hand at whist, and there had been no other opportunity to speak privately with him. As a farewell, it had been most unsatisfactory.

She thought now about what he had said about Pamela. He had not sounded in the least like a man who had ever had designs upon either his ward's person or her inheritance, and Gwenyth wondered if Pamela had honestly believed him capable of such conduct or if she had merely been waxing theatrical, as she had been wont to do at Miss Fletcher's. Gwenyth put the question to her when she found her in her bedchamber overlooking the courtyard.

"Do not talk to me of Marcus," Pamela retorted. "He is a beast. I'd never marry him, not if he were the last gentleman on earth." She rolled her eyes. "Gentleman? Ha! He is no gentleman, not if he can say the things he said to me, he isn't."

"What, precisely, did he say?" Gwenyth inquired. As she took her seat in the chair nearest the open window, she noted that the air outside had grown warmer and that a slight though not yet unpleasant scent of the stables drifted in.

Pamela flushed, unable to meet her steady gaze. "His words do not bear repeating," she muttered.

"You behaved badly," Gwenyth said gently. "He had every right to express his displeasure, you know."

Pamela's chin went up. "I had a right to express my feelings too, Gwen, and if he thinks he can force me to marry him after treating me in such a gothic manner, he had better think again.''

"I don't think he wishes to marry you at all.''

Pamela stared at her in astonishment. "I don't know why you say that. Why would he *not* wish to marry me?''

Deciding that it would not be precisely tactful to tell her the earl didn't even seem particularly to like her, Gwenyth was silent for a moment, trying to think how to put her answer into acceptable terms. Finally she said, "He is a good deal older than you are, my dear.''

"Pooh, nonsense,'' Pamela snapped. "What has his age to do with it. You are only two years older than I am, and you like him well enough. Moreover, in my opinion, a man ought to be a good deal older than his wife.''

"Good heavens,'' Gwenyth said, dismayed by the new thought Pamela's words put into her head. "You aren't looking in Sir Spenser's direction, I hope. The countess said you had been making sheep's eyes at him, but I'd not credited such a notion. Now here you are saying you want an older husband.''

Pamela heaved a sigh of exasperation and looked directly at her at last. "Don't be daft, Gwen. That man, dear and sweet though he may be, is old enough to be my grandfather.''

"But you do spend a great deal of time talking to him. He comes here, I thought, to pay polite attention to the countess, but he spends most of his time in conversation with you.''

"Only because she is always surrounded by decrepit old men who bore him. He told me. If you want my opinion, I believe he's always been in love with her and has never married because he has been keeping himself for her.''

"Pamela, you talk nonsense,'' Gwenyth said, laughing.

"Well, call it what you like, but I like to talk to him. He tells me things I like to hear about. He is a little like Papa, you know, and I like him very much, but I don't flirt with him.''

"You flirt with every man you meet,'' Gwenyth said,

laughing. "No, no, you goose, don't flash your eyes at me. I'll admit you don't treat him to the same nonsense that you practice on Davy and Mr. Webster."

"Oh, them," Pamela said, a note of scorn in her voice.

"I thought you liked them!"

"Well, of course I do, but they are just boys."

Gwenyth gave up that tangent and turned back to the primary issue, saying, "I think you had better wait until Lyford allows you to go to London before you look for a husband. He will, you know, because you are wrong about him. He doesn't wish to marry you, and he does want you safely married and off his hands."

Grimacing, Pamela said, "I do not know why you persist in thinking that he does not wish to marry me. He needs my money for this place, and every man I have ever met wishes to marry me. Why would he be any different?"

The conversation having come full circle with no good point having been made, Gwenyth suggested that they go down to the breakfast room. Pamela agreed at once, with undisguised relief, but just as Gwenyth was beginning to wonder what had ever possessed her to befriend the girl, Pamela turned impulsively on the stair landing and hugged her.

"You are so kind to me, Gwen. I don't know how I'd get on without you. I'm so glad you came with me."

Returning the hug, Gwenyth said, "I'm glad too, my dear." And she realized that the sentiment was a sincere one, although her reasons were mixed and certainly did not all have to do with Pamela. They descended the stairs and entered the morning room to discover the countess and Lady Cadogan in tense discussion.

"You are merely being contrary, Almeria, and that's the long and short of it," Lady Cadogan said tartly as they entered.

"Good gracious, Wynnefreda," retorted the countess, "but you are making a piece of work about nothing."

Gwenyth, having no doubt of the cause of their dissension, spoke over her shoulder as she moved to examine the dishes on the sideboard. "Then you do truly intend to go to town, ma'am?"

"Of course, did I not say so?"

Pamela caught her breath audibly. "You are going to leave us, ma'am?"

The countess glared at her. "Leave you? No, of course not, goose. I mean for us all to go. Doubt you'd stay here on your own anyway, and can't expect Wynnefreda to stay on if I go."

Gwenyth looked in dismay from her aunt to the countess and then to Pamela, whose face was aglow with delight.

"You'll take me?" Pamela's voice squeaked.

"Didn't I just say so? What a fuss you make!"

Gwenyth said sharply, "What about Lyford?"

The countess shrugged. "You sound just like Wynnefreda. Lyford is not here, so he can have nothing to say."

"But Pamela is his responsibility, ma'am."

"Fiddle faddle. If I hadn't been in mourning, he would have saddled me with her quick enough. I am no longer in mourning, so there you are."

Lady Cadogan shook her head and said to Gwenyth, "It is no use. I have been arguing with her for the past half-hour, to no avail whatever. She means to go, and I can think of no way to prevent her. Either we remain here without her, or we go."

"Then we shall remain," Gwenyth said flatly.

"We go," said Pamela at the same moment.

The discussion continued for some time, but there was little that either Gwenyth or Lady Cadogan could do in the face of the others' determination. Once it was pointed out that neither of them had the least authority over Pamela, Gwenyth knew they had lost. She appealed to the younger girl's reason and to what little fear she had of the earl. Neither accomplished a thing.

"He is not here," Pamela said flatly, "and if need be, we can be back again before he returns from Bristol. He ought to have taken me to London himself, but since he did not, I am very willing to go with her ladyship."

Harping on the point of her ladyship's state of mourning began to sound ridiculous even in Gwenyth's ears. To quibble over what amounted to a period of no more than two or three weeks was the sort of thing that only the stuffiest patroness of Almack's Assembly Rooms would do. That they would be running contrary to Lyford's wishes bothered Gwenyth a good deal more, but it bothered neither Pamela nor the countess one whit.

They spent the next few days in preparation for the journey, the countess sending Frythorpe and a number of servants ahead to prepare the London house for occupation. She was in high croak. The only blight on her enthusiasm, since she liked a gentleman companion when she traveled, was that Jared could not be convinced to accompany them.

Apologizing profusely, he explained that he had business of his own to attend to, and though he did not say so, Gwenyth at least believed that he felt guilty that it was Lyford and not himself who had traveled to Bristol. Laughing, she asked him if he really meant to attend to business for once.

His smile lacked its usual gaiety. "I confess that although I do have some things to discuss with Powell, I also want to give Pamela a chance to miss my winning charm."

She had no wish to encourage him in such a plan, for she knew Lyford would not change his mind about a match between his cousins, but she said nothing more, turning her attention instead to her packing. Though she thought more than once about the earl, the countess had no patience for delay, and in the flurry of activity surrounding her there was no much time for any of them to miss the gentlemen.

When Sir Spenser paid them a visit on Tuesday afternoon, Lady Lyford informed him with a placidity that belied all the bustle that she was off to town for a short spell.

He raised his quizzing glass and peered at her through it. "Are you, indeed, Almeria? How very brave of you. I quite admire your decision."

"I thought you would disapprove," she said bluntly.

"On the contrary," he assured her, lowering his glass. "I have every respect for your good sense and I am sure the decision to cast off your mourning in time for the king's celebration is the correct one. The royal family, though sticklers themselves, must be grateful to have in attendance a lady of your stature."

Gwenyth, an interested observer of their conversation, was certain that if Lady Lyford had had a fan she would have fluttered it at him.

"You will make me blush," the countess said, "and I am far too old to indulge in such girlish stuff."

Sir Spenser shook his head. "When a lady ceases to blush," he said, "she has lost the most powerful charm of her beauty, which is something that you will never do, Almeria."

"Fiddle faddle," replied the countess, but her tone lacked its usual snap. " 'Tis naught but a sign of foolish sensibility, and I've no patience with it."

"Such sensibility as blushing indicates may be a weakness and encumbrance in *our* sex," Sir Spenser said grandly, "but in yours I believe it to be peculiarly engaging. Pedants, who think themselves philosophers, may ask why a woman should blush if she is conscious of no crime, but I believe it is a sufficient answer that nature has made you blush and has forced us to love you because you do."

Gwenyth, suddenly recalling important matters to attend to and wishing Lyford might have heard the exchange, managed to stifle her amusement until she had reached her bedchamber.

They left for London on Friday morning, and although the countess refused to consider making the journey in a single day, it was not thought wise to burden Meriel with their party, so they passed the night at the Crown in High Wycombe instead, arriving in London on Saturday afternoon to find the town oppressively hot. Gwenyth sent word of their arrival at once to Davy at Tallyn London House, and he and Mr. Webster joined them for dinner that evening. No sooner had the two young gentlemen, dressed in nearly identical buff-colored breeches and long-waisted dark blue coats, entered the drawing room than the countess demanded to know if Davy had purchased her tickets.

He produced them at once from the pocket of his waistcoat, a stunning confection of red-and-white silk-striped quilting. "Got you a box in the third tier, ma'am. Most desirable location."

Mr. Webster, to everyone's surprise, since he rarely offered his opinion, muttered under his breath, "Mistake to go." When he realized that they had all heard him, he blushed.

The countess turned her piercing glare upon him, much to his increased discomfiture. "What's that you say? Speak up, young man, speak up!"

Since Mr. Webster only grew more tongue-tied than ever, Davy said, "He don't think you ought to go, ma'am. Daresay you don't know what's been going on, since you don't take the town papers and won't have heard recent gossip, but there's bound to be trouble when the new theater opens."

"Trouble?" Lady Cadogan, her knitting in hand as usual at this time of day, cocked her head a little as she looked from one young man to the other. "What sort of trouble, Davy?"

"The theater management has raised the prices," he said. "Those box tickets were all of seven shillings, but of course it ain't the private boxes causing all the riot and rumpus. The common folk want the old prices. Can't blame them, I suppose."

Pamela smoothed the skirt of her white muslin dinner frock with an artful touch and tossed her head. "Surely if they have had to build a new theater, they have reason to raise the prices a trifle. I cannot see why people should fuss."

"Perhaps," Gwenyth pointed out gently, "because they cannot now afford the price of a ticket."

Shrugging again, Pamela said, "The people who matter will not mind. What night do we go, and what shall we see?"

Davy grinned at her. "You aren't afraid?"

"No, why should I be?"

"Because I just told you there will likely be a bother of one sort or another, that's why."

"Well, if the people who are objecting cannot afford a ticket, they cannot get inside, which is where we shall be, and I have never seen a London play."

He looked at the countess. "And you, ma'am?"

She made a dismissive gesture. "I cannot believe there will be a problem, particularly inasmuch as we do not intend to go to the opening. These tickets are for Wednesday night. Surely all the fuss will have died away by then. *Richard III* is one of my favorite plays."

"Oh," Pamela said, her enthusiasm slightly dimmed, "Shakespeare, and not a comedy."

"But a very educational play, my gel, and one that will make you glad to be living in modern times."

"I am already glad to be living in them," Pamela said. "Miss Fletcher told us people were used not to have glass in their windows or chimneys for their fires, which sounds very unpleasant to me. But I do not know why we cannot see a comedy."

Gwenyth said, "Hush, Pamela. You ought to be grateful that the countess means to take you at all. Perhaps the farce will be amusing."

Davy chuckled. "I don't know. 'Tis something called 'The Poor Soldier,' which don't sound promising. Web and I are going again on Thursday to see 'The Widow's Choice,' which promises to be rather something. Opening night will be *Hamlet*, of course, but though I ain't partial to Shakespeare and nor is Web, we don't want to miss all the fun and gig there promises to be."

As the ladies quickly discovered, the two young gentlemen were not the only ones expecting fireworks. The newspapers were full of the debate over the new prices, with a record number of letters to their editors, and promises of disruptions if the management of the new theater did not change its ways. Since the management stubbornly insisted that it had no choice in the matter, feelings were running high by opening night, and the following morning the *Times* reported gleefully that the promised disruptions had taken place.

"People can be very rude," was the countess's only comment when Gwenyth, who had been reading aloud to the others, paused to express her dismay.

"But, ma'am, it says here that the mob outside were hissing and shouting."

"That was outside. Not much happened inside," the countess replied calmly.

Pamela wrinkled her brow. "It is a very long article, of course, but I thought you said they hissed inside also, Gwen."

Gwenyth chuckled. "That was because they mistook the Duke of Kent for the Duke of York, who has become rather unpopular lately. No, please don't ask why, Pamela. The matter is a complicated one having to do with his mistress and the fact that she was selling army commissions, and I don't propose to explain it all to you now. Matters did grow rather loud inside, ma'am," she said to the countess. "So much so that Mr. Kemble and Mrs. Siddons were unable to make themselves heard above the tumult."

The countess shrugged. "Mr. Kemble has ever had a knack for making himself disliked," she said, "and he has not grown more popular through becoming manager of the new theater."

Lady Cadogan said quietly, "Much of the discontent arises from the fact that Mr. Kemble, Mrs. Siddons, and others of their ilk demand such extortionate wages for their performances. And when the common folk see them in their finery and know the ticket prices have been raised to accommodate their vanity, well—"

"Fiddle faddle," the countess said, banging her cane against the floor. "I've no patience with such talk. If we expect such people to perform well, we must be willing to pay them well."

Gwenyth, who had been reading silently while the others talked, said suddenly, "If this sort of thing continues, perhaps we ought not to go on Wednesday."

Pamela exclaimed indignantly, "Not go? Oh, ma'am"—

she turned agitatedly to the countess—"you will not change your mind! Surely you will not."

"No, of course I will not," the countess said calmly. "In my opinion, 'tis no more than the veriest tempest in a teapot. By Wednesday, everything that can be said will have been said."

She remained adamant, and even Gwenyth ceased her objections by Wednesday evening, for although the disturbances continued, nothing dreadful had happened. By the time the doors opened for Wednesday's performance, not an extra seat was available, and the only shadow over her pleasure was the lack of young gentlemen to escort them. She would even have settled for her brother, but Davy had informed her that one Shakespeare play was enough for him. Thus, their only male escort was one of the countess's elderly swains, who was to meet them at the theater, since their coach would hold only the four ladies in comfort.

They drove to the Prince's Place entrance, where there were liveried footmen waiting to hand them from their carriage and direct them through the proper entrance, located beneath a noble stone portico. They had to pass through a mob of people, hissing and shouting against the high prices, waving placards and generally making nuisances of themselves, but inside the great lobby, a long and narrow but disappointingly small room, it was quiet by comparison. Turning to the left, they mounted a short flight of steps lighted by bronze Grecian lamps, to an anteroom dominated by a statue of Shakespeare and supported by pillars in imitation porphyry marble. Gwenyth thought the staircase rather narrow and the anteroom even smaller for its purpose than the grand lobby, but all in all, the theater was wonderful.

"How elegant it is!" Pamela exclaimed as they stepped into their box and took their seats. "Do you suppose those gold pillars are made of real gold?"

Seeing that each tier was supported by a good many of the gold pillars, from the top of each of which ran a gilt iron bracket suspending a superb glass-and-gold chandelier for wax candles, Gwenyth laughed. "Don't be nonsensical. Of

course they are not or the price of tickets would be even
higher. It astonishes me that the management would purchase
wax candles, for that matter. Goodness, listen to that din!''

The theater was crowded, and now that the initial impact
of its elegance was fading, she noted that placards demanding the old prices had been hung against the dove-colored
fronts of the boxes on either side of them and opposite. As
she took her seat beside Lady Cadogan, she saw that in one
part of the pit below a long banner was being raised aloft,
held by three sticks tied together. Inscribed upon it in large
capital letters were the words ''RESIST THE IMPOSITION
EVERY NIGHT, UNTIL ABATED.''

Lady Cadogan, having settled her knitting bag beside her
and taken her work into her lap, now took time to look about
her. ''Good gracious,'' she said, shaking her head, but whatever else she might have said was drowned out by the roar
that greeted the raising of the pit banner.

Gwenyth leaned near her and said into her ear, ''I doubt
we'll hear much of *Richard III* tonight, ma'am.''

Lady Cadogan grimaced, and since the roar died a little,
Gwenyth was able to hear her clearly when she said, ''We
ought never to have come here tonight. 'Tis common and
unbecoming.'' Her needles began to move swiftly in her lap,
but she didn't look at them. She was still watching the crowd.
''I believe they have nearly doubled the number of seats in
this place, but if they can get people to pay seven shillings
to sit in those little pigeonholes above us, as I'm told they
do, when the view there must be twice as bad as it is in the
one-shilling gallery, then the management are magicians. No
wonder so many are complaining.''

Lady Lyford rested her cane against the box partition and
turned to face them. ''I call this exciting,'' she said in a
carrying tone, ''so don't be putting your Friday face on,
Wynnefreda, for I've no patience with such stuff tonight.
You watch. They'll quiet down once the band begins to play.
Where is Sir Algernon, do you suppose?''

But her swain had not appeared by the time the band had
settled itself in place below the front of the stage, and

although the first notes of "God Save the King" were heard with perfect clarity, the rest of that patriotic tune was drowned out entirely by a theater orchestra composed of watchman's rattles, horns, and whistles, with which members of the audience had previously provided themselves. More placards appeared, and papers were thrown onto the stage itself, settling in little piles against the front of the drop curtain.

At last the curtain went up, and for a moment the roar subsided, only to begin again when the actors began to speak. It continued unabated, turning Shakespeare's famous play into a pantomime, but the actors went on to the end. In the middle of the third act the uproar became so alarmingly violent that Mr. Kemble, still in costume as Richard III, stepped forward, and after another volley of shouts, toots, rattles, catcalls, and shrieks, he was able to make himself heard.

"Ladies and gentlemen, I have at last comprehended that the cause of your displeasure consists in the small advance of prices on the boxes and pit." Encouraged by cries of "Yes, yes!" from his audience, he continued, "In the reign of Queen Anne the price of admission to the pit was three shillings. One hundred years ago, the galleries, ladies and gentlemen, were—"

But although he continued to speak, his listeners had heard enough. The roar grew louder than ever, until the men in the pit beneath the wide banner began shouting, "Get on the stage!"

Gwenyth saw to her shock that people were beginning to press forward, and suddenly a veritable posse of Bow Street officers in red coats erupted from the stage doors. First they opened trapdoors in the stage to catch any unwary person laying siege. Then they descended into the audience. People appeared cowed at first, but when Kemble stepped forward again to speak, pandemonium erupted. Soon men were fighting the Bow Street officers and each other everywhere and women were shrieking. Even as the four ladies prepared to take immediate departure, loud altercations erupted outside their box door.

Gwenyth looked at her aunt. "What do we do, ma'am?"

Before Lady Cadogan could reply, the door to the box burst open, and two men, clearly inebriated, surged in, stumbling into the extra chairs. "We'll have them seats, ladies," jeered one, reaching to pull Lady Lyford out of hers, only to yelp in pain when she cracked her cane down on his knuckles.

"Here, here!" exclaimed the second man. "Watch that damned thing!" His gaze shifted appreciatively to Pamela, but before he could say more, Lady Lyford whacked him hard across the backside.

He screeched and turned menacingly toward her, reaching out in fury, his purpose clearly to murder her, but Lady Cadogan slid the knitting from her needles and jabbed his hand. Crying out again, he snatched it back and glared at her.

There was movement in the anteroom behind them. "Get out of here," Lady Cadogan snapped at the two men. They hesitated, but when the countess lifted her cane menacingly, they rushed out again, stumbling over their feet and each other in their haste.

The old lady said sharply to Gwenyth, "Shut that door behind them, gel. Quickly, now, before anyone else gets in!"

Gwenyth made haste to obey her, pushing the door hard against a hand that pushed back from the other side.

"Here," said her aunt beside her, dragging a chair up. "Put the chair back beneath the handle. "That will help."

But as Gwenyth attempted to do as she suggested, the door was suddenly thrust harder from the other side, too hard for her to withstand. The edge hit the side of her head as she was thrown heavily against the box partition. As she slid to the ground in blinding waves of pain, she thought dreamily that she saw Lyford knock an unknown man to the floor with his bare fist. The thought was so ludicrous that she spurned all possibility of its reality as she sank into oblivion.

11

When Gwenyth came to, they were in the carriage. She had vague memories of being jostled, of loud noises that made her head ache, of being carried in strong arms against a muscular chest. Now, however, as the carriage rattled over cobblestones, she felt warm and safe and as comfortable as one could feel when one's head ached abominably, one's body felt as though it had been systematically pounded into one large bruise, and one was sitting rather awkwardly on a lumpy seat. There was silence in the carriage, although in the glow cast by the carriage lamps, she could see that her aunt and Pamela occupied the forward seat.

"Her eyes are open," Pamela said just then.

Lady Lyford spoke from a little behind Gwenyth. "Told you she'd be all right. No need to have made such a fuss."

Gwenyth, realizing that she was sitting sideways and forward of her ladyship, struggled to straighten, only to feel two strong arms tighten around her, making her squeak with pain.

"Don't try to move yet." The voice was Lyford's, and to her astonishment, she realized he was holding her on his lap.

She struggled more. "Put me down, sir." Her voice was weak, and her movements had no effect on him other than to make him loosen his hold a little when he realized he was hurting her.

"There is no room to put you down," he said quietly. "And you must be quiet. I fear you must have been badly hurt."

"I am perfectly all right," she lied, "and it is most unsuitable for me to be sitting on you like this."

"Hush," he said.

Pamela spoke again. "Really, Marcus, you ought to stop the carriage and hail a hackney for yourself. We are abominably crowded with five of us in here, and Gwen is right. You—"

"If I were you," he said harshly, "I should not open my mouth again tonight. I have a number of things to say to you, but I do not want to be plagued by your foolish prattle now."

"But—"

"Be silent!"

Since even Pamela could not fail to note the menace in his tone, she subsided, and the rest of the journey passed in the silence he had requested. Gwenyth would have liked to ask him several questions, but the effort required to put even one of them into words was too great. Relaxing her head against his shoulder, she sighed deeply and shut her eyes, falling asleep almost instantly.

When they reached Lyford House, she wakened and tried to free herself again, but without bothering to discuss her wishes, he carried her up to her room, ordering one of his footmen in passing to run for the doctor.

Only Lady Cadogan followed them upstairs, and as Lyford laid Gwenyth upon the bed, the viscountess said calmly, "You may leave her to me now, Marcus. I will ring for her maid."

"No," he replied, drawing up a chair to the bed. "We will wait together for the doctor."

"I am all right now," Gwenyth said feebly.

"No, you are not. Don't talk."

"How did you come to be there?" she demanded instead.

"I reached the house at nine, and Frythorpe told me where you had gone. Since the ructions have been fully detailed every day in the London papers, I could not credit my ears, but he insisted that you had gone to Covent Garden, so I hailed the first hackney coach that came along and went to fetch you home. Had all I could do to get into the place without a ticket, since there were none to be had, but all bedlam broke loose as I was attempting to explain to the money takers that I wanted only to fetch my family. Took me some time to push my way to the third tier and find your box. I had to break into two others before I saw you. Now, I have answered your question, so do not speak again until the doctor has seen you, unless, of course, you wish to explain to me how you came to do something so foolhardy.''

Since she did not think she had the strength just then to explain anything, let alone to justify her actions, she fell silent again, only moving at all when Lady Cadogan placed a cool, damp cloth that she had wrung out at the washstand on her forehead. Her headache began to subside a little.

Silence reigned in the bedchamber until Dr. Hastings, a round, twinkling little man, came a quarter of an hour later. Shooing a reluctant Lyford from the room, he examined Gwenyth carefully, beamed at her, and gave it as his considered opinion that she would live.

She smiled at him. ''I'm quite certain of that, sir.''

''Well, head wound, you know,'' he said. ''Tricky, some of them. You'll want to have a care, my lady.''

She frowned. ''How much care, sir? I am not much good at playing the invalid.''

Lady Cadogan, who had been hovering anxiously, said in a crisp tone, ''You'll do as you're bid, my dear. His lordship will see to that if I cannot.''

Gwenyth grimaced, having no doubt that she was right about Lyford. She began to turn her head to look at the doctor again, decided against it when a bolt of pain rewarded her effort, and shifted her gaze instead. ''Must I stay in bed?''

''Your head aches, does it not?''

''Truthfully?'' When he only twinkled, she sighed. ''Rather fiercely, I'm afraid.''

''I will give you some powders to take. If you take them as you ought, without thinking that you know better than I do, you will be much better by Friday. You need stay in bed only until your head stops hurting, though I warn you, your bruises will ache a good deal longer than that. You took quite a clout on your hip and shoulder, you know."

She didn't know. Her whole body ached, to be sure, but her head was the worst. She watched out of the corner of her eye while he stirred a packet of powder into a glass of water. As he turned to bring it to her, there was a hard knock on the door.

Lady Cadogan opened it to find the earl standing there impatiently. She smiled at him. "You may come in, Marcus. The doctor tells us there has been no great harm done. He is giving her some medicine now."

When Gwenyth tried to sit up just then to take the **gla**ss, only to fall back with a sharp cry in a wave of pain, Lyford hurried forward, stepping past the doctor without ceremony. He bent and slipped his arm behind her shoulders, lifting her before taking the glass from the doctor's hand to hold it for her.

She took a sip and made a face. "That is awful stuff."

The doctor chuckled, but the earl said, "Drink it, Gwen. If you drink it down quickly enough, you won't notice the taste."

"You have not tasted it, Lyford. You cannot know."

"Don't be troublesome," he said.

Glancing at him, she saw that he was looking stern, and remembering that he did not always consider himself bound by the normal codes of a gentleman, she could not doubt that he would tip the foul-tasting stuff down her throat for her if she did not obey him rather quickly. She tried another sip; then, holding her breath, she took the glass from him and drank the rest.

"Good girl," he said, removing the glass from her hand and laying her back against her pillows. "Lady Cadogan, you may ring for her woman now." He stood looking down at Gwenyth, and she felt comforted by the tenderness in his gaze.

The doctor said, "She will need to rest, my lord, but I can discover no real damage. She's got a bump on her head and a number of bruises, so she aches all over, but there's no real cause for concern. She'll be full of bounce in a week or so."

"Can she travel?" Lyford asked without taking his gaze from her face.

"In a few days, I suppose," the doctor said. "Dashed hot in town. No doubt she'll be more comfortable in the country. Wait until the headaches stop. Then you may do as you think best."

Lady Cadogan waited only until the doctor had departed before ringing for Annie, saying to Lyford as she did so, "Your grandmother might not wish to return to the abbey, you know."

"She'll do as I tell her," the earl said grimly, without so much as glancing at the viscountess, "or she may henceforth frank her own way. But in truth, I don't care whether she goes or not. You won't fail me, ma'am, and Gwen will recover more quickly in the country than here in the heat and bustle of London."

"Gwenyth would do as well with her sister in Maidenhead or with her brother Davy here in London," Lady Cadogan said in a tone that in anyone else would have suggested provocation.

Lyford dismissed her words with a gesture. "Davy won't look after her properly, and Lady Meriel must look after herself. Unless . . ." He looked more closely at the viscountess. "Are you telling me that you prefer to remain in town?"

She shook her head. "No, but have you considered Pamela?"

His countenance hardened. "Certainly. I will have much to say to Pamela." When Gwenyth moved as though to speak, he looked down at her again. "What is it?" he asked in a gentler tone than she had yet heard from him.

"You mustn't scold her, sir," she said. "She only accepted your grandmama's invitation when it was offered. Even you would not have expected her to remain obediently at the abbey with only my company or even my aunt's after the countess had invited us all to come to town with her.''

He was silent for a long moment before he said, ''I think we will not discuss just now what I ought to have been able to expect.'' The door opened, and he looked up. ''Here is Annie now. I daresay she was awaiting your summons. The doctor's instructions are on the table yonder, by your packets of powder. See that you follow them exactly.''

''Yes, sir,'' she said meekly.

He smiled then and leaned close to murmur for her ears alone, ''Practice those two words and that nice submissive tone. I shall expect to hear them more often in future.''

Her eyes twinkled. ''Expect what you like, sir. The reality may be rather different.''

''We'll see,'' he said, turning away to hand the doctor's instructions to Annie. ''She is to be very careful, Annie, and if she gives you any backchat about following these in-structions, I shall expect you to come to me. We must see that she gets well again as soon as possible.''

''Yes, my lord.''

''See, Gwen, that's how it ought to sound.''

She laughed, then wished she hadn't. Her ribs hurt, and her head ached. ''Good night, Lyford.''

He was soon gone, and Lady Cadogan followed him, leaving Gwenyth to Annie's tender care. Since this consisted of getting her mistress into her nightdress while muttering her candid opinion of folks who thought attending a riot to be a proper evening's entertainment, Gwenyth was glad when she, too, had gone. But, perversely, once she was alone, she found she could not sleep. The room was hot, and her head ached abominably, yet her brain seemed to buzz with activity. Her nerves seemed to have developed a life of their own, making her skin feel prickly all over, and she could not get comfortable in her bed. Whatever way she turned, she rested on a bruise. She was still wide-awake when her door opened and Pamela stepped hurriedly inside.

''Gwen,'' she hissed, shutting the door behind her.

''Yes, I'm awake.''

''Oh, thank heavens. I was afraid you'd go right to sleep.

What did the doctor say? I didn't want to ask Lady Cadogan, for fear Marcus would come upon us while we talked. I daresay I ought to stay out of his way for a bit, you know.''

"I know, Pamela, but I think that if you don't exert yourself to put him out of temper, he will not say much to you about tonight's activities. I told him the notion to come to town was the countess's.''

"Did you? Good. Then perhaps he will let me stay.''

"He has already said we are to return to the abbey,'' Gwenyth said, speaking carefully. Talking made her head ache.

"Well, if that is not the outside of enough,'' Pamela declared. "It is just like him to deny me pleasure, so I ought to have known he would spoil things now.''

"I believe he thinks it will be better for me to be at the abbey,'' Gwenyth said. "The heat in town—''

"Oh, that is just the sort of thing he would say to make his wishes more acceptable to others,'' Pamela said scornfully. "You can get better just as well in town as anywhere else.''

"Well, it is very hot—''

"Then you ought to go to your sister, but it is not fair to make me leave London just because you hurt yourself a trifle.''

Gwenyth said nothing to that, and the silence that followed grew heavy before Pamela said in a small voice, "That was a dreadful thing to say. I didn't mean it, you know. It is only that Marcus makes me so angry that I don't think about anything or anyone else. I hope you were not badly hurt, Gwen, and if you wish to return to the abbey, we will go, and I shall not say another word about it.''

"That's very kind of you, Pamela. The doctor has said I will be fine. Perhaps we might discuss all of this further in the morning.''

"Oh, are you very tired? I shall leave you to sleep, then. Is there anything I can do for you before I go?''

"No, thank you,'' Gwenyth said, rejecting the notion of having her ring for Annie to have the sheets on the bed changed. New ones would soon become just as wrinkled and uncomfortable.

When Pamela had tiptoed from the room after furtively checking to be sure the coast was clear, she tried to find a comfortable position but was no more successful than before.

Fifteen minutes later the door opened again, less furtively this time, and Lyford came in, carrying a book and followed by a chambermaid bearing a tray. In the glow of the corridor's candlelight, Gwenyth could see that the tray held a pitcher and two glasses. When the chambermaid had set it upon the table and lighted a branch of candles there, Lyford dismissed her.

Gwenyth nearly asked him if Pamela had told him she was still awake, but fortunately he spoke before she could do so. "I doubted you would sleep after so much excitement, so I asked the sawbones if lemonade would do you any harm. He assured me it would not. Would you like some?"

"Oh, yes," she said, trying to sit up in her bed.

"Be still. I'll help you as soon as I've poured out." He turned to attend to the lemonade, saying over his shoulder, "I'd do nicely at a tea party, don't you agree?"

She chuckled, content to wait for him to help her. First he opened the window.

There was no breeze, but just the fact of having the window open made the room feel less confined. Nevertheless, she said provocatively, "My aunt disapproves of night air, sir, and she would certainly disapprove of your presence here in my bedchamber at this or, indeed, any hour."

"I trust you do not hold similar views," he said, opening the curtains wider to let in as much air as possible. "This window overlooks the garden, you know, so you won't be disturbed by street noises, and it is as stuffy as a tomb in here. You must be sweltering."

Since she could not deny that, she said no more, having all she could do to affect an attitude of calm dignity when he moved close to the bed and bent toward her. He lifted her, propped pillows behind her, and settled her back against them. Then he handed her one of the glasses, drew up a chair to the table, and sat down, opening the book in his lap. Shifting his body so that the light from the candles would fall upon the pages, he looked up at her, his eyes twinkling.

"I thought about bringing something you would like, one of Mrs. Radcliffe's tales, or Fanny Burney's, but I decided that you would benefit much more from a truly improving work."

She grimaced. "Benefit?"

"It ought to put you straight to sleep," he said. "Now, drink the lemonade down and get comfortable. The first essay in this book is entitled, 'Self-Control.' How appropriate. No, no, do not speak. You are meant to sleep. I promise you, I shall not be offended if you nod off straightaway."

She smiled at him, thinking he was being singularly foolish, but once he began reading, she found herself listening to him with pleasure. Had she been asked to comment upon the content of the book, she would have been unable to do so, but the sound of his voice was pleasant. Low-pitched, calm, and very, very pleasant . . .

When she awoke it was still dark, but he was gone and she was lying flat in her bed again. That he had touched her without her knowledge gave her brief pause, but the feeling of concern soon passed, though the memory of his visit lingered teasingly. She had no idea what time it was, but the darkness made it clear that it was too early to ring for Annie, so she indulged herself by turning her thoughts to the earl.

The experience of three London Seasons told her that despite his obvious attraction to her, his interest might result from nothing more than that she had told him she intended never to marry. It was odd, she thought, the effect that declaration had on most gentlemen. Her attitude was a challenge to them. Even those who could have no earthly desire to marry her found it necessary to try to make her change her mind, for each wanted to be the one to win her, though she was certain that not one she had met before now would be satisfied with her as his wife.

Could she be satisfied with a husband? Certainly she had

discovered of late that a gentleman's presence in her life could be both stimulating and comforting, but the fact remained that marriage was another matter altogether. And Lyford wouldn't like being married to her either, she decided with a sigh. He thought her heedless about money, and his attitude toward extravagance was well-known to all who lived beneath his roof. And he disapproved of her notions about managing the abbey. No doubt, were they to wed, she would express her opinions far too often for his comfort. But they would not wed. She had not changed her mind about that. She would remain a spinster, in control of at least some aspects of her own life, and one day, when she had obtained her brother's permission to do so, she would set up her own household and hold interesting receptions there.

Not that Lyford had asked her to marry him, but he soon would. Of that much she was certain, if only because he doubted her desire to remain single and had a pronounced habit of assuming that everyone around him would do his bidding. Before she could decide whether she wanted him to propose in order that she might give him the set-down he would deserve for doubting her sincerity, she fell asleep again and did not waken until the sun was shining brightly through the open window.

It was Annie's entrance into the room that awakened her, for the abigail was muttering darkly under her breath as she strode to the window and shut it with a bang. "London air! Worst thing I can think of for a body trying to get well." Noting that Gwenyth was awake, she continued in a louder tone, "What was you thinking of, m'lady, to get out of bed like you did and open this window? Dangerous, it was. You might have got dizzy and fallen, and then where would you be? And night air too. Might of been the death of you."

"I was hot," Gwenyth said, feeling entirely unable to deal with the ramifications of telling Annie that Lyford had opened the window.

"Breathing that London air in the daytime must be right dangerous too," Annie went on. "It fair stings the eyes today. Dreadful. The sooner his lordship has us out of the city again, the better I shall like it, and no mistake.'' She moved to ring the bell for the chambermaid.

Gwenyth moved carefully in the bed. Her headache had subsided to a dull throb, but her bruises were still bothersome. Nevertheless, she had no intention of remaining in bed until Lyford decided she was well enough to leave town. ''I shall get up, Annie,'' she said decisively.

''That you'll not. His lordship said—''

''His lordship is not my master,'' Gwenyth retorted. ''I have no intention of dancing in the streets, but neither will I stay cooped up in this hot room. It will be cooler downstairs in the library or in the morning room, and I will be quite content to lie on a sofa all day.''

Knowing of old that it would do no good to argue with her mistress in this mood, Annie capitulated rapidly, insisting only that Gwenyth remain where she was until she had fortified herself with chocolate and toast. Perfectly content to obey, now that she had won her own way in the matter, Gwenyth even allowed her abigail to order a full breakfast and took her time afterward about dressing. Only when she swayed on her feet, attempting to walk without assistance, did Annie remonstrate with her.

''You'll let me send for a pair of footmen to help you down them stairs, Miss Gwenyth, or I'll send for his lordship and we'll just see who's master and who's not.''

Gwenyth agreed, not because she feared that Lyford would force her to stay in her room, but because she feared he would carry her downstairs himself. Agreeably as the fancy struck her, she could not allow him to do such a thing. Nor would she allow the footmen to form a chair for her with their arms, as Annie suggested when they arrived. Providing herself with a book that promised to be far more interesting than the one Lyford had read to her the night before, and with a footman on each side to lend her an arm, she managed to walk downstairs, her dignity intact. She was grateful, however, that although her aunt and Lady Lyford were in the morning room when she entered it, Lyford was not.

Lady Cadogan exclaimed in annoyance, "Gwenyth, you were told to remain in bed!"

"I decided, however, that I should prefer to sit down here, ma'am," Gwenyth said, settling herself on the sofa with her book. "My room is very hot and uncomfortable."

She had to repeat that argument when Pamela entered and again when her brother Davy, having been informed of her injuries in a note from Lady Cadogan, paid a morning call to determine their extent for himself. He was still sitting with her when Lyford entered the room, attired in riding dress.

Davy leapt to his feet. "This is a dreadful thing, sir! I have just been telling Gwen that she ought to be tucked up safely in her bed, but she will pay me no heed."

Lyford gazed at her searchingly for a long moment, while she stared defiantly back at him. Then, raising one eyebrow, he said, "Hot upstairs?"

Releasing the breath she had been holding, she smiled at him. "Very hot."

"Then you were no doubt wise to come down. Does your head still ache?"

"Only a little."

"I trust you will have the good sense to rest, then." He shifted his gaze to the book resting in her lap. "Reading cannot be good for the headache."

The countess snapped, "Let the girl alone, for pity's sake. All this fussing and fretting over no more than a bump on the head is what I have no patience with."

Lyford turned toward her and said gently, "Let us not discuss patience, ma'am. I have been exerting mine till it is stretched rather thin, and I would prefer—"

"You would prefer, you would prefer!" She banged her cane on the floor, but since it was carpeted, the thump was scarcely satisfactory to her outraged feelings. "I suppose you think you may call the tune whenever you like."

"Well, yes," he said, "in my own house, I do." His tone was still gentle, but Gwenyth saw a muscle tighten high up on his cheek and knew he was controlling his temper with difficulty.

Lady Lyford's lips had thinned into a straight line, but although she said nothing for a moment, she did not look away. Finally she muttered, "Things have come to a pretty pass when a young man may speak to his elders in such a fashion."

Lyford was silent, but his expression was grim.

The countess tilted her chin. "I expect you are vexed because we came to town without a by-your-leave from you, my lord." She laid unnecessary emphasis on the last two words.

"I have every right to be vexed."

"Fiddle faddle. I am old enough to do as I please."

"But Pamela is not. And don't tell me you only thought of bringing her at the last minute. You had to order your theater tickets, after all."

A sudden movement from behind him recalled the earl to Davy's presence in the room. Turning toward him ruefully, he said, "I forgot you were here. Hope you'll—" He broke off, staring at the younger man, who had flushed deeply. "What's this? You look as guilty as Judas, man."

Davy's color deepened, and he looked wretchedly at Lady Lyford, then helplessly at Gwenyth.

Her lips twitched. When Lyford looked at her, his brow knitting, she could see that he was thinking swiftly, and she nodded. "Davy bought the theater tickets for us, sir."

Lyford turned back to the younger man. "Not your fault," he said. "You couldn't have stopped my grandmother."

"By Jupiter, sir, that's decent of you." Davy pushed a hand through his hair. "I've been kicking myself, I can tell you, for having had anything to do with the matter, what with Gwen getting hurt and all, but when we first arrived in town and arranged for the tickets, of course we could not know how bad things would get. There is word now that they mean to close the theater."

Lady Lyford stood up, arranging her skirts and leaning a little on her cane. "I have calls to make, so I shall leave you now. Try to learn to control that temper of yours, Marcus. It don't behoove a man in your position to let the world see his emotions so clearly. Lend me your arm to my carriage, young Traherne, and I shall set you down wherever you like. Bond Street, I'll be bound.''

The only sound in the room when they had gone was the click of Lady Cadogan's needles, until Pamela said defiantly, ''I hope you do not mean to scold me, Marcus. You must see now that none of it was my doing.''

He said abruptly, ''You would do better to keep silent. I had every right to expect you to obey me. My grandmother may certainly do as she pleases, but you, my girl, must answer to me for your conduct.''

Gwenyth said calmly, ''Perhaps you would prefer to await a more private moment for this discussion, Lyford.''

He turned on her, his temper snapping visibly. ''You will have the goodness to keep out of this! I should have thought your injuries enough to prove how foolish you were to visit that theater last evening, knowing how dangerous it was—''

''But—''

''Dangerous!'' he shouted. ''You were a damned fool, and look what it got you. Bad enough that you should encourage Pamela to flout my authority, as you have, but to endanger yourself—''

Gwenyth threw her book at him.

12

The book glanced off Lyford's shoulder, effectively stopping his tirade mid-sentence. He leaned down to pick it up, then straightened and looked hard at Gwenyth.

Her own temper seething at the fact that he had dared to reprimand her in front of the others for something that had been none of her doing in the first place, she glared back at him, her lips folded tightly together in order to prevent the words that had leapt to her tongue from escaping them.

He bowed, handing her the book. ''Impulsive, too, m'lady?''

She replied carefully, ''I'll not apologize, Lyford. 'Tis you who ought to do so. You cannot have meant the things you said to me just now.''

He straightened, his countenance harder than ever. ''I meant them, all right. I trusted you to look after Pamela, and while I might have known my grandmother would play me false, I never thought you would do so.'' And with that, he turned on his heel and left the room, leaving her speechless, her bosom heaving, her emotions in a ferment. Her throat hurt, and she wanted to scream at him and cry at the same time. But she could not even speak.

When the door had shut behind Lyford with a decided snap, Pamela said explosively, ''That man! He had no right to call any of us to account. We have done nothing wrong! How, I ask you, were we to know that there would be a riot? Had there been riots before? No, there had not! And even if he were in the right of it, he had no occasion to rebuke you, Gwen. None at all!''

Gwenyth scarcely heard her, for her own feelings were threatening to overwhelm her, and she feared to expose them to the others. Never before could she recall responding to anyone's reprimands in such a way. She had felt resentment and fury before, certainly, but never such deep hurt as was mixed in with those emotions now, never such a strong desire to run after the one who had scolded her, in an attempt to make him see that she had done nothing so dreadful as he seemed to think, to coax him to behave tenderly toward her again.

After a pregnant silence it was Lady Cadogan who spoke. "Lyford," she said calmly, "has had much to bear from his grandmother, and something else is preying upon his mind too. I wonder if he did not find something sadly amiss in Bristol. Jared ought to have gone, of course, but I think Lyford learned something from Sir Antony that caused him to go instead, and with Sir Antony involved, the matter may be a serious one."

Since at that moment neither Gwenyth nor Pamela cared one whit about the earl's business in Bristol, neither was able to respond satisfactorily. Gwenyth soon picked up her book and opened it, effectively ending conversation, and Pamela, after gazing at her for a moment or two, announced that she had cards to write. "Not," she added with a grimace, "that I shall know what to tell anyone, now that Marcus seems determined to put an end to our pleasure and drag us all back to Berkshire."

"I should think," Lady Cadogan said matter-of-factly, "that you must refuse with regret any invitation you have received. To allow yourself to pretend that Lyford will change his mind at this point would be singularly foolish."

Pamela left the room with a near-flounce, and when the door had shut behind her, Lady Cadogan added in a gentler tone, "I hope you do not mean to sulk, Gwenyth. It don't become you."

Gwenyth, who had decided that she was refining entirely too much upon the earl's display of temper, looked over the top of her book with a sigh. "I won't sulk, ma'am, but I mean to explain certain things to that man and have an apology out of him before we leave London. He will soon discover that he cannot take me so unfairly to task without admitting his error.''

But despite her best intentions, when the party was finally settled in the Lyford traveling carriage on Friday morning, she still had received no apology from the earl. Her failure was not for lack of effort, however, for she had made it clear to him upon more than one occasion that she expected one from him. When he came to assist her down the front steps into the carriage, and she found herself alone with him for several moments before she joined the others, she came very near to wheedling.

"Come now, sir," she said, smiling up at him, "you know you were in the wrong to scold me. Can you not bring yourself to admit as much now that your temper has cooled?"

His manner had been pleasant until that moment, but her words acted upon him in precisely the opposite manner from that which she had hoped. His countenance hardened, and his eyes frosted over as she watched, his manner becoming not only cool but also remote. The distance between them widened in seconds to the point where it was suddenly as though she beheld a stranger, and she felt chilled to the bone as he handed her into the carriage without speaking and turned away again to mount his horse.

Lady Lyford had made no more objection to accompanying them once she discovered that Lady Cadogan would not remain in London while Gwenyth was at the abbey. Indeed, the countess appeared entirely reconciled to the journey and made no complaint other than declaring that men in London were thoughtless, and observing a number of times that Lyford was very like his grandfather in that he considered no one's wishes other than his own.

The journey was hot, dusty, and unpleasant. By the time they reached High Wycombe and the Crown, Gwenyth was exhausted and aching, but she would no more have admitted her discomfort than she would have walked naked in the street. Nor would she admit that she envied Lyford his freedom to ride instead of remaining cooped up in the closed carriage. Only once had she asked to have the windows let down, but discovering that the resulting dust storm inside made it impossible to breathe, let alone to be comfortable, they had quickly put them up again.

The following day was no better. Though they were away from the smells of the city, which must always be a benefit, the weather was even more oppressive, for the whole of England was suffering from a bout of the worst heat in years. Even traveling near the river made little difference, and everyone was glad to reach Molesford Abbey at last. Just seeing the thick green trees surrounding the house made the air seem cooler, but Gwenyth had scarcely settled into her bedchamber with its windows thrown wide when Pamela swept in, her face the picture of annoyance.

"I must have another room," she declared without ceremony.

Gwenyth stared at her for a moment, then realized what the trouble must be. "The courtyard?"

Pamela gave an abrupt nod and took her seat in the chair by the open window. "I cannot think why the stables have not been moved to a point more distant from the house," she said. "You cannot know how lucky you are to have a room overlooking the river. I might as well be in an oven. And the smell! You cannot imagine. Just come experience it for yourself."

"No, thank you," Gwenyth said with a grin, shifting in her chair. Her bruises were, if anything, more troublesome today, after two days of traveling. "I believe you. Ring for the housekeeper and tell her you wish to move. No one will care, and I daresay there are any number of rooms you might have instead."

Pamela followed this excellent advice and was soon settled in the room next door to Gwenyth's own. It was not so large as the one she had occupied before, nor so well-appointed, but it was well enough, and its air, as she told Gwenyth when she returned to report her success, was as fresh as a nosegay.

It was soon time for supper, and Gwenyth exerted herself

to go downstairs despite her aunt's suggestion that ordering a tray sent to her bedchamber would offend no one. She was glad she had made the effort, however, for Sir Spenser Newton had done them the honor of agreeing to sup with them. She soon discovered that the countess had sent for him at once to tell him they were again in residence and to plead with him to call.

"I could do no less," he said in his ponderous manner when they had gathered in the drawing room. " 'Tis the duty of a gentleman to serve such ladies as pass within his orbit, you know. And how did you like London, my dear Miss Beckley?" he asked, turning his quizzing glass toward Pamela and peering at her through it.

Blushing, she told him she liked London very well. "We did not go about so much as I had hoped," she added. "Only one dinner party and a musicale, but I met several young people."

"All handsome gentlemen, I expect," he said, nodding at the others as though expecting chuckles at what he clearly thought a sally. "And did you approve of them, my dear? I need not ask, you know, if they approved of you."

Lady Lyford said sharply, "Don't encourage her, Spenser. Her head is as big as a bell tower already. The lads swarmed round her like bees round a honey pot. And she . . . Well, the less said about that, the better."

Pamela swelled with indignation. "I did nothing for which I need apologize, ma'am. Goodness me, we scarcely set foot out of the house, and by the time we began to receive invitations to parties, Marcus was there, insisting we leave, so the only real entertainment we had was the evening we went to Covent Garden."

"Dear me," said Sir Spenser, turning his quizzing glass toward the countess. "I do hope you were not caught up in all that riot and rumpus."

"Well, we were," she retorted. "Not that we could have known from the outset how it would be, though Marcus would have it otherwise."

"No, no," Sir Spenser said loyally. "How could you?

I daresay you expected only to be entertained. Such goings-on! I read all about it in the *Times*, you know, and I cannot tell you how much I envy you being part of all that excitement.''

Gwenyth stared at him, unable to imagine Sir Spenser, always precise to a pin and never out of temper, in the midst of the Covent Garden riots; however, the countess seemed to approve of his attitude, for she actually smiled at him.

''A man tried to break into our box,'' she said, lifting her chin and looking down her nose. ''We soon sent him to the rightabout, I can tell you.''

He nodded. ''Only thing to do. Pray, Almeria, you must tell me all about it.''

She complied, and soon talked herself into an excellent humor, dampened only when Pamela attempted to interpose some detail or other that she had forgotten to mention. But Gwenyth frowned at her friend, and Pamela fell silent again until Sir Spenser exclaimed at hearing that Gwenyth had been injured.

''She is all right now, sir,'' Pamela said when he looked at Gwenyth in astonishment and expressed his hope that she had not been seriously injured.

''Who is all right?'' Jared asked from the threshold of the drawing room. They had not noted his entrance, and since they had not seen him since their arrival, his grandmother greeted him with enthusiasm, declaring that she had not realized he had returned to the abbey.

''I quite thought you meant to be away some time on business,'' she said. ''You said you could not go with us to town, but had I known you intended to finish your business so quickly, I would have invited you to ride down as soon as it was done.''

He smiled as he bent to kiss her cheek. ''Then I would have passed you on the road and got to town to find you gone, ma'am, so 'tis as well I stayed here, is it not?''

''You could scarcely pass us without noticing,'' she said, shaking her head. ''I am sure the Lyford crest is quite as well-known to you as your own face, and it is painted a foot high or more on both doors of the carriage. And surely you know our livery and our coachman. And he would recognize you too, you know. And truly, if only you had—"

"Yes, yes, ma'am," he said, laughing. "I ought to have told you that my business would occupy me for only a few days, and had I known as much at the time, I certainly would have done so."

"I cannot imagine what sort of business you might have had anyway," she said fretfully.

"Dull business," he said, "and I was most surprised, for that matter, to learn that you had returned so soon. Surely you did not tell me you meant to do so."

She snapped, "We did not mean to do so! Marcus would have it that Gwenyth must recuperate at Molesford."

"Recuperate from what?" Jared inquired, looking at Gwenyth. "Were you ill, ma'am?"

At the same time, Pamela exclaimed, "He would have made us come back anyway!"

"Fiddle faddle," retorted the countess, as Gwenyth, in an undertone, attempted to put Jared in possession of the bare facts of their visit to Covent Garden. "If you think, miss," Lady Lyford went on severely, "that anyone but you would have returned with Marcus, had it not been for Wynnefreda's thinking her duty lay with Gwenyth rather than with me, you much mistake the matter. Ah, here is Marcus now, and not before time, I must say, sir. You might have considered the fact that others are hungry."

"I beg your pardon, ma'am," the earl said quietly. "I was delayed and certainly knew better than to come down to dine in all my dirt."

She did not respond, but noting the butler's entrance at that moment to announce that dinner was served, she stood and held out her hand to Sir Spenser to take her in. Since he was speaking to Pamela, who was smiling up at him, the countess found it necessary to speak his name sharply before he looked at her and saw that she was waiting for him. With another smile at Pamela, he hurried to escort her, leaving the others to follow in what order they pleased.

The earl was quiet during the meal, leaving conversation to the others, and although he escorted Sir Spenser to join the ladies in the drawing room afterward, explaining that Jared had had letters to write, he soon made his own excuses, and left them listening to Pamela play upon the pianoforte.

Gwenyth, finding that his mood strongly infected her own, pleaded her aches and pains in order to leave before the tea tray had been brought in. Intending to retire early, she rang for Annie to plait her hair and help her into her nightdress, then dismissed her and lay in her bed with the covers pushed off, pretending that it was cooler in the darkness.

Through the open window she could see the moon rising over the eastern Chilterns, at first no more than a glow, then a brilliant halo outlining a small section of the crest. The halo grew larger, rounded into a half and then a full bright orb, lighting her room, setting shadows to dancing. Gwenyth got out of bed and moved to the window to look out.

At the bottom of the garden, the moonlight touched the water of the Thames, making it look as though an artist had outlined its ripples with silver. There was no traffic on the river. A nightbird called, but other than that the stillness was absolute for several minutes. Then she heard a horse's whicker, low and muted, from the direction of the stables. The air at the window was cooler than it had been earlier, but still warm enough so that she was not chilled in her thin lawn nightdress. Indeed, she was still hot, and looking at the river, she remembered the evenings before, when she had watched the gentlemen going down to swim. The water would be blissfully cool. Just thinking of it made her feel her bruises more than ever.

Swiftly, before she could change her mind, she tugged off her nightdress and donned her shift, a simple morning frock with a drawstring bodice that she could fasten herself, and a pair of sandals. Then, snatching up a towel from her washstand, she slipped out of her room, down the corridor to the rear stairs, and out through the east-wing door. Walking rapidly downhill toward the garden, she glanced back over her shoulder to see if anyone was watching her.

The windows of the east wing, except for the earl's library, were all reassuringly dark. And no dark figure watched her from the library window.

She could see the garden path clearly in the moonlight, and soon she was running, holding her skirt in one hand, her towel in the other, down the brick path to the beaten ride beside the river. There was better cover farther along, where the trees came down near the river, but it was also darker there. She decided that if she hunkered down to remove her dress, the willows and other shrubbery along the bank at the bottom of the garden would provide her with sufficient concealment.

In minutes, her dress was folded beside a shrub, her sandals sitting next to it with her towel. Glancing about again, she noted that the trees which formed such an admirable backdrop for the abbey by day looked like towering black walls at night, obscuring the lines of the house. What was to be admired was the river, silvery and alive in the moonlight, whispering to itself as it flowed past the abbey grounds. Barefoot, in her shift, she waded carefully through the willows into the water, testing the current as she went, feeling for obstacles beneath the surface.

The Thames was a good deal cooler than she had expected, as chilly as ever, in fact, despite the weather, and the mud on the bottom squished between her toes. There was more silt here than in her little cove or, indeed, in her rivers at home. She had bathed from the machines at Barmouth, and the sand there had a tendency to move in a similar fashion beneath her feet. The feeling was not altogether unpleasant, but a moment later the thought of the creeping, crawling things that might inhabit the mud sent her splashing toward the center of the river.

When the water was up to her waist, she remembered the possibility of being seen from the abbey and quickly, with a fleeting glance over her shoulder, submerged her body so that only her head was above the water. The shock of the cold robbed her of her breath, and for some minutes she remained where she was, gasping, but once the initial shock passed, she found the water's temperature to be very pleasant. Her bruises seemed to have vanished, and she felt no pain.

The current made itself felt now, pushing and tugging at her body, but it was gentle and didn't frighten her. She thrust her arms forward, put her face down between them, and lifted her feet, floating, letting the current take her where it would, rolling onto her back a moment later to watch the moon. Only when she felt the sharp chill of the water against the back of her head and the heaviness of her plaited hair did she wonder what Annie would have to say if her hair was still damp in the morning. Not that it mattered. At the moment, Annie's feelings didn't matter to her in the least. She was too intoxicated by moonlight and the moving river to care about consequences. She felt weightless, and the solitude, after spending the greater part of the past two days cooped up in a coach with three other women, was blissful.

She was sorely tempted to remove her shift. That thought and the accompanying mental image of a passerby's reaction upon seeing her floating naked on the Thames doubled her up, gasping with suppressed laughter and choking as she swallowed a mouthful of water. When she regained control of herself, she swam a few strokes with the current; then, discovering that she had drifted nearer the Oxfordshire bank than her own and had moved much farther downstream than she had meant to, she began swimming at an angle with the current as her father and brothers had taught her, so as not to fight its full force with every stroke.

The current was inconvenient rather than troublesome, for there had been no rain for several months and the river was lower than normal. Then, too, the Molesford lock and its counterparts at Streatley were closed. But even as she began to congratulate herself that she would make landfall near the bend in the river and thus not more than half a mile from where she had started, she heard a muffled creaking sound and a thump downriver and felt the water undulate around her. Knowing at once that the lock had been opened, she stroked harder, well aware that she could not follow her instinct to fight for shore, that to fight the powerful surge would be dangerous, perhaps even fatal.

The chill of fear nearly paralyzed her when she remembered the river at Streatley, foaming and boiling beneath the bridge after the lock had been opened. Telling herself that with luck she would not be swept into the white water below Molesford lock, that the waters above would not become such a vicious torrent, she forced herself to concentrate on swimming. Still moving at an angle, but having to fight the current to keep her direction as the water moved faster and faster, drawing her with it, she stroked as hard as she could until, hitting something slimy in the water, she jerked her hand away instinctively and overset herself, submerging.

Losing control, she was carried along for several moments, thrashing and twisting as she fought for the surface and tried to regain her balance. She was nearing the bend and knew the lock was just beyond. Her mind worked rapidly. She knew, for the information had formed part of her father's lessons, that the water on the inside of the curve, the Berkshire side, ought to move more slowly than the water on the outside and that it ought to be shallow there, as well. She began feeling with her feet, trying to find bottom and at the same time to keep what control she had of her movements, to keep moving at an angle, however small, toward the bank. The fear of being seen by the men at the lock gave her great motivation, greater strength. She was in her shift, after all, not a presentable sight.

As it happened, she found bottom with her knees before she managed to touch with her feet, which proved to be singularly unmanageable in the swift current. Grabbing at the weeds of the riverbed with her hands, she took in a large mouthful of water, but she knew she was safe. She was a short distance past the bend in less than three feet of water. Seconds later, she was leaning against the overhang where the river had eroded the dirt away, her body, up to her shoulders, still in the water. She did not dare stand up to get out for fear of being seen and also because she did not at the moment trust her legs to support her.

How long she remained sitting there, gasping, waiting for her thudding heart to regain its normal rhythm, she had no idea, nor was she aware of when she first began to hear voices. They came from the direction of the lock, not more than thirty yards away from her now. The roar of the river had eased, and the voices carried distinctly over the water to her sharp ears.

"Get that gate shut proper now," a man said. "Old Nat'll be fit to be tied if you split another paddle."

"That ter Nat Philps," retorted another. His gesture, clearly visible in the moonlight, drew her attention to his dark figure on the catwalk.

She couldn't see the first man, but he chuckled. A moment later he said, "That lot will make London safe enough, but I'm wonderin' about the next, what with the abbey as full as be damned again. Young master's gettin' right nervy on us."

Gwenyth's attention was riveted now, her mind working madly to make sense of what she heard. Surely they spoke of the earl.

The first man spoke again, and there was a familiar sound to his voice, but she could not think where she had heard it before. "The next may be the last, for a while," he said. "'Taint's safe, with so many folks about and young Joey always searching for his treasure. Mayhap one day he'll know he's already found it, and then the lot of us'll be for it. That gate shut proper now?"

"Aye. Won't no one know nothing about this little trip. Let's be gettin' upriver, though, afore we're seen by someone who'll split."

Gwenyth fought the panic rising within her. They would pass right above her and surely would see her if she stayed where she was, for her white shift would show beneath the water in the moonlight. Sliding upward, hoping they were concerned more with getting away from the lock than with watching for observers, she lifted herself onto the bank and swung her feet around, then stood up. The sound of a footfall from the trees behind her startled her as she took her first hasty step. She stumbled, only to be caught from behind as a large hand clapped over her mouth, muffling the little scream that was the only sound she was capable of making. A strong arm wrapped around her, lifting her from her feet.

"Keep silent, damn you!" her captor whispered fiercely.

She knew at once that it was Lyford and was sorely tempted to bite his hand, but he must have known her temptation, for he shifted its position, cupping it over her mouth so that she could not do so. Silently he carried her into the cover of the trees, squatting behind a large one and forcing her to keep low.

When she struggled again, trying to free herself, he muttered savagely into her ear, "Keep still. They'll hear you!"

His reminder instantly renewed her panic and froze her in place. A few moments later she heard the men pass by.

When the last echo of their footsteps had passed into the distance, Lyford got to his feet, hauling her up beside him with a heavy hand and forcing her to face him. "You," he said, glaring down at her furiously, "deserve to be soundly thrashed, and I've a very good mind to see to it myself."

13

Gwenyth stared up at the earl, shivering, her breath coming in gasps. The moonlight filtering through the branches overhead played on the rugged planes of his face, revealing his angry expression, making it clear that his threat was no idle one. Had she been a weaker woman, she'd have cringed at the sight.

Lyford glared down at her silently, as though he dared her to answer him back, but when she did not, his gaze shifted lower to her heaving bosom, and his lips parted slightly. Realizing where he was looking, she tried to cover herself and was immediately reminded of her near-naked state. Warmth surged through her and she raised her free arm in an attempt to cover herself.

Her movement recalled Lyford to his senses. Releasing her, he shrugged out of his coat and flung it around her. Then, resting both hands on her shoulders, he looked down at her.

"I am angry with you," he said harshly, but there was another note in his voice that made her wonder if he was informing her of that fact or reminding himself.

"I know," she said, hearing her own voice as if it were that of a stranger. All her awareness was centered upon his hands and the feeling in her shoulders where they touched her. He was too close, and she was more vulnerable than she had ever been. His coat didn't help. If anything, it made matters worse, for she could feel the warmth of him in the material of his coat, and it was thus as though her whole body were being embraced.

"You ought not to swim alone," he muttered. "It is dangerous. And you promised me—"

"I know," she said, looking at his top shirt button, "but I was hot. I didn't think."

"It is a hot night," he agreed. His voice was ragged.

"Very hot."

"Yes." His hands moved on her shoulders as though he would let her go, but then suddenly they clenched tightly, making her gasp and look up at him again. He gave her a little shake. "You never think, Gwen. You just act. If you had thought about how wrong it was to take Pamela to London after I had said—"

"That was not my doing," she said, looking him straight in the eye. As always, she wished immediately that she had not done so foolish a thing, for she could not look away, and her whole body seemed to swell with new sensations that made her forget his anger, forget the chill of her damp shift, her bare feet, forget everything except his nearness and her awareness of him.

He drew in a sharp breath, then let it out slowly, but he did not take his eyes from her. The tension in his body made her more aware than ever of the fact that she had on only her thin shift, reminding her that in the moonlight, when he had first seen her, she might just as well have been naked. When he bent his head toward her, she knew she ought to step away, but she could not move. Mesmerized, she stood silently, waiting, anticipating, her lips invitingly parted, her eyes wide.

His mouth touched hers, and when she did not resist, his hands moved from her shoulders to her back, and he drew her nearer, kissing her harder. The coat slid off one shoulder, and he pushed it impatiently off the other, moving his hands exploringly over her shoulder blades, down to her waist and hips.

The night air touched her again, chilling her arms and shoulders, as well as the skin beneath the damp shift, but instead of bringing her to her senses, the feeling stirred a heat within her that matched Lyford's. She did not know herself. It was as though some other young woman stood there on the riverbank experiencing a host of new feelings, discovering within herself a hunger and passion that she had never known she possessed. Lady Gwenyth Traherne watched that strange young woman from a distance, enjoying the scene and the resultant sensations vicariously, and thus shamelessly.

She did not want him to stop. When his tongue pressed inquiringly against her lips, they opened for him as though she had done such things many times in the past instead of only once before, with him. And when his hands caressed her hips, then moved upward along her sides to the soft swell of her breasts, she stirred against him as though to urge him to take even greater liberties. When the fingertips of his right hand traced an outline along the lacy edge of her shift above her breasts, she waited, breathless, for those fingers to slip beneath the cloth to caress her soft bare skin.

He held her closer, his left arm around her waist, his right hand cupping her breast gently, tenderly, warmly, making the nipple tingle with a sensation she had never experienced before. When Gwenyth moaned deep in her throat, Lyford went still. For a long moment he did not move. His lips pressed against hers, but they no longer demanded. His right hand still rested against her breast, but it no longer caressed her. Slowly, gently, he moved it away and stepped back, his left hand moving back to squeeze her shoulder for a brief moment before it dropped to his side.

She stared at him, wondering why he had stopped. Her senses were whirling, uncontrolled, still part and parcel of the strange young woman, not Gwenyth's senses at all.

"Foolhardy," he said, the word barely audible as he bent to recover the coat and drape it about her again. She did not know whether he meant himself or her. Then he muttered, "You have no understanding of the foolish risks you run."

When he said nothing more, but just stood there looking sternly down at her, she began to collect her wits, to realize that there had been no fantasy, that what she had been allowing him to do had been real. No less pleasant, merely real. Biting her lower lip, she looked again at the top button of his shirt.

"I don't think," she said slowly, careful not to look up, lest she find herself trapped again in the depths of his eyes, "that what just happened between us was altogether my fault."

"Nor will it be altogether your fault, I suppose," he said grimly, "if I make good my threat to put you across my knee and teach you the lesson you deserve for what you did tonight."

"You would not dare." But she moved both hands protectively to her hips.

"Don't tempt me. I ought not to have done what I did just now, either. But the temptation was too great to resist, and the temptation now is nearly as great, for there is no one else to deal with you. Or will you tell me that Tallyn would not dare, had he come upon you as I did tonight?"

"That," she said with careful dignity, "is different. He has the right; you do not."

"But he is not here," he reminded her, "and I am. Surely you have learned by now that I do not always follow the rules."

She had learned that much of him, to be sure. Biting her lower lip, she watched him warily, noting with relief when he took visible, rigid control of his temper.

After a moment of silence he said evenly, "You have a knack for stirring my anger, Gwenyth. Indeed, I cannot remember ever being so angry with anyone as I was when I saw you alone tonight in the river, or before, in London."

"But I did nothing in London to warrant—"

"You did!" he snapped. "You might have been killed. Supposing that instead of being thrown against the partition, you had been knocked over the balcony. You would never have survived such a fall. And all because you decided to do as you pleased instead of what was sensible. Why are women never sensible?"

She straightened indignantly. "Of all the crackbrained things to say! Of course we are sensible, and even with all that was written in the papers, I saw nothing to suggest that violence would prevail that evening. The only thing that happened before then was that the noise of the crowd made it impossible to hear a word the actors said. No one in the theater was hurt, for heaven's sake. And you blamed me for taking Pamela to town! That was not my doing at all."

"Perhaps not," he said, abandoning that argument, "but your swim tonight can scarcely be blamed upon anyone else, and here you are now, standing about in a wet shift, bandying words with a man who could as easily seduce you as look at you."

"Could you?" she asked, a note of defiance, even of daring in her voice.

"Dammit, Gwen, I am not made of stone. Do not challenge me like that, or we'll both be sorry."

"Very well, but do not try to convince me that I should be afraid of you. I do not understand everything that's happening, but I do know that I need not fear seduction from you."

"By God, you need a master," he growled. "Someone who will curb your extravagance and keep you from doing such idiotic things as must endanger both your life and your honor. What your brother has been thinking of to give you your head these past years, I cannot imagine. He ought to be horsewhipped."

Her lips folded tightly together, and the only emotion she was aware of at that moment was anger. "You clearly want to hit someone, my lord, but I am cold. I am going back. We ought not to be standing here like this, anyway. We might be seen."

Lyford glanced about, then looked ruefully at her again. "I can't believe I forgot those men for even a single moment," he said. "Did you see what they were doing?"

His attitude was suddenly a little too casual, and Gwenyth struggled to regain her wits, to remember what she had seen and heard. He had told her he'd seen her from the library window, and she knew that that was entirely possible. But she had not seen him, and she had looked. Moreover, it was equally possible that he had been near the river all along, that he was the "young master" the others had mentioned, that dark deeds were being done and that he knew all about them. In any event, his question was not so casual as he would have her believe. He wanted to know how much she had heard. Remembering the death of Silas Ferguson, she knew she did not dare follow her instinct to trust him until she had had time to think. She took refuge in her anger.

"I have no more to say to you tonight, Lyford," she said icily. "If you do not desire to escort me back to the house, I will go alone."

For a moment he looked as though he meant to press her for answers to his questions, but something in her expression must have convinced him that such an inquisition would prove futile, for he shrugged and reached out to adjust the coat over her shoulders instead. "Little idiot," he murmured, but there was warmth in his voice again, and she was glad to hear it.

They found her dress and sandals and then did not speak again until they reached the house, entering through the east wing and taking the back stairway, as Gwenyth had done earlier. Upstairs, as they walked along the corridor toward her room, she might almost have predicted the moment he would speak.

He said very quietly, "We must talk, you know. There are matters that must be discussed."

She glanced up to see that he was watching her intently. She wanted to trust him, to discuss the possibilities suggested by the events she had witnessed that night. But she could not forget that he might be part of whatever was happening, that a man had already been murdered for knowing too much.

As she opened her mouth to tell him that she was tired, the door next to her own opened suddenly, startling them both, and Pamela put her head out.

"There you are, Gwen! I couldn't think where you had gone. Goodness, your hair is all wet! And your dress."

Lyford said sternly, "You go to bed."

"Well," she said indignantly, letting the door swing wide

as she placed her hands upon her hips, "of all the things to say when you come strolling along in a wet coat with a lady whose hair is dripping! I daresay your grandmama and Lady Cadogan would be vastly entertained to hear of it."

"They will hear nothing about it," Lyford said grimly.

"No?" Pamela retorted with a saucy smile. "Perhaps they will not if you will promise to take me back to London before the king's Jubilee celebration has ended."

"By God—" Lyford reached for her, but Gwenyth grabbed his arm with both her hands.

"Do not, my lord," she said sharply. "I will talk to her, I promise, but leave us now, if you please."

He looked at her angrily, then glanced again at Pamela, who merely stood watching him as though she observed an exotic beast at the Tower of London. Returning his gaze to Gwenyth, he said, "Very well, but you and I will talk tomorrow."

"Yes, sir." She was conscious of deep relief when he turned on his heel and strode away from them, but she still had Pamela to contend with. "Come into my bedchamber," she said. "You can help me get the tangles out of my hair. I dare not ring for Annie. She would drive me to distraction with her scolds."

Pamela followed with alacrity, demanding to know the whole even as the door shut behind her. "And do not think to fob me off with some Banbury tale, Gwen, for I won't have it. Where have you been? And why were you with Marcus?"

"I was swimming," Gwenyth said shortly. "I was hot, and my body ached. I thought a swim would—"

"You weren't swimming with Marcus!"

"No, he found me," she said, sitting on the stool by her dressing table. "I swam from the riverbank at the bottom of the garden, but I drifted too far down the river. He had seen me from the library and came to fetch me, that's all. And really, Pamela, you would do better neither to refine too much upon it nor to tease Lyford. You will only make him angry."

"He will have to do as I wish now," Pamela retorted, beginning to unplait Gwenyth's tangled hair.

"You know better than that. He will allow you to prattle what you know to whomever you like and then he'll have us both to suffer the consequences." That Pamela would accept her first argument was too much to hope. Finally, in exasperation, Gwenyth said, "Lyford is already vexed with me, Pamela. And my aunt and the countess will be both shocked and displeased if they come to hear of it, as they certainly will if you continue to tease him."

Pamela frowned, then said quietly, "I don't wish to cause you further distress, Gwen, though I do mean to make Marcus take me back to London. If he has been scolding you . . . well, I know what that is like. Not," she added with a grimace, "that you do not deserve scolding. Why, if I had been so foolish as to swim alone at night—if I could swim, that is—you would—"

"I know," Gwenyth said, laughing in relief. "Lyford asked me what my brother would have had to say if he had seen me, and I can tell you, the very thought set goose bumps to dancing on my skin. I am very glad that Tallyn is many miles away."

When Pamela left her to her own reflections at last, Gwenyth found it hard to sleep, for her thoughts were busy ones. The more she thought about the things she had learned since coming to Molesford, the harder it was to imagine the earl being party to anything underhanded. Still, he had never denied that he needed money, and if, as her aunt supposed, there was something amiss with the Hawtrey Shipping Company, it was possible that the earl had been part of it for a long time and that it was somehow connected with whatever was happening at the abbey.

On the other hand, Silas Ferguson had been killed, and she could not believe the earl a murderer. She might believe many other things about him, but not that. It was true that she had come to Molesford to keep him from forcing Pamela into marriage, but she had seen at once that he had had no such intention, and everything else she had learned of him had been to his credit. So much so that she had fallen in love with him.

Instead of making her task easier, that last notion, leaping to mind as it had, had frightened her, for she knew she could not be thinking clearly. As she tried to put her thoughts in order, she tossed and turned uncomfortably, the sultriness of the air around her turning her bedclothes into a wrinkled mess. By the time she finally fell into exhausted slumber, she had come to the conclusion that the only thing to be done was to put the business into hands more experienced with such matters than her own.

The following morning, as soon as she had dressed, she found paper and pen and wrote to Sir Antony. The letter was not one of her better epistolary efforts, by any means, for she decided at once that it would not do to write everything down, lest it fall into the wrong hands. If he was away, she could trust Meriel to send it on to him and hope that he would comprehend it well enough to advise her. Still, there might well be need for action soon, before Sir Antony could arrive. After some thought, she realized that she had to trust Lyford. There was no one else.

Taking time only to entrust her letter to Frythorpe for posting, she hurried to the breakfast parlor, where she found her aunt eating in solitary splendor.

"Where is his lordship?" Gwenyth demanded without ceremony.

"Gone to the stables," Lady Cadogan replied, regarding her with curiosity. "You look big with news, my dear. What is it?"

"I must speak with him first," Gwenyth said.

"Well, it might not be the best time now," Lady Cadogan said, "because he's bound to be out of temper. What must that idiotish Pamela do but get up betimes only to tease him to take her back to London. She sat here at the table with us, casting the oddest looks at me while she talked nonsense to him about what she might say if only she wished to say it. I can tell you, dearest, 'tis a wonder the man didn't strangle her. And then what must she do but follow him when he left, still prattling of balls and parties and the king's Jubilee."

"If Lyford does not strangle her," Gwenyth said grimly, turning toward the door, "I shall attend to it myself."

She pushed past a young footman entering the room and hurried downstairs and across the courtyard to the stable entrance. There was no one inside except for Joey Ferguson, who waved at her, and another groom who did not look up from the bridle he was polishing. Hearing an angry scream outside in the yard, and recognizing Pamela's voice, Gwenyth quickened her pace, emerging into the sunlight in time to see the earl take his cousin by her shoulders and give her a hard shake.

Pamela shrieked at him to stop, and he snapped something at her that Gwenyth could not hear. Neither of them heeded the sound of approaching hoofbeats or saw the broad-shouldered horseman bearing down upon them. He was upon them in seconds, leaping from his saddle to grab the earl by the arm before Gwenyth could do more than gasp in astonished dismay.

Startled, Lyford released Pamela and whirled to face his aggressor, but a sharp right jab to his chin felled him to the ground before he could so much as open his mouth to speak.

"Joss!" Gwenyth cried, rushing forward.

"Oh, thank you, my lord," Pamela breathed, clasping her hands at her bosom and regarding the Earl of Tallyn with shining eyes. "He frightened me so!"

"Are you quite all right, Miss Beckley?" Tallyn inquired, turning toward her solicitously as he rubbed the knuckles of his right hand against his leather coat. "Good thing I came along. No one out front to take my horse, you know, which don't say much for the way this place is run, if you ask me. That fellow didn't hurt you, did he? By God, if he did—"

"Joss, look what you've done," Gwenyth cried, falling to her knees beside Lyford and feeling for his pulse, her heart hammering with fear in her breast. "You might have killed him!"

"Might yet if he's hurt Miss Beckley," Tallyn said grimly. "Who is the fellow, anyway?"

"He is Lyford," Gwenyth snapped. "Our host."

"Well," said Tallyn, unimpressed, "he ought not to go about molesting defenseless young females. Are you sure you have not been harmed, Miss Beckley?"

Pamela began to assure him that she was unhurt, but Lyford groaned just then, and hearing him, Gwenyth sighed in relief and turned quickly back to him. "Thank heaven, he is coming round. Lyford, wake up." Glancing up a moment later, she noted that Tallyn and Pamela were still involved in their own conversation and that the incident had drawn an audience.

"Joey," she called as the boy emerged from the stable with the clear intention of joining the grooms and stableboys already in the yard, "fetch his lordship a damp cloth."

"Aye," he shouted back.

"Don't try to sit up yet, sir," she told Lyford when he opened his eyes. "You will be better in a moment."

"Damn," he muttered, ignoring her and trying to sit, his hand to his jaw. "I think he loosened a tooth. Who is that damned maniac?"

"My brother Tallyn," she said briefly, taking the damp rag Joey handed her and attempting to apply it to the earl's chin.

He took it from her, eyeing Tallyn and Pamela with disfavor. "Your brother, eh. What's his interest in my cousin?"

"None, sir. He met her once, that's all, and he seems to have misunderstood your intentions toward her just now."

"No, he didn't. I was ready to murder the wench."

"Can you get up?"

Tallyn turned back to them as the earl got shakily to his feet, and the two men glared at each other for a long minute before Gwenyth said, "Joss, you must apologize. You misunderstood. Lyford is Miss Beckley's guardian."

"Don't refine too much upon that," Lyford said with a sigh, extending his hand to Tallyn. "I'd no doubt be thanking you if Pamela had been struggling with anyone else and you'd intervened. You didn't know me."

"Good of you to say so," Tallyn said, shaking his hand.

His manner was still reticent, but he relaxed when Lyford began to smile, only to grimace in pain instead. Tallyn smiled ruefully. "Sorry about that."

"You've got steel in that fist," Lyford told him. "You must practice."

"I do," Tallyn agreed. "Spent time in America, where it don't do for a man not to be able to defend himself. Once had to dust three fellows at once, but that's another tale. Guess I ought to be thanking you for looking after my sister. Trust she's behaved herself." When Gwenyth looked guiltily at Lyford, remembering a portion of her conversation with him the previous night and what she had said to Pamela afterward about being glad Tallyn was not at hand, the look was not lost on her brother. "See she hasn't. Care to tell me about it?"

Lyford looked at her, and for a fleeting moment she feared that he would, but then she saw the teasing amusement in his eyes and her fear vanished.

He said, "Nothing at all. We'll go inside, shall we? Have you breakfasted, Tallyn? You've come at a dashed early hour, you know, for paying a call."

"Came late's what I did," Tallyn said, interrupting himself to give brief instructions regarding his horse to one of the grooms before adding, "My man's coming later with my gear. I put up in Pangbourne last night and rode on this morning. Had breakfast near about sunup."

Lyford glanced at the group of stableboys and grooms, and the look was enough to empty the yard at once. "You'll stay for a few days, I trust," he said.

Tallyn nodded. "If you haven't had your fill of Trahernes."

"I haven't." Lyford looked at Gwenyth again, and the tender expression in his eyes made her blush. As she turned, she found her brother regarding her rather oddly. He opened his mouth as though he would say something, but shut it again and offered his arm to Pamela instead.

"Don't look at me like that again," she muttered to Lyford

under her breath as they followed the other two around to the front and into the house.

She heard him chuckle. "Why not? I like to look at you."

"Lyford, don't be nonsensical, or that sore jaw of yours won't be the only consequence of my brother's genius for misunderstanding."

"Whatever do you mean, my dear?"

"And don't call me your dear!" she hissed.

"Very well, my love."

"Lyford!"

"I think," he hissed back, "that I shall take a leaf from my little cousin's book."

"What do you mean?" she demanded.

"Blackmail."

"Blackmail?"

"Yes, surely you know the sort of thing. If you are not kind to me, I shall have a nice long chat with the estimable Tallyn. I'll wager he won't think highly of your liking for the water, my love, or of your visit to Covent Garden."

"You wouldn't," she declared flatly.

He grinned at her. "We'll see."

14

Denied immediate opportunity for private conversation with Lyford, Gwenyth found herself occupied for some time with her brother. She considered confiding in him but decided almost at once that to do so would require rather too much explanation for her comfort. Indeed, she was grateful that Tallyn did not question her, and he did not do so for the simple reason that Pamela managed to accompany them wherever they went.

Under ordinary circumstances, Gwenyth might have wished her at Jericho, but as it was, she had no wish to be alone with Tallyn. Nor did she stop to consider why he did not demand a few moments alone with her, for she had other matters on her mind. There was one task, at least, that she wanted to see to at once.

When she offered to take Tallyn over the house and grounds, Pamela announced cheerfully that she would go too, and it was an easy matter for Gwenyth to guide them toward the stables. Leaving Pamela to accompany Tallyn while he looked the place over, she went in search of Joey and found him in Cyrano's empty stall, only to discover that Lyford had been ahead of her.

"Said he'd dust me jacket hisself if he heard I were treasure-huntin' again or even talkin' 'bout it," he said, grinning at her. "And Mr. Powell were here this morning too. He done told me ter keep clear or e'd tell me dad. Don't like Mr. Powell much, I don't, but I do what me lord tells me."

Gwenyth thought about Mr. Powell for a moment. He was

Welsh, which was certainly a point in his favor, but she wondered why he would concern himself with the boy. No doubt, she decided, he had been acting on Jared's orders.

They met Jared himself in the stableyard, and when Gwenyth had introduced Tallyn to him, he said he had been searching for Pamela to invite her to ride. Assenting at once, Pamela promptly asked Tallyn if he wouldn't like to join them. Her invitation, Gwenyth noted, did not much please Jared, but he rallied quickly, extending his own to include Gwenyth.

She refused without a qualm, having no worries about Pamela so long as she had two escorts, and certain by the way the two men looked at each other that neither would leave her alone with the other. She had hoped to take the opportunity to speak with Lyford, but he was nowhere to be found. She did not see him until dinner, and by then the lines of battle between Tallyn and Jared had been clearly drawn. The two men looked daggers at each other throughout the meal.

Sir Spenser had not called that day, a fact that the dowager commented upon at length over dinner, and afterward, when the ladies retired to the drawing room, she wondered aloud more than once if Tallyn might not enjoy a hand of whist. Gwenyth, knowing he was not fond of cards, suggested several alternatives, but the countess was not enthusiastic about any of them. Lady Cadogan drew up her tapestry frame and began sorting through her threads, casting her niece an occasional glance of sympathy but offering no suggestions for the countess's entertainment.

When the three gentlemen joined them half an hour later, Gwenyth saw that Lyford was amused. The other two went to speak to Pamela, and Gwenyth was surprised to see that, rather than encouraging them with her customary flirtatiousness, Pamela behaved rather oddly. When Jared addressed a comment to her, she smiled and laughed in a near-parody of her normal style. But when Tallyn spoke to her—in a far gentler tone, Gwenyth noticed, than any his sisters had ever heard from him—Pamela blushed and stammered shyly in the manner of a schoolgirl, albeit not the manner Pamela herself had ever displayed at school.

"Much," Lyford murmured at her ear, "as I should like to enjoy the excellent farce being enacted for us by my idiotish cousins and your brother, I should like even more to enjoy some private conversation with you, my love. Shall we leave them to their amusements?"

Glancing at him, she encountered a look of calm intent and promptly decided that the last thing she wanted to do was to be private with him. Not, in any case, at that particular moment, with Tallyn frowning at her as he was, and with the dowager glancing from Jared to Pamela and then at Tallyn with much the same scowling expression.

"Lottery tickets!" Gwenyth exclaimed, moving rather quickly away from Lyford. "I have not played for months, and we have a good number, if everyone will play."

To her surprise, Lady Lyford approved her choice, and Lady Cadogan obligingly set her fancywork aside. Tallyn shook his head as though he would prefer not to play, but when Pamela exclaimed in pleasure, he promptly assured everyone that it was one of his favorite pastimes. Jared said nothing, but helped find the box containing the game pieces, and Lyford was left with little choice but to help set things up.

The dowager soon proved that she was without peer in her mastery of the game, but the rest were sufficiently entertained by her shrewd maneuvering that they played late, and Lyford made no further attempt that evening to engage Gwenyth in private conversation.

The following morning, knowing that she could no longer put off talking to him, she went down to the breakfast parlor early in search of him. Only Jared and Lady Cadogan were there.

"Good morning," she said to them. "Has Lyford been down?"

"An hour ago," her aunt told her. "He has gone riding on the downs with Joss." When Gwenyth sighed with disappointment, she added, "Did you not speak with him yesterday?"

"I couldn't," Gwenyth told her. "Joss arrived just as I was about to do so, and I never had another chance."

Lady Cadogan cocked her head to one side, regarding her shrewdly. "I thought the matter was of some importance."

Gwenyth nodded, biting her lip and turning to serve herself from a platter of Smithfield ham. As she reached for the toast, Jared said casually, "Perhaps I might be of some assistance with this so important matter."

Glancing at him over her shoulder, she smiled. " 'Tis nothing, really. Only some things I wished to discuss with him." When he continued to look steadily at her as though he expected her to continue, she turned back to the sideboard, put several pieces of toast on her plate, and moved to sit beside her aunt. "What do you mean to do today, ma'am?"

Lady Cadogan replied that she had no particular plan, and glancing at Jared, Gwenyth noted with relief that he had returned his attention to his breakfast.

A moment later he said, "I wonder if Pamela would like to take a little trip along the river today. It is possible, you know, to ride a barge from Streatley through the Molesford lock, and there are some excellent bits of scenery along the way."

"You must ask her," Gwenyth told him. "No doubt she will be down to breakfast soon."

"Would you like to go too?" he asked in what was clearly an afterthought.

"No, thank you," she replied, thinking of how best to separate Lyford from Tallyn's company when they returned from their ride, without arousing Tallyn's brotherly curiosity.

Lady Cadogan said to Jared, "You must take a groom with you. It will not do for you to escort Pamela without one."

"It would be dashed inconvenient, too," he said, laughing. "Someone must lead our horses back, after all. And," he added hastily, "there will be bargemen with us on the river, so everything will be as right as rain, ma'am."

When Pamela entered the room twenty minutes later, he informed her of the treat in store for her, and if she did not exclaim with enthusiasm, at least she did not reject his offer outright. "A ride will be pleasant," she said musingly. "Perhaps Lord Tallyn would like to come with us."

"Well, I don't intend to wait for him," Jared said, "so I hope you aren't bent upon his company."

She looked at him more sharply then. "But why should you mind if I want him to come?" When he only looked at her, she shrugged. "Very well, but I wish to call upon Sir Spenser along the way, so I hope you won't object to that."

"Can't think why you'd wish to do such a thing," Jared said.

"He did not visit us yesterday," Pamela replied, "and I wish to know that he is not ill."

"Well, I don't mind. We'll look in on the old fellow on our way to Streatley and then wave at him on our way down-river."

Pamela's brilliant smile gave Gwenyth the distinct impression that it was she who had got her way rather than Jared, but he left at once, and in a very good humor, to arrange for their horses to be brought around. Pamela ate her breakfast in a leisurely manner before going up to change into her habit, and Lady Cadogan and Gwenyth adjourned to the morning room, where the dowager countess found them half an hour later.

"You look as fine as fivepence in that rig, ma'am," Gwenyth said, looking up from the magazine she was reading.

The countess looked down complacently at her bright blue morning frock. " 'Tis a good dress, isn't it? Dratted weather's gone chilly again, though. Brought my shawl." Leaning slightly on her cane, she hefted the brightly colored Norwich shawl she carried over her free arm. "Where is everyone?"

Lady Cadogan glanced up over her tapestry frame. "If you will refuse to leave your bedchamber until noon, Almeria, you cannot express wonder at the fact that everyone else has gone on about his business in your absence. Lyford and Tallyn have been up since dawn and are out somewhere gazing at barley and tenant farms. Jared has taken Pamela to call at Newton Park before—"

"What!" The countess banged her cane upon the floor. "What did you say?"

Lady Cadogan grimaced. "You will have a fit of apoplexy if you exert yourself with such suddenness, Almeria, and pray, what is it to you if Pamela allows Jared to accompany her? From all that I can see, you have encouraged that relationship. Have you done so only to spite Lyford?"

" 'Tis an excellent match," the dowager snapped, "but why does he take her to Spenser? Don't he realize his error?"

"What error?" Lady Cadogan asked, pausing to remove the sky-blue wool from her needle and rethread it with red. When Lady Lyford still had not replied, she looked at her, frowning. "Well, Almeria? What is it?"

"That fool chit may have pulled the wool over your eyes, Wynnefreda, but she has not bamboozled me. You may choose to think she has an eye to poor Jared, but much as I would like to see it, I can tell you her interest lies elsewhere."

"Well, yes," Lady Cadogan agreed, "I believe you may be right. I didn't wish to say anything, because—"

"No doubt, but I cannot think why you should wish to encourage a match with a man old enough to be her father—"

"Surely not her father, Almeria!"

"Oh, very well," Lady Lyford said tartly, "although I am sure that older men have fathered girls her age before now."

"*Older* men!" Gwenyth exclaimed, stifling laughter. "Good gracious, ma'am, do you mean Sir Spenser?" She looked at her aunt and saw at once that that lady looked quite as astonished as she felt. "I know you have suggested before that Pamela has an interest there, but I can assure you that she does not."

"And what can you know of such matters?" demanded the countess. "I tell you that where a gentleman like Spenser is concerned, there is nothing that can happen that would

surprise me. Women of all ages have been on the catch for
that poor man for as long as I have known him, which has
been a very long time indeed. He has never chosen to cast
his handkerchief, but that does not mean that he will never
do so. I will, however, do my possible to make sure he does
not cast it in Miss Beckley's direction.'' Turning on her heel,
she moved swiftly and without making use of her cane to
pull the bell. When a footman entered in response, she
ordered her carriage brought around directly.

''Where are you going, Almeria?''

The countess retorted abruptly, ''I recall that Spenser
mentioned having noticed a book on the shelf in the drawing
room that he admired very much. I shall take it to him.''

''But,'' Lady Cadogan said reasonably, ''a book on the
drawing-room shelf must by rights belong to Lyford, and
he might not—''

''Good gracious, Wynnefreda, I suppose I have a right to
give a book to Spenser if I wish to do so. I am still mistress
of this house, I'll have you know, and that book belonged
to my husband. Not that I ever saw him read any book, but
that does not signify. Spenser will read it. Pray, what has
Marcus to say to anything?'' Without awaiting a reply, she
left the room.

Gwenyth grinned at her aunt. ''Do I detect a touch of
jealousy, ma'am? Is it possible that the dowager wants Sir
Spenser for herself?''

Lady Cadogan shook her head in sardonic amusement. ''I
am sure I cannot say. She has looked over every decrepit
prospect in the county, and a good few others in London.
Sir Spenser is no more decrepit than she is herself, but I
believe she does have a fondness for him. Even if she would
consider the match, however, she is perfectly right in saying
that he has successfully avoided every lure ever cast his
way.''

''But I think he likes her,'' Gwenyth said. ''Pamela thinks
so too.''

Lady Cadogan shrugged. ''Perhaps, but liking is not

marrying, my dear, and we must hope that her activities these past weeks have not given him a disgust for her.''

"I think her efforts have amused him. They certainly have not kept him from haunting this place.''

"He does that,'' Lady Cadogan agreed. "Oh, dear, I have snagged this thread.'' She bent to her work, and Gwenyth returned to her magazine.

A short time later, she put her magazine aside and decided to stretch her legs. She had reached the door when she heard voices approaching and knew Lyford and Tallyn had returned.

They saw her and came into the morning room, whereupon Gwenyth noted with amusement her brother's swift glance around and his disappointed expression when he saw only their aunt.

"Miss Beckley,'' Gwenyth said sweetly, "has gone riding along the river trail with Mr. Hawtrey. I believe he means to indulge her in a trip down from Streatley on a barge.''

"What?'' her brother exclaimed. "That damned scoundrel! She ought not to be traipsing about the countryside with him at all, let alone on the river.''

Her evil genius prompted Gwenyth to say, "I cannot think why they should not go to Streatley together, sir. They have got to know each other rather well these past weeks, you know.''

She had forgotten Lyford. "What the devil were you thinking of, to let her go off alone with him?'' he demanded.

Turning swiftly to face him, she said, "They did not go alone, sir, they took a groom. And they are calling at Newton Park on the way. Your grandmama is also calling there,'' she added. "She may even have arrived ahead of them, since she took her carriage and went by the road. I would not have let Pamela go alone. Nor would my aunt. Surely you know that.''

But if he was satisfied, Tallyn was not. "Damn fool thing to do, to go with that fellow. A loose screw if ever I saw one, begging your pardon, Lyford.''

"No need to beg my pardon, but she is perfectly safe in his company, I assure you. He knows he will have to answer to me." He glanced back at Gwenyth, frowning. "Did you say my grandmother also went to Newton Park?"

"She said something about taking a book to Sir Spenser," Gwenyth told him with a limpid look.

His expression relaxed. "She did, did she?"

"Yes, I hope you will not object."

"No, why should I? 'Tis rather Sir Spenser who might object, if she creates a Drury Lane drama on his doorstep."

"Where is this Newton Park?" Tallyn demanded.

Gwenyth started to tell him again that he had no need to be concerned about Pamela, but before she spoke she remembered that Lyford would very soon insist upon private conversation with her and that he would not easily be put off again. Nor did she want to put him off. But to speak with him at all would be far easier with her brother out of the way. Thus it was that instead of trying to discourage Tallyn, she willingly gave him the direction he sought and expressed no surprise over his decision to depart as soon as he had tidied himself.

When he had gone to ring for his valet, Lyford grinned at her. "I wondered how you would manage to be rid of him. His presence here makes it difficult for us to be alone. Of course, I could formally seek his permission to request your hand in marriage. That would make matters easier."

Gwenyth looked swiftly at her aunt to see if she had heard him, but Lady Cadogan appeared to be immersed in her fancywork. In any event, she did not look up.

"We'll go to my library," Lyford said.

"I don't think I want to talk to you, after all."

"Well, you've got to. And we cannot talk here. Nor are we likely to get a better chance. You're going to tell me what you saw and heard the other night, and then we are going to decide what to do about it."

With a sigh, she nodded and allowed him to slip her hand into the crook of his arm, wondering why it was she felt like a lamb going meekly to the slaughter.

Inside the library, Lyford took his place behind the desk and gestured toward the tapestry armchair beside it. "Sit down."

As she obeyed, she watched him a little warily, certain now that he would not like some, at least, of what she had to tell him. "There is something you ought to know at once, sir. I ought to have told you before that I wrote to Sir Antony. You see, at first I was afraid that you might be part of whatever is going on, but I have since realized that you are not."

He rested his elbows on the desk and pressed his fingertips together, making a tent and peering thoughtfully at her over it. "Would you mind telling me how you came to that conclusion?"

"I'm not certain. I was trying to write enough to alert Antony without giving everything away if it fell into the wrong hands, so I thought carefully about it all. I believe that whatever is happening has something to do with the shipping company, and I thought at first that that must mean you were involved, because of your long association with the company. But your uncle trusts you, and you are not a man to betray a trust."

"You are certain of that?"

She looked at him for a long moment, then said slowly, "I am no doubt being foolish, since your uncle can have no real reason still to trust you, now that you have the abbey to look after."

"He has every reason, but that is not important now. Tell me what you saw the other night."

"First, you tell me if you really saw me from the library."

"No."

"No, you didn't see me, or no, you won't tell me?"

"No, I didn't see you. Not until you had been carried by the river nearly to the lock. Seeing you then well nigh frightened me out of my wits."

"Then you know how I felt when you grabbed me from behind!"

"You deserved to be frightened. Of all the idiotic—"

Gwenyth leaned forward in her chair. "If you want to discuss this further, Lyford, you had better not make me angry."

"If they had seen you—"

"Who were they?"

"I saw only one of them, and his name wouldn't mean anything to you. He's one of my tenants. I don't care about him or the other one, for that matter. It's their leader I want."

"He wasn't there," she said. "They talked about him. 'The young master' they called him, and I thought for a moment they meant you. Didn't you hear them?"

"Only bits. I had come from the ruins. Thought I saw activity there and hoped to catch them, but they had already loaded up and gone by the time I arrived. I heard the lock opening a moment or two before I saw you, and then I wasted time trying to decide whether to risk their seeing me by jumping into the water to rescue you. I might have heard the two manning the lock sooner but for focusing all my attention on you until I saw that you were safe." He looked hard at her for a moment.

She glared back. "Did you wish to say more, sir?"

His lips twitched, and the expression in his eyes softened. "You know very well that I'd like to say a great deal more, but you are right to remind me that it would waste time. Unless," he added grimly as a new thought struck him, "you dare to tell me you knew beforehand that they would be there. Is that why you were in the water, Gwen—trying to sneak up on them?"

"Good gracious, no! I am not totally devoid of good sense."

"Well, I wondered. Tell me what you did see."

She did, pausing now and again to search her memory, trying to see everything again in her mind, to repeat to him what she had heard as she had heard it. When she had finished, he leaned back in his chair.

"Is that all, love?"

"Don't call me that."

"I think you will soon have to change your mind about some of your future plans," he said gently.

"You're demented, Lyford."

"Perhaps," he agreed. "Was that all?"

"Yes, except . . ." She frowned. "They said something about Joey Ferguson. It worried me, and I—"

"He'd better not have been hunting for his uncle's treasure again. I warned him."

"That's it. Oh, not that he's been looking again," she added hastily when the frown returned, "although now I come to think of it, he may have done before you spoke to him. The men said he didn't know he'd found it, which I thought was odd. He once told me he'd found nothing but a pile of barley husks in the ruins, no treasure at all. If he has found something else—"

"He hasn't found anything else." The way he said it made her look at him narrowly.

"You mean that's it?"

He nodded.

"But how can that be? Barley husks!"

"That's why I went to the ruins when I thought I saw activity there. Remember the day I tried to explain to you about customs duties and the excise tax?"

Gwenyth bit her lower lip, searching her memory. "I remember talking about it, but I don't remember much of what you said. Something about paying two taxes and then getting some back if the goods went out of England."

"The drawback. That's how they work it. The company ships goods from Bristol to London that are meant to be shipped to the northern part of the Continent. The cheapest way to move those goods from Bristol is by canal to the Thames. They pass right by Molesford, and along the way the number of bales of tobacco changes. Forty bales leave Bristol, but sixty arrive in London. If anyone were to examine them all closely, they would find a number with tobacco leaves baled around barley husks and other worthless stuff. But no one can check that closely, and at the London end, once the goods are loaded and away, the drawback is paid according to the number shipped. Davies discovered certain discrepancies before he came here. My own agents had discovered similar inconsistencies, but when we double-checked, it appeared that numbers might have been misread. I thought no more about it until Davies showed up here, making it clear he thought I was part of it. I fancy I was able to convince him of his error.''

"How?'' she asked.

"That isn't important now. What is, is putting a stop to the practice. I'd have been hard put to have stopped them by myself the other night, and I'll confess I meant only to see how they went about it, but I'll wager we can do something next time. Did they say when the next shipment is due through here?''

She shook her head. "You are not the master they spoke of, so who is?''

"There is only one person it can be,'' he said, and there was weariness and pain in his voice. "Only one other person has the authority and knows enough to have organized this.''

Gwenyth stared at him. "Your cousin Jared?''

He nodded.

"But surely he would not have killed Silas Ferguson!''

"I don't know. I wouldn't have thought him ruthless enough, but if he did not do it himself, he knows who did, and that's very nearly the same thing.''

"What will you do?''

"Wait. They were forced to move the last shipment sooner than they meant to, because we came back unexpectedly. I believe they've moved their operation away from the ruins, so they may have some difficulties with the next one, as well.''

"Can you not send to Bristol to discover when it is due?''

"I doubt there's time. It would not have been far behind the other, because they can't have counted on having a great deal of time alone here. I'll have to think about what is best to do. I don't know whom I can trust.'' He looked up as the door opened just then to admit one of the footmen. "Yes, what is it?"

"Mr. Lacy is below, my lord, and asks to see you."

Lyford nodded and said for Gwenyth's benefit, "One of my tenants. We visited his farm that day. You may tell him I'll be with him directly," he said to the footman. When the man had gone, he got to his feet. "We'll talk again later," he said, adding bitterly, "Who knows? Your brother may solve my problem by killing Jared over that idiotish young cousin of mine."

15

Gwenyth left the earl and went upstairs to change into her habit, then walked to the stables, where she found Ben Forbes talking to two of the grooms.

"You meanin' t' ride out, ma'am?" he asked, dismissing the others.

"I was hoping you might allow Joey to ride with me again," she said, smiling at him. "Where is he?"

Ben's mouth twisted into a wry grimace. "Just as well he ain't here, ma'am, 'cause it'd be worth my place an I was ter let him ride out again wi' ye. As it happens, he and Ned rode with Mr. Jared and Miss Beckley to play gooseberry and ter bring their horses back, 'cause they be meanin' ter come back on the river. Joey and Ned should be home soon now, I reckon."

Gwenyth nodded. Defeated in her plan to make sure Joey had done no more searching, she decided she didn't really wish to ride after all, and walked down through the garden to the river instead. Traffic was light, and the weather had turned cooler, so her walk was a pleasant one. She strolled to the lock and back again, and as she neared the ruins, she looked up and saw a horseman riding toward her along the river, waving madly.

It took her a moment to realize it was Joey. He drew up before her in a flash of hooves, hanging over his mount's neck to ask urgently, "Where be the master, m'lady?"

"Up at the house. What's wrong, Joey? Where's Ned? And where are Mr. Jared's and Miss Beckley's horses?"

"Mr. Jared, Miss Beckley, and m'lady Lyford all be on

yon barge, m'lady Gwenyth! I've got ter get me lord!''

"Well, I'm surprised to hear that her ladyship went with them, but you knew they were going—''

"You don't understand," he interjected. "He's got hisself a pistol, and there's others aboard, bad men—men me dad said I warn't ter go near, not never.''

Gwenyth's stomach tightened. "Who's got a pistol, Joey? Mr. Jared?''

"No, Mr. Powell. We passed a barge what had been pulled into a backwater, with bales o' tobacco, and when we got ter Sir Spenser's, Miss Pamela told 'im straightaway. Sir Spenser said they was on 'is land and 'e'd see 'em gone. Mr. Jared tried ter stop 'im, said they was bad men, but 'e wouldn't listen. The countess were there, and 'e told 'er ter stay, but she wouldn't neither. The barge were on the river by then, but Mr. Jared seen Mr. Powell and shouted for 'im ter come back. When 'e did, 'e 'ad a pistol and said Mr. Jared and the ladies was ter get aboard quick. They knocked Sir Spenser down when 'e tried ter stop 'em takin' the old countess, and then they knocked Ned down too. I rode off, and run bang into Lord Tallyn. I told 'im, and 'e was mad as fire that he didn't have his pistols by 'im, Said 'e'd foller 'em downriver, though, and said I was ter get me lord.''

"Then get him," Gwenyth said, "and go as fast as you can, Joey. Where is Lord Tallyn now?''

The boy had begun to turn the horse, but he shouted over his shoulder, "He's follerin' the barge. Like ter be 'ere any minute, too.'' He kicked his horse and was off.

Gwenyth peered upriver and soon saw her brother and a long narrow barge, loaded with what looked like bales of tobacco. Atop the bales sat Jared, three other men, Lady Lyford, and Pamela. She heard Pamela shriek and saw one of the men slap her.

Seeing Tallyn react but knowing him to be helpless against the armed men, Gwenyth saw also, on the other side of the river, that Big Joe Ferguson and several other scufflehunters were following the barge. How Powell thought he could succeed in getting away, she couldn't think. There were locks ahead, after all. The thought spurred her to action, and she turned, snatched up her skirts, and ran along the beaten path as fast as she could.

She was out of breath when she reached the Molesford lock, and Nat Philps scratched his head at the sight of her.

"There's a barge coming, Mr. Philps," she cried. "There are three men with pistols, and they have taken Lady Lyford, Mr. Hawtrey, and Miss Beckley captive. You must stop them!"

"Pistols!" exclaimed Mr. Philps. "They've got pistols?"

"Please, sir, say you won't open the gate to them. You mustn't. We've got to stop them."

"I ain't going ter do nothing," snapped Mr. Philps. "They can do as they likes, but ain't no part o' my job ter get m'self shot. You'd best get out o' the way too, m'lady."

"No, we can't do that! They will open the gates themselves, as they have done before. It was they who broke your paddle that time, and they went through again only a few nights ago!"

"Then they can do it theirselves now," declared Mr. Philps, jumping down off the catwalk that ran along the top of the swing gate. A moment later he had disappeared from sight, and Gwenyth could see the barge coming around the bend. There was little time to think, but a sudden memory of the first time she had watched the lock, when Lyford and Jared had explained how the locks worked, flashed through her mind. She had watched often enough to know how the business of opening was accomplished, and she jumped onto the catwalk to draw the lock tackle free herself.

"It might already be too late," she muttered under her breath as she struggled with the first paddle. It wasn't nearly so easy as it had looked. Though she pulled, the river held the thing in place. Looking up, she saw her brother riding toward her. "Hurry, Joss!" she shouted. "I can't do it alone."

"What the devil are you trying to do?" he demanded, flinging himself from his saddle.

"We've got to open the gate!"

"The devil we do! We've got to stop them. Come down from there at once."

She bit her lip in exasperation, trying to think of a way to convince him swiftly enough to help her, but then, seeing Lyford behind him, pounding along the ride on Joey's horse, she sighed with relief. "Lyford, help me!" she yelled when he was near enough to hear her. "If we can open it soon enough . . . No, Joss!"

Tallyn had reached her and was trying to pull her off the catwalk. "Get down, you idiot," he snapped. "They'll shoot!"

Lyford hauled him unceremoniously out of the way and leapt onto the catwalk beside Gwenyth, grabbing paddles and beams and pulling them free of the frame. When he signed to her, Gwenyth released the latch, and moments later the catwalk, which was counterbalanced, swung back on the pivot post set into the riverbank, carrying the two of them with it. Lyford jumped to the ground and lifted her down beside him.

Tallyn was furious. "What the devil do you think you are about? We might have stopped them here!"

Lyford looked at Gwenyth. "Yes, love, what have we been about, if I might ask?"

She was still out of breath, but she stared at him. "I thought you knew what I was doing."

"Didn't really think about it," he said. "Saw you'd thought of something and needed help, that's all."

She opened her mouth twice before the words would come. "I hoped they would run aground. You said if the gate was opened too soon, the heavier barges often ran aground because the river dropped too quickly to allow them to reach the opening on the swell. But we were too late. Look!"

The barge was moving more swiftly, riding the fast current. Pamela screamed at them as it swept past into the white water, and Gwenyth watched in dismay, but before Tallyn had opportunity to tell either her or Lyford what he thought of them, there was a heavy, grating crunch, then louder screams from Pamela, and the barge ran aground on the huge bar of gravel that had been thrown up by the back currents below the gate. When the barge tilted crazily, Gwenyth watched in shock as Pamela was flung head over heels into the water.

"Joss," Gwenyth screamed, "she can't swim!"

Both men began to run, but Tallyn was ahead and, without a word, ripped off his coat and boots and flung himself into the swiftly moving river. Across the way, Big Joe Ferguson was also in the water, swimming powerfully toward the barge. On the barge itself, only one man was still armed. It was the same one who had slapped Pamela, and Gwenyth decided he must be Powell. Two of his men had fallen into the river, and the third seemed to have lost his pistol. Jared was bending over the countess.

Powell lifted his gun, but even as Gwenyth drew breath to shout a warning to the swimmers, she saw the old countess push Jared aside, raise her cane, and bring it crashing down upon Powell's wrist. The pistol went flying, and Powell and the third man turned angrily toward her, but Jared knocked Powell's man into the river just as the countess whacked the length of her cane with all her considerable strength across Powell's midsection. Doubling in pain, he crumpled against one of the bales of tobacco, and the old lady stood over him, triumphant, her cane held aloft, clearly daring him to move.

Just then Lyford shouted, "This way, Tallyn, to me, man!"

Gwenyth snatched up her skirts and followed him, arriving as Tallyn reached the riverbank, where Lyford helped him carry the gasping, choking Pamela to shore. As Tallyn knelt to lay her upon the ground, she clung to him.

"Don't leave me!"

"I won't," he said calmly, "but we must get you warm, and we've got to bring those fellows to shore, as well."

"No need to bother your head about them," Lyford said. He had been watching the water, and Gwenyth, following his gaze, saw that Joe Ferguson and the scufflehunters had Powell and his cohorts well in hand. A rowboat was approaching the barge, and a rope had been thrown to Jared.

"Good," Lyford murmured. "Barge seems pretty well stuck, but it's as well to have them off quickly. Don't want to lose the countess, or Jared either."

Gwenyth glanced up at him. "The countess, sir? Not Grandmother?"

He shook his head, grinning at her. "Seeing her like this, I'd say she's earned the right to be called whatever she likes."

Gwenyth smiled back at him, but she could see little humor in the situation. "What will happen now, sir?"

"They'll row them over here, of course, and I aim to have a few choice words with Jared. Good God, is that Newton?"

Turning, Gwenyth saw that the old gentleman was nearly upon them. To her astonishment, he was on horseback, and if his mount was not galloping, it was certainly maintaining a respectable canter. "What's toward, Lyford?" he shouted as he drew rein. "Where's Almeria? And Pamela? Oh, there you are, child. Didn't see you at first behind Tallyn's bulk. You are all wet!"

Pamela was still clinging to Tallyn, but she managed a watery smile. "I shall be better directly, sir, if I can only get warm again."

"Well, Spenser," snapped the countess, as the rowboat bumped against the riverbank behind Gwenyth, and one of the scufflehunters helped the old lady to disembark, "I might have known you'd concern yourself with that idiotish young female!"

"Good gracious, Almeria, that you? Whatever are you doing there?" As Gwenyth watched with increasing amusement, he dismounted and strode to take the countess's hand. "Allow me to assist you. What a remarkable woman you are, to be sure!"

Lady Lyford raised her eyebrows at him. "And you, Spenser, did you truly ride all this way? I cannot credit it. Watch that Powell fellow, Marcus," she added with a snap, as the boatman helped the man, still clutching his midsection, to the riverbank. When Lyford, assuring himself that the boatman had Powell well in charge, stepped forward to speak to Jared, the countess turned back to Sir Spenser, her plump countenance softening. "Tell me what happened after that jackanapes abducted us."

"Tallyn found me moments later and commanded me to let my servants look after me," he said, returning her smile and continuing to hold her hand in his. "But I've taken more than one knock in my life, my dear, and I could not simply sit there and wait, not knowing what had become of you."

"Of young Pamela, I suppose you mean to say," she said with an unsuccessful attempt at wry humor.

"No, my dear. I cannot imagine why you must persist in thinking I've a particular tenderness for Miss Beckley. She has done me the honor to beg my advice from time to time, seeing in me something of her own father, I daresay."

"You would have me believe that she came to you today to ask your advice?"

"Indeed." He glanced at Pamela, now covered with Lyford's coat, but still reclining against Lord Tallyn. "Not that I think she really needed my help. Her own feelings appear to have led her aright." Looking at Gwenyth, who was also watching the pair, he said, "I daresay you will have guessed her mind, my dear."

She nodded. "I'm afraid it was a case between them from the start, sir," she said.

Lady Lyford looked from one to the other. "You mean that idiotish wench wants Tallyn? Good gracious!"

"You ought to have known, Almeria," Sir Spenser said, looking fondly at her. "I have been steadfast these many years."

Pamela stirred in Tallyn's arms and said with a wan smile, "What did I tell you, Gwen?"

"See here," Tallyn said, "we must get Miss Beckley to the house before she catches her death!"

"You are a trifle damp too, Joss," Gwenyth pointed out.

"Never mind me," he retorted. "I'll take her up myself."

"What about those impudent men?" the countess demanded.

Lyford joined them in time to hear her question. "Ferguson

and his lads have them all in charge," he said. "Jared tells me Powell killed Silas Ferguson, so we may trust Big Joe to keep them close until a constable can be sent for."

"Or Antony," Gwenyth murmured.

"I'll deal with Antony," he told her.

"And what about Jared?" the countess asked in a more subdued tone. "I cannot think he had much to do with all this, but he said more than once on that barge that it was all his doing!"

"We'll sort it out at the house," Lyford told her gently. "Tallyn, you're soaked, man. Let me carry her."

But this Tallyn would not allow, so they all followed him back to the house, making such a commotion when they entered that Lady Cadogan heard them and hung over the wrought-iron railing of the soaring stair to demand to know what was going on.

Jared looked pleadingly at Lyford. "May we speak privately?" he asked.

The countess, hearing him, banged her cane on the floor. "Try it, and see how far you get, my lads. I want an explanation, and you aren't either of you setting a step out of my presence until I get one!"

Sir Spenser beamed at her. "Good for you, Almeria. We'll have a round tale yet."

Lady Cadogan called down to them, "Are you coming up or shall I come down?"

In the end, except for Tallyn and Pamela, who went to their bedchambers to get dry, they all adjourned to the Chinese drawing room, and Jared, with more courage than anyone might have expected from him, did his best to explain. "I don't know how it started," he said. "When Grandpapa died and Father said I was to take over Marcus's duties, I didn't want them, so when Powell offered to look after things, I leapt at his offer. I never knew that he and our London agent had cooked up the scheme with the drawback. Powell began slipping me money from time to time without explaining where it came from."

"You didn't ask?" Lyford's tone was grim.

Jared shook his head, looking shamefaced. "I'd never learned enough about the business to know it wasn't customary. Always had someone else do the work."

Gwenyth remembered Lyford's having said Jared had been the sort of schoolboy who made his fags do all the work. She remembered, too, that anyone who asked him about his business was referred to Powell.

Lyford had clearly been thinking along similar lines, for he said, "I didn't think Powell had enough authority to have pulled all this off, but I collect you had given him such authority."

Jared nodded. "Not until Sir Antony showed up here did I realize that something was seriously amiss. You had suggested that Silas Ferguson's death was no accident, Marcus, and there was Sir Antony asking me a lot of damned awkward questions about possible mishandling of customs and excise money. I got the wind up, and when you went to London, I confronted Powell. He said the money I'd accepted made me party to the whole. Said if I didn't keep my mouth shut, I'd go to prison. Shall I have to go now?"

The countess declared acidly, "I am not quite nobody, I hope. No grandson of mine is going to prison."

Jared smiled weakly at her, but turned to Lyford for reassurance. "Marcus? I swear I didn't know before that, but I was criminally stupid, I suppose."

Lyford put a hand on his shoulder. "I think we can keep you out of prison, coz, but this might be an excellent time for you to learn a good deal more about the business."

"I want to! I never want anyone taking advantage of me like that again!"

Gwenyth looked at Lyford. "Travel, sir?"

"Barbados first, I think," he said. "There's a ship setting sail from Bristol within the week."

"Barbados!" Jared exclaimed. He did not look as though the prospect of an ocean voyage thrilled him, but when Lyford nodded, he did not argue. His ordeal was not yet finished, however, for the countess and Lady Cadogan had more questions to ask him, and Sir Spenser added his mite as well.

Under cover of their conversation, Lyford leaned closer to Gwenyth. "I want to talk to you, my love, about a matter of grave importance. If you insist, we can attempt it here, but I confess I'd prefer a quieter place. Will you walk with me to my library? They will not miss us, I think, for some moments."

Looking at him in astonishment, Gwenyth chuckled. "Do you truly think this an appropriate time for private conversation, sir? I cannot credit it."

He grinned at her. "I do not intend to let you put this off, Gwen, so make up your mind to it that I shall have my say. I have let you put me off before and then found I did not get you alone for days afterward."

"Not days, Lyford, only one day."

"Nevertheless, do you come, or do I speak here?"

Glancing at the others, still involved in their conversation, she said quietly, "I'll come, sir."

In the library, she took her seat in the armchair, but he went to stand beside the fireplace, looking rather uncertain of himself for once. She was glad to see it. It would not do for him to be too sure.

He looked down at her. "I believe you must know what I wish to say, for I have hinted at it often enough, but until now I was persuaded you would not hear me."

"Oh, no, sir," she said, smiling at him. "I had determined to hear you, so that I might give you a well-deserved setdown."

"Ah, then you do know my mind?"

"Do I?"

"I want to marry you, Gwen, but I've a small confession to make before I do."

"You wanted to marry Pamela, after all," Gwenyth said on a note of satisfaction. "I have cut the minx out."

He stared at her. "I never had any intention of marrying my idiotish cousin. Indeed, I ought to be offended that you could ever have thought such a thing of me."

"Well, I only thought it until I met you," she told him, "but why on earth did you insist she remain at school?"

"I didn't know what was going on here," he said. "I, too, was misled by my ignorance. I didn't see the things that were happening right under my nose, but I did know I needed to learn about the place quickly, and that left little time for Pamela."

"Well, if it is not that you were crazy in love with her or wanted to marry her for her money, then what must you confess?"

He hesitated for a long moment, then said, "You choose to make light of this, Gwen, and while that gives me hope, it also frightens me witless. I'm not by any means certain that what I'm about to tell you won't alter things considerably."

"You're going to take up your duties with the company again," she said complacently.

"Not exactly, although there is a good deal to be cleared up before this business is behind us, including replacing my London agent. The fact is, I own half the damned company. I earned it, worked for it, and I don't believe I want to put it behind me. But having been taught by my grandmother that one does not so much as mention even a slight connection with trade, and having been advised by you that any connection must remain firmly in my past, I was afraid to tell you about it. What do you think?"

In reply, she clasped her hands to her bosom in Pamela's favorite gesture and, imitating the countess's severest tones, said, "Lyford, you have grossly deceived me! Are you very rich?"

Instead of casting him down, her words made him grin and step nearer. "You will forgive the connection in return for riches, is that it?"

"Certainly, though I cannot think why you do not spend more on this place if you have the money to do so. I heard Jared say that several of Powell's men are your own disgruntled tenants."

"I meant what I said about making things pay for themselves. Whether the men were disgruntled or not makes little difference. When one gives a man something he has not earned, he does not appreciate it. Consider Jared himself, if you will."

"I won't. I have had my fill of Jared. If I yield to your wishes, sir, I suppose you will carp every time I spend a groat."

"Certainly, but I hope that question means you do not intend to give me a set-down and that you will marry me in spite of my nipcheese notions and my despicable connection with trade."

"Well, I'm very much afraid I will," she said.

He stepped near to her, pulling her up from her chair and putting his arms around her. Then he said in a tone very different from the one he had been using, "What made you change your mind, Gwen?"

She looked into his captivating eyes and wondered that he could ask. "You trust me," she said simply. "No man has ever truly done that before. I noticed it first when you not only allowed me to swim but also arranged a place for me to do so. There were other such instances too, but today when you leapt to help me when my own brother would not, and when you hadn't the slightest notion of what I was trying to do . . . well, no one has ever done such a thing before. I knew I cared for you long before that, of course. I think you know that."

"I do. 'Tis why I dared to tease you."

"Well, perhaps I would have succumbed to your wishes in any event, sir, but now I no longer fear marriage, not with you."

The next thing she knew, she was being thoroughly kissed and enjoying it very much. Neither of them heard the library door open, but both jumped nearly out of their skins when the countess banged her cane sharply upon the floor.

"So this is where you have got to! What on earth are you doing, the pair of you?"

Lyford recovered his composure first. "You may be the first to wish me happy, ma'am. Lady Gwenyth has done me the honor to agree to be my wife."

"Oh, she has, has she?"

Gwenyth eyed her warily, but Lyford chuckled. "No doubt you do not think her a proper person to take your place at Molesford, ma'am, but I assure you that you may remain with us as long as necessary, to teach her everything you know. No doubt Newton will be content to hang about for another year or two."

"Fiddle faddle!" snapped the countess, turning on her heel and slamming the door behind her, leaving them to return to what they had been doing before she interrupted them.